SOMETHING WAS IN THE WOODS.
SOMETHING DARK AND EVIL.

The music grew louder, beckoning to her. She noticed a light shining between the trees.

Hidden by the underbrush, Gabrielle crept closer until she reached the clearing. The bizarre chanting grew louder, encircling her head, burning her ears. When her eyes finally adjusted to the light, what Gabrielle saw caused them to stare in terror.

Hooded figures circled around a woman who knelt on the ground. The woman rocked back and forth.

And in her lap she cradled the skeletal remains of an infant. . . .

WHAT ABOUT
THE BABY?

WHAT ABOUT THE BABY?

Clare McNally

BANTAM BOOKS
TORONTO · NEW YORK · LONDON · SYDNEY

WHAT ABOUT THE BABY?
A Bantam Book / September 1983

ISBN 0-553-23670-9

Published simultaneously in the United States and Canada

Bantam Books are published by Bantam Books, Inc. Its trade-
mark, consisting of the words "Bantam Books" and the por-
trayal of a rooster, is Registered in U.S. Patent and Trademark
Office and in other countries. Marca Registrada. Bantam
Books, Inc., 666 Fifth Avenue, New York, New York 10103.

For my second mother and father,
Michael and Marta Pastore—
for the Sunday dinners.

Prologue

The infant was sleeping peacefully, oblivious to the dark figure who stood above him with a pillow clutched in his fists. The man stared down into the cradle, lovingly placed near the warm fire of a hearth. But he felt no love for this child, who at eight months of age already resembled him. There were dark curls and thick lashes, and· indications the boy would one day have his chiseled features.

Yes, if anyone were to see this child, there would be no denying who the father was.

"Your mother threatened to reveal you to my wife and family," the man said, speaking to the baby as if he could be understood. "Were she to do that, all that I have done to better my life will be in vain. I can not allow that wench to destroy me!"

He heard a noise, and turned abruptly to face the front door of the little house. But there was no one there; he reasoned it must have been the wind. He berated himself for having been startled, for he knew full well that he was alone. Hadn't he dismissed the child's nurse, bribing her with more money than she had ever seen? He smiled to think that everyone had a price.

"Except, perhaps, for your mother," he whispered. "But she shall rue the day she defied me!"

Slowly, he leaned down towards the cradle, the pillow bunched in his massive fists. . . .

*   *   *

1

The man was so caught up in his thoughts (the desire for a good strong rum at the best tavern in London) that he did not notice the young girl who watched his figure as it retreated down the dark, puddle-covered street. She stopped a few yards from the house, her heart fluttering. Was it possible he had come to visit her? That he had come to tell her of his love, only to find her not home?

"Please, let it be true!" she breathed, starting for the small half-timbered house that sat wedged in a row of similar dwellings. A mangy dog brushed past her legs and ran into a dark alley, but she paid no attention.

The very sight of him sent her mind flying through time and space, and suddenly it was two years ago; she was on the road leading from her father's country farm. She wore a simple cotton dress of pale, pale blue and a bonnet decorated with delicate blue flowers. She'd been picking berries. . . .

"May I buy some?"

She'd been speechless, looking up at the handsome man who sat astride a huge black stallion. It had been the beginning of their love. They would meet in secret, sharing each other's passions and dreams as they shared their bodies in love.

"My sweet one," he'd breathe. "One day, I will make you my wife, and I will give you diamonds and rubies, and emeralds greener than your eyes."

"You know that you can't marry me," she'd protest, although not too strongly. "I'm from a very poor family, while your father is a rich doctor. Let this moment be ours alone, and let's put the future from our minds."

But she wanted to marry him. Oh, how she wanted it. Yet months went by, and he never even attempted to introduce her to his family. Finally, when she became pregnant, she wondered if this might be the answer. Surely, he would marry her now!

He did not return to her after hearing the news, and she soon learned the horrible truth:

Her lover had married another woman, a woman of his own class.

The young girl had been crushed—even more so when he refused to give her financial help. Her family disowned her, branding her a "harlot" and sending her from their home with only a few belongings. But she was determined to care for herself and her baby. She found work as a scullery maid, and even put aside a few pennies a week so that an elderly neighbor could take care of her baby while she worked. Finally, in desperation, she had gone begging to her former lover. But he had denied knowing her, even when he saw how the baby much resembled him. She threatened to tell his wife everything. But her threats were hollow, for in her young heart she still loved him.

She opened her front door, her heart still pounding, and hurried to look for a note. She didn't even notice that her baby's nurse was missing.

Seeing there was no letter, she turned at last, and saw the empty room.

"Millicent?"

The baby was sleeping in his cradle, the light of the hearth dancing on his face.

"Millie probably went to gossip with the woman in the back alley," she decided. "I'll certainly give her a talking-to!"

She bent down to lift her son in her arms.

There was something wrong with him. He did not stir, nor did he make a sound. She moved closer to the fire, and in the light noticed a tiny drop of blood on the baby's mouth. She shook him gently, but when he did not respond she began to shake him furiously.

"What is wrong with you?" she screamed. "Little Brett, open your eyes!"

The child did not move.

The girl set him down in his cradle and backed away, covering her mouth as she screamed, a scream that rang through the house and shattered the very air around her. But in the darkest alley of London's poorest slum, no one heard. She went on screaming, until at last her voice was too hoarse to continue. Then, she lifted the infant in her arms, rocking him even though he could not feel her loving embrace.

What a fool she had been, to think he'd come to profess his love! To think he had *ever* loved her! Well, she hated him now—loathed him!

For a long time she stared into the flames of the hearth, her emotions running from confusion to fear to anger, then finally to a hatred so consuming it would possess her for the rest of her life.

"I will make him pay, my little Brett," she whispered. "I swear by God I'll make him pay!"

The American Southwest, 1976

Naomi Hansen stood behind the counter of her little diner, turning over the hamburgers she had working on a grill. Behind her, Pat Rukeyser, owner of the local drug store, slurped loudly on his coffee, swivelling his chair back and forth. Naomi winced to hear the squeaking noise, then sighed at her annoyance. Just a week ago, she wouldn't have minded it at all.

But a week ago, Paul had been standing right here, chattering so happily that she was unaware of anything else. A week ago, Paul was alive.

She turned and served Pat another cup of coffee and a piece of pie, staring into his blue eyes as if to admonish him to be still. She was so tired. She shouldn't even be working this soon after Paul's funeral. But Naomi had two little mouths to feed, and the diner was her only source of income.

"Hey, where's my food?" a voice demanded.

"Right here, sir," Naomi said, forcing a polite tone. She recognized the man from the gas station across the street, Joe Allman, and had to fight an urge to cover her nose when she approached him. The smell of grease and gasoline on his coveralls nauseated her. So much was hateful to her these days.

Last Friday, the sheriff had come to tell her that her husband was dead—torn apart in the desert by a pack of wild dogs. Naomi closed her eyes and saw a vivid picture of Paul's mutilated body, lying on a slab at the coroner's. She had fainted after making the identification.

The sound of a baby's cries brought her out of her trance. The half-dozen customers had now all been served so she was free to hurry into the kitchen. A little girl with long dark braids was trying to comfort the wailing infant.

"Mommy, Kerry's wet," she said.

"Gabrielle, you are ten years old," Naomi said wearily. "You know how to change a diaper!"

"Yes, ma'am."

"The Pampers are in the left-most cupboard," Naomi said. "On the bottom."

Gabrielle crossed the big kitchen, passing rows of pots and utensils that hung on metal racks suspended from the ceiling. As she bent down to retrieve the box of diapers, the necklace she was wearing slipped from her neck and fell to the floor with a soft twang. Gabrielle, busy getting the box out, made no immediate attempt to pick it up.

"No!" Naomi cried. "NO!"

Gabrielle straightened up, the box in her arms.

"Mommy?"

Naomi snatched up the necklace, and, with a jerking movement, put it around her daughter's neck again.

"Didn't I tell you never, *ever* to take that off?" she demanded. "Didn't I tell you bad things would happen if you did?"

"It just fell off, Mommy," Gabrielle whimpered, her violet eyes huge. "I didn't mean to lose it!"

Naomi saw the frightened look on her daughter's face, and realized she must sound like some sort of witch. Pulling Gabrielle close, she kissed her a few times, then said:

"I didn't mean to scare you, lovey. But you do know that the amulet carries a special blessing to protect you."

"Why do I need to be protected, Mommy?"

Naomi shook her head.

"You're too young to understand," she said.

"You're sad because of Daddy, aren't you?" Gabrielle asked.

A lump filled Naomi's throat.

"Why did those dogs attack him?"

"I don't know, sweetheart."

Naomi let her daughter believe, as everyone else did, that Paul's death had been an accident. But she knew better. There never were any dogs. She was certain Paul had been murdered. But how do you explain murder to a ten-year-old?

"Mommy has to get back to her customers," she said softly.

Out in front, Joe Allman felt something hard scrape against the back of his teeth. Spitting into his palm, he was shocked to see speckles of blood in his saliva. He started to pick up his sandwich, to see if he could find something in the tuna salad. But suddenly, the sandwich fell out of his hand, as a sharp pain sliced through him. He doubled over, coughing violently, choking up blood.

"What the hell is wrong with you?" Pat Rukeyser demanded, setting down his cup of coffee.

Down the counter, a woman began to gasp. She clutched the chair next to her and croaked:

"There's something in the—the—"

The word "food" was lost in a rush of blood. Without warning, the other customers in the diner began coughing and choking. Pat jumped to his feet with a curse and ran outside in search of help.

At that very moment, Naomi pushed through the doors, meeting Joe face-to-face. He was holding his throat with one hand, and reaching towards her with the other. His mouth was stretched into a hideous grimace, his eyes bulged, his face was a terrifying purple color. Naomi watched in horror as blood spurted from his mouth, staining the front of his green coveralls.

"Someone help him!" Naomi screamed.

But the others only gaped at her with terrified looks on their faces. Two young boys fell into puddles of blood and were silent. The woman at the counter gasped something unintelligible, then fainted.

Within a few moment's time, the diner had grown deathly silent. Naomi gazed around herself in dismay, sweat staining the pink cotton of her waitress uniform, a chill rushing over her fair skin.

It was horribly quiet.

"Mommy?"

Naomi had not heard the kitchen door open. She turned around and grabbed her daughter's arm, pulling her back into the kitchen.

"What was wrong with those people, Mommy?"

"Nothing!" Naomi insisted. She bent to her daughter's height. "Lovey, we've got to leave this place. Go upstairs and get your and Kerry's things together."

"Mommy, why?" Gabrielle asked, tears brimming.

"Gabrielle, *please!*"

They're after me, Naomi thought in panic. *They murdered Paul and now they want me, too!*

"Go upstairs, Gabrielle!"

Her daughter obeyed her, but when she heard the kitchen door open she stopped on the stairs to look. The sheriff was there, walking slowly towards Naomi, holding out his hand.

"Pat Rukeyser called me," he said. "Don't worry, Naomi. I'm sure it was all an accident."

"No," Naomi whispered. "It was no accident."

"Pat said there was something in the food. Maybe something fell from a shelf . . ."

"NO!" Naomi screamed, unaware that her daughter was hidden in the shadows of the staircase. "I'M NOT A MURDERESS!"

"Naomi, it's okay!"

As the shock wore off and reality hit her, she fell to the floor, kicking and tearing at her hair. Gabrielle watched her, sickened, trying to tell herself this wasn't her sweet, pretty mother. It was another woman who had invaded the little kitchen, another woman who was acting crazy.

Naomi went on screaming. Gabrielle backed slowly

up the stairs, covering her ears. A black film came down over her vision, cutting off the sight of her mother. Unable to accept the sound of Naomi's screams, the sight of blood, the chill of the air, Gabrielle's senses were numbed.

She wanted to block it all out, forever.

One

"You are a vile, despicable creature," the old woman hissed, staring through thick-lensed glasses at the teenage girl in front of her desk. Her grotesquely pale eyes were cold. "Why do you do such hateful things?"

Gabrielle Hansen folded her arms around her small waist, wishing she could squeeze herself into something so small that she would disappear. A tear fell from one violet eye, caught on the edge of a sculpted cheekbone, then rolled to the corner of her trembling lips. She gazed past Mrs. Macon to the yard outside. Children were playing softball or climbing on monkey bars or chasing each other, laughing, unaware that Gabrielle was here with the orphanage director. She spotted Charlie Taylor, a good-looking teenager she had once had a crush on; now he was holding hands with another girl. She turned away. "I didn't do anything, Mrs. Macon," she said finally, wishing she were outside with the others.

"What did you say?" the old woman asked. "Speak up, girl!"

Gabrielle swallowed hard, and tightened her arms again until she could feel the hardness of her ribs through her sweater.

"I said I didn't do anything," she repeated.

"Don't lie to me," Mrs. Macon said. "This isn't the first time this has happened. Why did you kill that kitten?"

I didn't kill it, Gabrielle protested in her mind. *It*

9

was in my room, all bloody and horrible, but I didn't kill it.

She remained silent.

"You have been in the care of this orphanage for seven years," Mrs. Macon said. "When you were younger, you were quite a delightful child. But for reasons I can't imagine, you've become something evil. Mrs. West, your foster mother, found that innocent creature in your bed—with its throat cut! This sort of thing has happened repeatedly over the last two years, in every home where we've placed you. Rabbits, hamsters, dogs—you don't care what you hurt!"

Gabrielle sniffled, then raised a hand to push back a lock of black hair that had come loose from her layer-cut tresses. Her head ached, partly from her tears, partly from trying to remember what had happened to cause the old woman's fury. Her mind whirled back to the last moments she'd spent at the West house. It had been morning, and she had been awakened by the sound of her foster mother calling her to breakfast. But the bed was so cozy that she didn't want to get up just yet.

She had stretched her legs and arms, trying to wake herself up, until her foot had thumped against something small and hard. But the bed had been empty the night before. . . .

Groggily, she had hoisted herself up on an elbow to look at the foot of the bed. The kitten had been there, lying with its four paws crossed, its head supported by a fold in the blankets. A white kitten. White, and red with blood. Slowly, Gabrielle had pulled her knees up to her chest. It had happened again, just the way it had happened in every foster home in the past two years.

Instinctively, her eyes had been drawn to the mirror over the room's dressing table. Someone had used the kitten's blood to draw on the glass. Someone had scribbled a picture of a skull with a snake running through its eye sockets.

It was the same symbol Gabrielle had found in the other homes.

"Hansen!"

Mrs. Macon's shrill voice brought her back to the present. Startled, Gabrielle looked up at the old woman.

"We have tried our best with you," Mrs. Macon said. "Analysis, medicine, and a good deal of patience. I have had enough! You are simply bent on destroying any chances you have to lead a normal life!"

Mrs. Macon sighed. "Never in all the years I've directed this orphanage have I experienced such an evil girl. It's no wonder, though," she said, taking off her glasses to clean them. "I should have seen this coming when I brought you here. I should have forseen that your mother's wickedness would one day rub off on you!"

"My mother," Gabrielle said. "Everyone says she was bad. But *why?*"

Mrs. Macon slapped the top of her desk, making Gabrielle cringe.

"You have been told that you are not to discuss your mother," she said, shaking her glasses at the young girl. "What she did was horrible, nothing for a child to think about!"

I'm not a child, Gabrielle thought. *I'm seventeen, and I have every right to know what happened to my mother.*

"The time has come to forget sympathy," Mrs. Macon said grimly. "Despite what our doctor says about patience, I am going to punish you for what you did."

Gabrielle's stomach soured, and she brought a hand up to clutch the pendant she wore. Mrs. Macon did not speak for a moment, knowing the fearful anticipation might be more effective than the punishment itself. Gabrielle's trembling hand rubbed the smooth amulet. Mrs. Macon wondered why the girl always wore it. She had tried to remove the thing when Gabrielle first arrived at the orphanage, but the child had thrown such a tantrum that the staff decided she should be allowed to keep it. It was a crude thing, just a silver equilateral triangle within a golden circle. Hardly the sort of jewelry a normal teenager would like.

Gabrielle squeezed the amulet, and wished her mother were here now to help her. But Mrs. Macon had told her Naomi was dead, killed in a prison fire two years ago.

"All right," Mrs. Macon said finally. "You are hereby grounded for one month. That means no activities, no television, no letters. No sports."

Oh, God, Gabrielle thought. *I wish my brother were here right now. I sure need him!*

"In addition," Mrs. Macon continued, "you will scrub down all the bathrooms. And you won't be permitted to go to bed until you've finished. Perhaps some hard work will give you time to think about what you've done!"

"Yes, ma'am," Gabrielle said.

"You may go now," Mrs. Macon told her. "Report to the janitor after dinner. If you don't delay you'll be finished by lights-out."

Eager to be out of the stuffy office, Gabrielle turned and pushed through the door to the hallway. Her eyes stung from her tears, and she closed her lids to rest them a moment. In the distance, she could hear someone playing a piano, and the sounds of children reciting to a teacher. Someone's laughter echoed along the empty hallway.

As she stood there, a pair of small arms snaked around her waist. Gabrielle opened her eyes and looked down at her seven-year-old brother, Kerry. He returned her gaze with a solemn one of his own. He resembled his sister with his fair skin and curly black hair but the pronounced cheekbones were still hidden under the soft layers of his baby fat.

"What are you doing out here?" Gabrielle asked.

"I thought you might need me," Kerry said. "I just had a funny feeling about you."

"That's weird," Gabrielle said. "I was kind of wishing you were there."

Kerry wrinkled his pug nose and asked:

"'What's old Owl-eyes do to you?"

"I'm grounded for a month," Gabrielle said. "And I have to scrub down the bathrooms. It's not so bad."

"It's lousy," Kerry growled, pulling away. He hooked his thumbs through the belt loops of his jeans and threw back his shoulders. "I'll fix her, someday!"

"Shh, Kerry!" Gabrielle hissed.

"I'm not afraid of her," Kerry insisted.

He swaggered towards the door to Mrs. Macon's office, his bright yellow t-shirt coming loose from his jeans to expose a baby-potbelly. Making his eyes small, he said through his teeth:

"I'll fix you, Macon-Bacon."

Gabrielle shushed him again, and reached to grab his arm.

"Kerry, don't!"

"My sister didn't kill no dumb kitten!"

He lifted both hands and pointed his index fingers like guns at the silver letters on the door that read "IDA MACON, DIRECTOR." No one would hurt his sister and get away with it! Then, without warning, the door opened. The scowl on Kerry's face dissolved into a sweet smile of innocence as he gazed up at Mrs. Macon. She frowned at him.

"Kerwin, what are you doing out here?"

"N-nothing, Mrs. Macon," Kerry said, his smile and his bravado instantly gone.

"Behave yourself," the old woman said. She looked at Gabrielle. "Are you still here? I suppose you've been filling this child's head with your lies."

Gabrielle shook her head and took hold of the amulet.

"My sister doesn't tell lies," Kerry protested.

Mrs. Macon regarded him a moment.

"Kerwin, you are too attached to your sister," she said. "You're only seven, aren't you?"

"Yeah?"

Kerry backed away and stood closer to Gabrielle.

"I think it's time you two were separated," Mrs. Macon said. "I feel that Gabrielle may be a bad influence on you."

Kerry looked at her for a moment, unable to comprehend what she had just said. And then it became apparent that she wanted to take him away from his sister. That could never happen!

"No!" he cried. "NO! I won't leave Gabrielle! I won't!"

His screams brought a rush of blood to his face, and reddened his fair skin as he waved his fists at Mrs. Macon. Setting her teeth, the old woman stepped towards him and delivered a slap to his cheek that stunned him into silence. Kerry gaped at her, then turned to hug his sister as his tears began to flow.

"Why did you do that?" Gabrielle asked softly. "He's just a little boy."

"I will not have him talking that way to me," Mrs. Macon said. "That's your influence, Gabrielle. You taught him to behave that way."

"I don't control my brother, Mrs. Macon," Gabrielle said evenly, anger at her brother's mistreatment giving her strength.

Mrs. Macon raised her hand again, then dropped it.

"You are such a monster," she whispered. "You, with your black hair and pretty face. What makes you think . . ." She stopped herself, then turned to storm down the hall. After she had disappeared around the corner, Kerry grabbed Gabrielle's hand and asked:

"She isn't really gonna send me away, is she?"

Gabrielle shook her head. "Of course not. She's always making threats like that. Besides, I don't think she has the authority to do it. She may be director here, but she has to answer to others."

Gabrielle was grateful for that fact, since it was only Mrs. Macon's lack of full authority that kept her here. If the old woman had her way, Gabrielle would have been in a detention home long ago. But she pushed the thought aside and smiled at her brother.

"If you can't go out," Kerry said, "I'll come up to your dorm and play with you."

"You aren't allowed there."

"Nobody'll know," Kerry said. "Want to get out the Scrabble game that old rich guy gave you last Christmas?"

Gabrielle laughed—Kerry's cheerfulness always turned her moods around. Perhaps there was a decade's difference in their ages, but he was her only family, and that meant a lot to her.

"I always beat you at that game," she said.

"If you let me use famous names I'd win," Kerry pouted.

His sister smiled again. "Okay!"

She took his hand and led him towards a flight of wide, tile-covered stairs that led to the second floor. A group of younger children passed them, keeping close to the iron railing as if afraid to come in contact with Gabrielle. They whispered to each other behind chubby hands and stared sideways at her. The news about Gabrielle's latest "crime" had spread like wildfire and the other children had decided her guilt. She was an outcast.

Now Kerry jumped out a little, waving his arms and making weird noises. The other children squealed and raced down the stairs. At that moment, Gabrielle thanked God for Kerry. At least there was someone in the world who loved her.

Artie Raven had worked as a janitor for the Macon Orphanage for ten years, yet he had yet to get used to Mrs. Macon's ways of disciplining the children. It irritated him that the girl Gabrielle Hansen was now busy scrubbing the bathrooms. That was *his* job, and he didn't like the idea of the old woman making him out to be the "heavy."

He watched her lean over one of the sinks, pushing a sponge across the white ceramic surface, and was tempted to tell her she could quit. But he knew better than that. Artie had once tried to intervene when Mrs. Macon had been this strict with another child, and it had nearly cost him his job. At sixty-eight years of age, he knew jobs that paid this well were hard to come by.

So, like everyone else here at the children's home, he was stuck under Mrs. Macon's thumb.

"Why don't you rest a few minutes?" he asked the young girl. "You'll wear yourself out."

"Thanks," Gabrielle said. "But I want to get this done so I can go to bed."

Artie shrugged and walked from the lavatory; Mrs. Macon would probably find fault with the girl's work anyway. As he left the room, two teenaged girls entered. They looked at him sideways, giggled, then pushed further into the room. Artie glowered at them on his way out.

"Hey, Hansen," one girl said. "Heard you killed another one."

Gabrielle sprinkled Ajax on the counter and ignored them.

"What was it this time, bitch?" the girl pressed. "A puppy? Or maybe you've moved on to bigger things."

"Maybe it was a baby this time," the second girl said.

Now Gabrielle turned to them, her eyes flashing.

"That is so gross," she said. "I didn't kill anything, and you know it."

"I only know what Mrs. Macon told Mr. Breslin, the math teacher," the first girl replied.

Gabrielle clicked her tongue and turned back to her work. Why did she bother defending herself? All the kids here hated her; they believed the rumors. If no one would give her a chance to defend herself, then the heck with them.

But still, sometimes, she felt so lonely. . . .

She smelled smoke, and in the mirror she saw the reflection of one girl lighting up. That figures, she thought. These two are really breaking the rules, but I'll bet *they* don't get caught!

"Say, did you hear about Teddy Avenelo and Andria Kline?" she heard one girl say. "They broke up last night!"

"No!"

"Yeah, it's true," came the reply. "Teddy's got the

hots for some other girl, I think, but no one'll say who it is!"

They both giggled, and Gabrielle felt the back of her neck tingle. She sensed they were staring at her.

"Imagine a hunk like Teddy Avenelo going out with that bitch?" one girl said, nodding towards Gabrielle.

"Imagine *any* guy going out with her?"

"Maybe Harry Dickens."

The giggling became louder. Gabrielle knew Harry Dickens was the homeliest boy in the orphanage. He'd tried flirting with her, but even a guy as desperate as that turned against her after all the rumors. Gabrielle thought, *It would really make heads turn if someone did ask me out, somebody really nice.*

She sighed as she packed up the cleaning gear, for that was just wishful thinking.

When, Gabrielle had first come to the Macon Orphanage, seven years ago, she was so withdrawn that she would sit for hours with her thumb in her mouth, staring. Social workers who had spent time with her decided this was a natural reaction to separation from her mother, and felt she'd eventually break out of the shell. Since she never mentioned the murders, it was assumed she knew nothing of them. And so, Naomi's alleged crime was never discussed. Gabrielle and Kerry were sent to numerous foster homes, where they would live for several months at a time. Things seemed to be going well, until Gabrielle turned fifteen. Mrs. Macon had received word that Naomi had died in a fire— leaving Gabrielle and Kerry available for adoption. That was when the trouble began; foster parents began to report dead animals found in Gabrielle's rooms.

"I'm not a monster," Gabrielle whispered. "I didn't touch one of those animals. No matter what anyone says, Mrs. Macon!"

She pressed her cheek against the window near her bed and watched the children playing in the yard below. Today, six weeks after she'd left the West home, she was going to live with another family: the Brodys.

All Gabrielle knew was that they had a teenaged son named Keith and lived somewhere in the northern part of the state.

Somewhere in the building, a clock chimed the hour, telling Gabrielle it was time to go downstairs. She turned from the window, and in doing so nearly bumped into Mrs. Macon. With a gasp, she grabbed for her amulet and backed away.

"Don't act so frightened," Mrs. Macon said. "I've come here to have a talk with you."

She picked up Gabrielle's valise and handed it to her.

"The Brodys are waiting downstairs," she said. "But before you go with them, I want to make something perfectly clear. This is your last chance to find a home. If anything happens—if you so much as pull a cat's tail—I will not be held responsible. You'll be eighteen in a few months, and once that happens I'm no longer responsible for you. So, if you have any ideas about performing one of your wicked little stunts, just imagine what it will be like on your own. And Kerry won't be with you!"

"Yes, ma'am," Gabrielle said. "May I go downstairs now?"

"Please," Mrs. Macon said. "And I hope this is the last I see of you!"

Keith Brody turned his ten-speed around a sharp corner, and shifted up the gears so that he could easily climb the hill before him. Only one white package remained in the wire basket over his back wheel; his work as a drugstore delivery boy was almost over for the day. The climb made him sweat despite the chill of the February evening; at the crest of the hill he paused to run the sleeve of his down jacket across his forehead. As he did so, he noticed an unfamiliar black dog across the street. It seemed the animal was watching him. Its dark eyes followed his every move, making Keith feel a little uneasy. He didn't like dogs very much.

After delivering the last package, Keith walked to

his bike, shoving his hands into his pockets and tucking his chin into his scarf to fight the bitter wind. To his relief, he saw that the dog was gone. He mounted the ten-speed, turning it around to head for home. Thoughts of the upcoming night were on his mind as he pedalled down the town's main road. He planned to introduce Gabrielle to his friends at a film the community college was presenting. She'd been here a week, but had always refused his invitations. Still, Keith kept insisting, figuring she ought to be making some friends. Then he wouldn't be obligated to entertain her. He thought Gabrielle was very pretty, but he had not known her long enough to develop even brotherly affection.

He noticed the black dog again and, wondering how it came so far in such a short time, skirted carefully around it. Suddenly it stood up and ran in front of his bike. Keith swerved, but the dog kept with him.

"Look, pest," Keith yelled. "I don't want to play with you!"

But he saw now that the dog was not wagging its tail. It began to walk slowly towards him, its ears laid back, its jaws bared. Saliva dripped from its jowls, and a soft growl rumbled from its throat. Keith felt his heart begin to hammer as his phobia overtook him, and forced his legs to pedal faster.

In spite of his efforts, he lost control of the bike. There was no chance even to cry out as he flew over the handlebars, tumbling onto the hard ground. Darkness swirled around his head, purple twilight changed instantly to deep black night. Keith felt something touching him, but could not move in response. Tiny chilling beads of sweat broke out over his skin.

His body was flipped over, and he found himself staring up at a half dozen figures in black robes. His head felt light, his vision was blocked by a strange, filmy haze. Keith tried to raise a hand, but it was as if his fingers were frozen to the ground.

He wanted to cry out, to get up and run away, but he couldn't. The figures leaned down towards him, chanting something over and over, the monotonous tone of their words pulling Keith into an evil trance. Hands pressed against his head, shoulders, groin, knees, and feet. A pair of icy green eyes bore into his, cutting through to his subconscious, overpowering him.

Leave me al . . .

Even his thoughts were numbed.

The pressure increased over his body as the hands squeezed his flesh.

"You will help us," a voice said. "You will take Gabrielle tonight, and fill her with your seed so that the cycle may continue unbroken."

Keith's head was too heavy to shake. Unable to move or scream, he simply lay still, lost in a spell, slave to the strange powers that had suddenly overtaken him.

"Take Gabrielle . . . Take Gabrielle . . ."

Help me . . .

Without warning, the chanting stopped, the figures disappeared, and the sky turned violet-gray again. Keith found himself lying flat on his back, a dull pain in his head, with no memory of what had happened. With a groan, he sat up and rubbed his eyes.

"I must have fallen," he said, shaking his throbbing head. He stood up slowly. His bicycle was resting against a tree. The front wheel was still spinning; he couldn't have been out for very long.

He remounted and started for home, only thoughts of dinner on his mind.

Two

Every morning since her arrival, Gabrielle had to force herself out of bed. Not that it was particularly comfortable, but as long as she stayed tucked under its covers she wouldn't have to face another day.

She hated the fear that gnawed at her, fear that another dead animal would appear. As long as she kept her eyes closed, she could pretend all was well.

A week went by without incident, the longest trouble-free time since the horror began two years ago. Was it possible a new life was starting for her? A happy life? Gabrielle could almost begin to believe it. Just this morning, Keith had asked her to go with him to a film at his college. Gabrielle had been reluctant to accept. Not that she didn't like Keith. He was cute, and as nice as any boy she had ever known. Well, not that she knew very many boys. In the orphanage she had tried to be friendly to some of the guys. But they had never reciprocated, though Charlie Taylor had kissed her once. But then he had run away from her as if afraid. All the boys seemed afraid of her.

No, Gabrielle didn't want to go out with Keith because she was afraid to meet new people. But Mrs. Brody had been standing right there, and Gabrielle didn't want her new foster mother to think there was something wrong with her. She had said "yes," but had spent this whole day brooding about it.

Then, to her surprise, Keith had announced a change in plans; the film had been cancelled. They would have to make it another night. Gabrielle pretended to be disappointed, but was secretly grateful. Still, there was something funny about all this. Keith's tone of voice was all wrong throughout dinner, and worse than that he seemed to be staring at her every time she looked his way.

But, of course, she was being paranoid.

The Brodys had been invited out that evening, and after they left, Gabrielle and the boys settled down to watch some TV. Keith said very little, but on occasion Gabrielle would catch him watching her with a strange look in his eyes. She shared a loveseat with Kerry, somehow glad she wasn't alone with her foster brother. Though she knew she should be flattered by the attention, he made her nervous. But Kerry had had a busy day, and by ten o'clock he was fast asleep. Carefully, Gabrielle picked him up and carried him to his bed.

Keith was sitting in Kerry's place on the loveseat when she returned to the den. Gabrielle hesitated a moment in the doorway, then walked to the lounge chair.

"I don't bite," Keith said.

"I'm more comfortable over here," Gabrielle replied. She fixed her eyes on the TV screen.

"I thought your brother would never fall asleep," Keith said. "I've been waiting all day for this."

When Gabrielle didn't answer, Keith stood up and walked to her, reaching into his pocket to pull out a small golden box. He held it out to her, the light of the television playing on the white cuff of his shirt. Gabrielle looked at the box for a moment, her lips turned down. Finally, she shook her head.

"I can't take that," she said.

"You don't even know what it is," Keith replied. He pressed it into her hand. "Go on, open it."

It was a small golden ring set with three chip diamonds. Gabrielle looked at it for a moment, unable to speak. Was this a joke?

"I see doubt in your eyes," Keith said. "Don't be worried. My aunt willed that ring to me, to be given one day to the girl I love most. That girl is you, Gabrielle."

Before she could answer, he took the ring out and placed it on her finger.

"Someday," he whispered, "I'd like to replace that with an engagement ring."

"You're my foster brother," Gabrielle protested, her voice hardly audible over the muffler commercial that blasted on the TV.

"But I noticed you from the moment you came here," Keith said. "And I *knew* you were the one for me. I love you, Gabrielle. I love you and I want you."

Gabrielle's eyes stung, and her thick lashes glistened with tears. The idea that he might really care was almost too much for her. She'd often been told she didn't deserve to be loved, and yet here was Keith, tenderly kissing each of her fingers, telling her *he* loved her.

"Stand up," Keith said.

Slowly, Gabrielle rose from her seat, though every fiber of her being told her this was wrong. How could she let Keith love her when it was just a matter of time before she was sent away? Still, she didn't break away when he pulled her close to kiss her. His embrace was crushing, his neck warm as she rested her head on his shoulder. Just for the moment she would let herself believe this was really happening.

What Gabrielle didn't see was the sudden change in Keith's expression. Eyes that had been filled with rapture a second earlier were now dull and robot-like. There was no love there, only coldness, only an unprotesting obedience to a command that chanted over and over in Keith's mind.

Take Gabrielle . . . Take Gabrielle . . .

"Come upstairs," he said.

"My brother . . ."

"He's fast asleep," Keith replied.

"But your parents will be home soon," Gabrielle said. She was fighting a trembling that rose inside of her, trying to stop this. *It was wrong!*

"They won't be home until midnight," Keith said. "Gabrielle, let me show you how much I love you. I've been waiting all week for this chance!"

She couldn't fight it. All the years of rejection, all the need for love had built up a wave of desire in her that came crashing down now. Keith loved her. He wanted to marry her someday. And he had given her a ring to prove it.

Gabrielle knew a little of what she was expected to do. Several years earlier, when she had still been on speaking terms with the other girls, someone had smuggled a porno magazine into the dorm. The men and women were doing strange things with each other, and it had taken the adolescent girl a long time to understand their actions. Now, she herself was doing the same thing. And somehow, it didn't seem dirty any longer.

In the darkness of Keith's room, she undressed, her need to please him overpowering her shyness. Keith laid her down on his bed, crawling over her to kiss her face and neck.

Suddenly, the closet door flew open, banging hard against the wall. Gabrielle sat up with a gasp, but Keith simply laughed and pulled her down again.

"Just a draft," he said.

Gabrielle's heart went on pounding, but within a few minutes it was no longer from the scare she had gotten. Keith gave himself to her, grunting words of passion. It was beautiful. The act of love made her want to cry out for joy. Someone wanted her. *Keith* wanted her.

But Keith, lying next to her now on the rumpled sheets, had no such thoughts in his mind. He was staring into the dark void of the closet, meeting a pair of icy green eyes that seemed to float there. They stared at him for a long time, then vanished.

"Keith?"

He did not answer.

"Keith, are you awake?"

Gabrielle wanted to talk to him, to ask if she had done everything right. But Keith had fallen into a deep sleep. Gabrielle bit her lip and resisted an urge to wake him. After all that excitement, how could he be asleep now?

She decided finally that she would dress and head for her own room. Her foster parents were due home soon, and she didn't want to be in Keith's room when they came upstairs. The lovemaking would be their secret alone. . . .

As she was stooping to retrieve her clothes from the floor, the light flashed on. Gabrielle yelped and turned around, her robe and nightgown bunched in front of her. Her foster mother was standing in the doorway! Mrs. Brody's mouth dropped open, and she turned away.

"Oh—my—God," she stammered.

Mr. Brody came into his son's room as Keith sat up in bed with a loud moan.

"What the hell is going on in here?"

"We—we didn't know you'd be home so early!" Gabrielle choked.

"Obviously!" Mr. Brody yelled. He jerked his hand at her. "Get your damned clothes on and go to your room!"

Trembling, looking to Keith for support, Gabrielle did as she was told. Keith only stared at her, as if he didn't know what she was doing here. His passion of just minutes earlier was gone. Fighting tears of hurt and humiliation, Gabrielle ran from the room.

No one came to see her that night. But she could hear yelling down the hall—her foster parents demanding an explanation, Keith's insistence that *she* had seduced him. Tears streamed down Gabrielle's face as she whispered to herself that he was lying. But she didn't make any attempt to get up and defend herself. What good would that do?

"Well, she's not a fit daughter for this household!" Mrs. Brody snapped.

Gabrielle turned on her back. A fit daughter. Though she remembered very little about her mother, she was certain that she had been loved once. If only her mother were here now, to understand and comfort. Gabrielle rubbed her eyes, surprised at how often she thought of Naomi these days.

Clutching her amulet in a white-knuckled fist, she cried herself to sleep. Morning came all too soon, household noises permeating the thick blankets that covered her. Gabrielle tried to shut them out.

Something was dripping in her room. Gabrielle listened to the noise for a long time, letting it lull her back to sleep again. Even when she heard the door open, she didn't move.

"You might as well get up, young lady," Mrs. Brody said. "You have a lot of ex—"

The woman's sentence was cut off by a scream that made Gabrielle throw her covers aside. Mrs. Brody had her hand to her mouth, and she was pointing at something on Gabrielle's dresser.

It was a rat, big and black, its tail curled up over a small wooden jewelry box. Blood dripped onto the carpet from a gash in its throat. Its teeth were exposed in a snarl, and one eye stared unseeing.

"You monster!" Mrs. Brody gasped. "You sick, sick monster!"

"I didn't do that!" Gabrielle cried.

Mrs. Brody only shook her head and ran from the room. Gabrielle fought the revulsion in her stomach and got out of bed, crossing the room to the dresser. Just like all the other times, she found a skull-and-snakes symbol painted on the mirror in the dead animal's blood. It encircled the reflection of her distraught face.

Suddenly, Gabrielle herself began screaming, more in anger than in fright.

"NNNNOOOO!!!!!"

With a cry, she leaned over the dresser and rubbed hard at the dried blood with her fist.

"I'm not a monster," she whimpered. "I'm not. . . ."

Three

Gabrielle put her arm around her brother as they sat in the back of Mr. Brody's car, heading back to the orphanage. Keith had watched them go, his hands shoved into the pockets of his down jacket as he stood in the driveway. Gabrielle felt a chill realizing she had believed his lies. The love she had thought she'd seen the night before was gone in the light of morning, replaced with cool indifference. Keith hadn't even flinched when she took the ring and threw it at him. This wasn't the kind of love she saw in the movies and on TV. Was it her fault? What was wrong with her?

Kerry kept silent all the while. He wouldn't tell his sister how disappointed he was. This home had been the nicest of all, and now they had to leave because the Brodys said Gabrielle did a bad thing. Kerry wondered why people were always saying mean things about his sister. She was always really nice to him. But then again, he had lost count of the foster homes he had been sent away from on account of Gabrielle. He wasn't sure if he would ever be adopted.

Still, he clung to Gabrielle as the only constant thing he knew. She was the only family he had in the world, and for that reason Kerry was able to believe in her innocence. Someone else was doing all these terrible things, of course. He wriggled closer to her and put his head on her lap to fall asleep. Absently, Gabrielle stroked his hair, hating herself for having once again ruined things for him. She wondered how much longer he'd go on loving her.

When at last they arrived at the orphanage, Brody took Gabrielle by the wrist and pulled her out, bringing a groggy protest from Kerry.

They waited outside Mrs. Macon's office as Mr. Brody launched into a loud and angry description of what Gabrielle had done. In reply, Mrs. Macon's tone was so even that Gabrielle couldn't make out what she was saying. Suddenly, the door to the office swung open, and Mr. Brody stormed down the hallway. Gabrielle's stomach knotted, and her heart pounded as she waited for Mrs. Macon to call her.

But minutes ticked by with agonizing slowness, and nothing happened. Why was Mrs. Macon waiting?

Kerry flung his arms at the door.

"Aww, forget her," he said. "Let's just go upstairs and unpack."

"What if she's waiting for me?"

"So, she'll come find you!" Kerry cried, his gray eyes rounding. "Come on, let's go upstairs."

Gabrielle decided it was the right thing to do.

There were two girls in the dorm when she entered, one of whom she didn't recognize. She walked to her bed without a word and placed her valise on the mattress. As she unpacked, she tried to ignore what they were saying.

"That's the bitch I was telling you about," one of them said.

"She's creepy, all right," said the second girl.

"Positively gross!" the first replied. "I'll bet she's got a chopped-up cat in that suitcase!"

Her friend giggled. "Just waiting to eat it for dinner!"

The two girls put their arms around each other and headed towards the door.

"Let's hurry," one said. "Everyone's waiting for us to go to that new Harrison Ford movie!"

Gabrielle turned to carry her only dress to the closet, hiding her tears. It bothered her to know she would not be invited to join the others. She knew she should be hardened to it by now, but it still hurt. If only they would listen to her, and believe that she was innocent! If only she could have some friends, too.

Her trembling hand found the amulet.

For some reason, Mrs. Macon did not say a word to her. That worried Gabrielle more than any threat, for she had no idea what the woman was planning. Kerry, in his usual brazen way, eavesdropped at her door, but could learn nothing. Finally, he decided everything was okay. Mrs. Macon had not said anything about separating them, and to the seven-year-old that was all that mattered.

Winter turned into spring, and Gabrielle saw many of the other children adopted or placed in foster homes. There were numerous people who looked in Gabrielle and Kerry's direction, commenting on their good looks. But nothing ever came of their attentions. Gabrielle quickly came to realize she and her brother would not soon be adopted.

But that was fine with Gabrielle. Maybe Mrs.

Macon thought ignoring her was a form of punishment, but Gabrielle found peace in being left alone. She started thinking about her future, that she'd soon be eighteen, and decided she'd try to earn money so that she could get Kerry out of this place. They would live together, and everything would be fine.

Just before dawn one April morning, Gabrielle was awakened by a sharp stomach pain. She couldn't help groaning, and her voice seemed very loud in the room. But the others girls did not stir.

I could scream "fire" and they'd ignore me, Gabrielle thought.

She tried to sit up a little, but a sudden dizziness overcame her. The walls seemed to waver before her eyes, the other beds floated like apparitions in the light that seeped through a rip in the old yellowed shade.

Gabrielle pulled her knees up to her chest. Maybe, if she let herself fall asleep again, she'd wake up later and feel fine. But the pain only worsened, until it was all she could do not to cry out. Suddenly, she felt as if her insides had leaped up a few inches. She barely made it to the lavatory in time to be violently ill. But she felt tremendously better, and by the time she returned to her room she was drowsy enough to fall asleep.

When she woke up, the pain was completely gone. She headed for breakfast, passing groups hanging out in the halls. Gabrielle guessed she'd just had a bug of some sort, but as soon as she saw the carefully-portioned trays of breakfast food she felt something rise in her.

"Is something wrong, dear?" the woman behind the counter asked as she filled a plate with a hefty serving of scrambled eggs.

Gabrielle shook her head abruptly, and turned to run to the nearest bathroom.

After being sick, she limped over to the mirror, clutching her stomach.

"What is wrong with me?" she asked her reflection.

Her skin, usually delicately fair, was so pale now that she was sure she could see the contours of her skull. Dark circles ringed her eyes, and though she'd just washed her hair that morning, it looked dull and lifeless. She felt trembly all over, but for the moment her stomach had settled.

Fresh air—that was what she needed. It was a beautiful day. Forgetting breakfast completely, she hurried from the building. Under the April sun, the woodlands surrounding the orphanage were filled with buds that carried a fresh, sweet scent. Passing the gardener Gabrielle strolled towards the trees, thinking how much she loved nature. It never judged, never ridiculed. It allowed everyone, even a lonely young girl, to enjoy its beauty.

A path marked by a long-dried-up creek twisted through the trees, littered here and there with old branches and pine cones. Gabrielle followed it, listening to the light song of birds. She was glad she'd come outside, because she felt a lot better. But her thoughts came too soon, for when she bent to pick a flower a new wave of nausea rushed over her. She straightened up slowly and closed her eyes, waiting for the feeling to pass.

When she opened her eyes again, she noticed a woman standing just a few yards away. She wore dark glasses and had covered her hair with a kerchief. Gabrielle frowned at her, wondering what she was doing here. But before she could speak, she suddenly felt dizzy. In a moment she hit the ground, unconscious.

As she fell the amulet slipped from her neck and dropped into the weeds. The woman pulled off her glasses to reveal a pair of green cat's eyes and started walking towards Gabrielle's body, a smug expression on her face. She kicked at the amulet, sending it flying into the trees.

There was a scent of pine in the air. Gabrielle turned her head to one side, but did not open her eyes. She had passed out in the woods, and the aroma of the trees had brought her to her senses. Slowly though, she came to realize there was something light and cool on top of her. She opened her eyes and saw her pale reflection in the polished metal side of a nightstand. She was in the infirmary, under the light blanket and the pine scent was disinfectant.

"Hello," a friendly voice said. Gabrielle turned and recognized Dr. Grolier. "You really shouldn't wander through the woods in your condition. Fresh air is fine, but not when you're going to go passing out on the damp ground."

He shook down a thermometer, then placed it in her mouth.

"I'm going to keep you here a few days," he said. "If, for anything, to make sure your baby's okay."

Gabrielle shook her head.

"Baby?"

The doctor looked at her.

"You're pregnant, Gabrielle," he said. He watched her eyes go round. "You didn't know, did you?"

Gabrielle straightened herself and pulled the thermometer from her mouth.

"No, I'm not pregnant," she said.

"As a matter of fact," Dr. Grolier said, "you're in your second month. Your baby is due some time in October. Didn't you notice when you skipped your last menstrual cycle?"

"I—I had a lot on my mind," Gabrielle whispered.

She felt a numb sensation rush over her as the doctor replaced the thermometer. *Pregnant*. The word echoed over and over in her mind. She was pregnant? She, who had never even gone steady? But that was impossible! She only did it once with Keith, and everyone knew you couldn't make a baby the first time. The other girls had said so! No, the doctor had made a mistake. It had to be a mistake!

"Hey, don't worry," Dr. Grolier said. "We'll take good care of you."

Gabrielle didn't want his consolation. He was a stranger to her. She wanted her brother Kerry—but Kerry wouldn't be able to help her. He was barely a baby himself! If only her mother were here. . . .

Rocking herself, she reached through the opening in the front of her nightgown for the amulet.

It wasn't there.

Opening her eyes, Gabrielle said in a choked voice:

"Where's my necklace?"

"Necklace?"

"My gold and silver necklace," Gabrielle explained. "Where is it?"

"I'm sorry, dear," the doctor said. "But you weren't wearing any such necklace when the gardener brought you here."

"Yes, I was!" Gabrielle cried.

Panic filled her as she searched the bed, hoping it had just slipped off while she was sleeping. For the moment, the worry about her pregnancy was overshadowed by a feeling of raw dread. She needed that amulet! She had to have it!

"It's not here!"

"I'm sure someone will . . ."

"You don't understand," Gabrielle said. "I have to have it! Terrible things will happen if I don't!"

Tears spilled over her sculpted cheekbones. Now Dr. Grolier put a hand on her shoulder to steady her.

"Easy!" he cried. "You're in no condition for hysteria!"

"I have to have my necklace!" Gabrielle blubbered. *"Please!"*

"All right," the doctor said, standing up. "But it's obviously not here, is it? Now, you lay back down and try to get some sleep, and I'll go out and look for it. Okay?"

Unable to do anything else, Gabrielle nodded in agreement. Dr. Grolier shook his head, feeling sorry for her. These poor kids were always getting messed up. It made him glad he had had two parents while he was growing up.

Well, the least he could do was try to find the necklace. But the amulet had mysteriously vanished. Dr. Grolier couldn't figure out why Gabrielle had wanted it so badly. Was it a family heirloom? Something from her past, to remember her parents by? No, he remembered that she said terrible things would happen if she didn't have it.

She'd just been hysterical, of course. Still, he couldn't afford another display of emotion like before. It wasn't safe. So he decided to soften the blow of his news by letting her little brother Kerry come visit her. He hoped the child's presence would help.

Gabrielle seemed delighted to see her brother the next morning. Dressed in jeans and a bright green sweat shirt, he ran to jump on his sister's bed. Dr. Grolier didn't stop him, even when Kerry threw his arms roughly around her and gave her a big kiss.

"Gosh, I missed you," he said. "I kept feeling like you needed me. I wanted to see you so bad, but no one would let me!"

"I've been very sick," Gabrielle said.

Kerry frowned.

"Why are you sick, Gabrielle?"

The young girl hesitated a moment, looking up at Dr. Grolier. He nodded his head slightly.

"Kerry," she said. "I'm going to have a baby."

"You are?" Kerry asked, wrinkling his nose. "But Gabrielle, you aren't married. You have to be married to have a baby."

"No, you don't," Gabrielle said. "Kerry, I'll explain it to you someday, but you're too little to understand now. Just trust me."

Kerry shrugged, quickly losing interest in the topic. He began to tell his sister all that happened the previous day, beginning with his latest project in arts and crafts and finally telling her how hard Dr. Grolier had been searching for her necklace. Gabrielle turned to him.

"Did you find it yet?"

"I'm afraid not, dear."

"Someone stole it, I bet," Kerry growled.

Gabrielle sighed and laid her head back down on her pillow, losing the happy glow that had been on her face just a moment earlier. The amulet had been a part of her since she was a little girl, and she felt empty without it. How could it have just disappeared?

But she'd spent the night thinking about it, and had tried to steel herself for the possibility it was really gone. Now she ran those same thoughts through her head once more: maybe there was no use in brooding about it; her mother had said terrible things would happen if she lost it, but things weren't so great now. Maybe it was a good omen, a sign that things would change.

"I—I guess I'll be okay," she whispered.

"Of course you will be," Dr. Grolier assured her. "You just wait and see. Everything will be all right."

The very next day, something happened that made Gabrielle believe this might be true. She was released from the infirmary, and as she was changing into fresh clothes in her room, Mrs. Macon entered. She stopped and stared at her.

I should have known it would happen, she thought. *I should have known a pretty young girl like that would get herself in trouble! Just like that little tramp my husband . . .*

She cut that thought off.

Well, her mind continued, *at least I have a chance to get rid of her now.*

Gabrielle knew the old woman had been told of her pregnancy, and wondered what she'd say now. But even a lecture would not have shocked her as much as these words:

"Put on your dress, girl. There's someone downstairs who wants to adopt you."

Four

When Gabrielle entered Mrs. Macon's office, she saw a woman standing near the window, looking out at the grounds. Her heart beat with anticipation, for she could not imagine who'd want to take her in. She must be a very kind person, since Mrs. Macon said she insisted Gabrielle's condition didn't matter. Wanting to know her, Gabrielle said:

"Hello?"

The woman turned around, smiling. She seemed to be in her mid-thirties, with white-streaked brown hair and green cat's eyes. She was tall, a stunning figure. Her black dress was accented with gold jewelry that glittered brightly, even in the dim office light.

"This is Flora Collins," Mrs. Macon said.

"Hello, Mrs. Collins," Gabrielle said, uncertainly.

"Good afternoon, my dear," Flora said, a slight British accent to her voice. Her smile broadened. "My, but you do look like your mother."

"I do?" Gabrielle's heart fluttered. "You knew my mother?"

"Yes," Flora said. "I went to school with Naomi— with your mother. She was very dear to me, but we parted company when you were very small. I heard nothing from her for years, and only through mutual acquaintances did I learn that you had lost her."

Gabrielle brought her hand to her mouth, rubbing her lips. She could hardly believe she was talking to someone who had known her mother. Someone who might be able to tell her the truth about Naomi.

"Do you—do you know what happened to her?"

"Hansen!" Mrs. Macon cried, slapping the top of her desk.

Flora waved a hand at her, the gold bangles along her wrist jingling melodically.

"It's perfectly all right," she said. "But, my dear Gabrielle, I'm afraid I know very little of your mother's story. You see, I've been in Europe for quite a number of years. When I returned, I decided to look up my old friends. Imagine my horror to learn that dear, sweet Naomi had died!"

Gabrielle waited for her to continue.

"Now," Flora said, "I made it my business to find you, and I'm delighted to say Mrs. Macon has given me permission to take you home."

Flora studied Gabrielle, looking for some sort of reaction. She hardly expected the girl to throw her arms around her in gratitude, yet there wasn't even a hint of emotion. Gabrielle was deep in thought, wondering why a total stranger would suddenly show up to adopt her after all these years. Especially under the circumstances! It was almost as if Flora was heaven-sent. Confused, Gabrielle looked at Mrs. Macon.

The old woman looked smug, glad she would be getting rid of Gabrielle once and for all. She and Mrs. Collins had made arrangements privately, so that the woman wouldn't have to bother with the papers and interviews that took months to complete. Mrs. Macon just wanted Gabrielle out of here.

"I see you're confused," Flora said. "But there's no need. I'm simply doing what I feel is right, and wish that I had come back to the States sooner!"

"But—but won't I be trouble for you?" Gabrielle asked, finding this all too hard to believe.

Flora held up a hand, and Gabrielle noticed she had a ring on every finger.

"Hush!" she said. "You'll be no trouble at all. I live on a huge farm, where you'll have your own room and all the privacy a young girl needs."

Gabrielle smiled for the first time.

"A farm? Kerry will love that!"

"Kerry?" Flora echoed, looking at Mrs. Macon.

"Kerwin Hansen is Gabrielle's seven-year-old brother," Mrs. Macon explained. "He was an infant when they were brought here."

Flora's expression turned sad, and there was remorse in her voice when she said:

"I didn't realize you had a brother. I'm afraid I simply can't take him in. My house has only one spare room."

"We'll share it," Gabrielle said quickly.

Flora shook her head.

"Then I won't go," Gabrielle said. "My brother is more important to me than *any* home."

Mrs. Macon's eyes grew cold behind the thick lenses of her glasses. When she spoke, her voice was grim.

"Gabrielle, you will go with Mrs. Collins," she said. "Remember, you're still a minor, and have no say here. You will do as you are told and that is final!"

"But my brother..."

"Are you arguing with me, young lady?"

Gabrielle shook her head and clenched her teeth to fight tears of disappointment. Tears would not move that old bitch. But now Flora put a hand on her arm and said:

"Maybe we can arrange something. You come with me tonight, and we'll see about getting your brother to my farm as soon as we can."

Gabrielle looked at her.

"He's really a good kid," she said. "He wouldn't be any trouble at all."

"I'm sure," Flora said. "But I'll have to go through some procedures, and I'll have to rearrange the sleeping quarters at my house to accommodate him. That will take some time."

Gabrielle considered this, then realized there was no use in arguing. Mrs. Macon was right—as a minor, she had to do as she was told.

"I think I'll go upstairs and tell my brother the

news," she said, her voice softened by the numbness she felt after such a quick turn of events in her life.

"I don't want you to go!"

"Kerry, please listen to me..."

"You're my sister and we're supposeta stay together!" Kerry wailed, snatching a stuffed raccoon from his bed to fling it across the room. "My birthday's comin' up and I want you to be here! You can't go!"

"Kerry, it's only for a while," Gabrielle said. "Mrs. Collins's going to arrange to adopt you, too!"

When Kerry just stood there pouting, Gabrielle tried harder.

"Mrs. Collins knew our mother," she said. "There are so many things she could tell me about her."

"I don't care about our mother," Kerry said. "She went and died and left us alone!"

Before she could stop herself, Gabrielle swung her hand out and slapped the little boy's cheek. He stared at her in disbelief, then burst into tears. Gabrielle was shocked too, and felt immediate remorse.

"Oh, Kerry!" she cried, pulling him to her. "Oh, Kerry, I'm sorry! I didn't mean to do that!"

"You did!" Kerry yelled. "You're mean and rotten like everyone says and I hate you!"

"Kerry!"

He jerked away and jumped from his bed, running across the room to retrieve his toy raccoon. He turned to Gabrielle, his face reddened and wet with tears. Clinging tightly to the animal, he said:

"Go ahead an' go to Kansas!"

"I have no other choice," Gabrielle said sadly.

"Yes, you do!" Kerry said. "You coulda been nicer! You didn't have to kill those animals like you did. The Brodys were real nice, and so were the Wests and the Macrays and those other people. And *they* wanted both of us!"

Gabrielle backed towards the door, shaking her head. It wasn't her brother speaking! Kerry had never believed she was guilty of those horrible things! He was just upset and frightened!

"Kerry, I love you," she said. "We'll be together soon, I promise."

"Go away."

Not knowing what else to do, Gabrielle lifted her bag from the floor, opened the door, and left the room. By the time she reached the top of the stairs, Kerry was running up behind her.

"Gabrielle!"

She stopped, put the suitcase down, and opened her arms to him. As she held him close, Kerry squeezed her tightly and said:

"I didn't mean all that stuff. I love you too, Gabrielle."

"I know you didn't mean it," the young girl said. "You're just scared."

"Am not!" Kerry cried.

"Sure," Gabrielle obliged. "Listen, I really wish you could come with me. I wish this wasn't happening so fast. But Flora Collins is the last chance I have to find a real home. And she'll take you in as soon as she can."

"I just hope they hurry up," Kerry said.

"So do I, Kerry," Gabrielle replied, kissing him again.

The sound of Mrs. Macon calling her downstairs forced Gabrielle to let go of her brother. She smiled bravely for him, then hurried down to the main floor. Kerry watched her go, trying to believe Kansas wasn't really that far away.

As she sat in the back of Flora's car, Gabrielle tried to straighten out her emotions, to make herself feel more sure of what she was doing. Flora seemed very nice, and yet Gabrielle still couldn't believe anyone would want to bother with her. She already missed Kerry. Whatever sunshine there was in her life came from him; and now they were going to be separated.

Through her tears, the passing countryside became one long blur of mountains and wheat fields and lakes.

Flora sat staring straight ahead, seeming as oblivious to the scenery as Gabrielle. Once in a while, she'd lean forward with an instruction for her chauffeur.

"This is all very surprising to you, isn't it, my dear?" she asked, after a long silence.

"Yes, ma'am," Gabrielle said, not turning from the window.

Flora touched her shoulder.

"My, but you are a polite young lady, aren't you?" she said. "Darling, I would prefer to have you call me 'Flora.'"

Gabrielle nodded.

"You're just like your mother," Flora said. "She was well-mannered, too."

"She was?"

"Oh, by all means," Flora insisted. "The very personification of etiquette."

Not a monster, Gabrielle thought.

"Tell me about my mother," she said.

"Oh, now," Flora replied, "there's plenty of time for that. Right now, I'd like you to try to take a nap. We have a long ride ahead of us."

"I'm not tired, Flora."

The woman held up a bejewelled hand.

"Please, my dear," she said. "Do as I tell you."

Suddenly Gabrielle realized she *did* feel tired. With a sigh, she slid down on the seat and rested her head in her arm. In moments, she was asleep. Flora watched her carefully, with a slight smile on her face.

It was nearly dusk when the black car swung onto a dirt road, and covered the half mile to the house. Gabrielle was startled awake by the car's bumping and pitching, and felt slightly disoriented when she sat up to look around.

"This is your new home," Flora announced.

In the distance, a cow let out a long, low moo. Gabrielle looked in its direction, trying to find a barn, but she could not see beyond the cluster of apple trees that hugged the corner of Flora's house. Their white blossoms took on a silvery quality in the twilight, and seemed to shimmer.

She followed her new mother into a brightly lit foyer that smelled faintly of lavender. Sprigs of the purple flowers burst up from a white vase that sat in the corner of the room, adding a pretty touch to an otherwise dull entrance. Stairs led to a darkened second floor. She followed Flora into the living room.

"This house has been in my family for many generations," Flora said. "I find it quite cozy, and hope you will, too."

Gabrielle stood near the doors and took in the room's details. Dark wooden beams accented white stucco walls; there was massive furniture of leather and wood. Three arched windows let moonlight flow into the room, casting a glow on the brass screen covering a huge fireplace. Gabrielle suddenly noticed the animal's skull that hung over it.

"Oh!" she exclaimed, startled.

"My grandfather found that many years ago," Flora explained. "It's quite fascinating, don't you think?"

Gabrielle, who knew all too well about dead animals, thought it was hideous. But she nodded in an effort to make Flora happy. After all, the woman had been very kind to her, for no apparent reason other than having been a friend to Naomi. It was only right for Gabrielle to be polite.

"Come, my dear," Flora said. "I'll show you the rest of the house."

None of the rooms made much of an impression on Gabrielle, and they were quickly forgotten once she reached the huge kitchen at the back of the house. When Flora turned on the chandelier, the light seemed to bounce off the white porcelain tile walls, making the room look bright and cheerful. It was bisected with a peninsula-style counter, into which a stove and a sink had been built. To one side, there was a long wooden table, and to the other an oven, a refrigerator, and other appliances. A round copper ring held pots and

pans and utensils over the counter. A border of painted
blue flowers ran around the rim of the ceiling.

"This is really nice," Gabrielle exclaimed.

"Yes, I enjoy working in here," Flora answered. "I
have plenty of counter space, as you can see."

Gabrielle thought of the diner, with its hanging
utensils and gleaming counters, but the memory quickly
dissolved away. She wouldn't let herself dwell on that
tonight, not at the start of what could be (what *had*
to be) a happy new life.

Gabrielle was surprised to find a back staircase to
the house. Flora explained that this was used by her
farmhands, whom Gabrielle would meet in the morning.

"Your bedroom is at the end of the hall," Flora
said.

Gabrielle followed her, but stopped when she noticed
a shorter hall branching from the main one. There was
only one door at its end, and in the yellowish light
Gabrielle could just barely see that it was somehow
decorated. She took a few steps towards it, so intent
that she nearly screamed when Flora called her name.

"Please don't go in there," Flora said. "It's my
room, and I'll show it to you in the future. But right
now it's being painted, and as you know, paint fumes
are dangerous to women in your condition."

"I didn't know that," Gabrielle said, exiting from
the little hall. "There are a lot of things I don't understand about having a baby. Am I going to talk to a
doctor about it?"

Flora stopped.

"Well, yes, of course," she said, a faint hint of
uncertainty in her voice. "Yes, but why don't you give
yourself time to settle in here first?"

"Okay," Gabrielle said.

"Now, let's see your room, my dear."

It was bigger than anything Gabrielle had ever
seen, even the dorm. Cream-colored carpeting warmed
the wooden floor, and large pieces of hickory furniture
were set against the walls. The fourposter bed had a

pale green and white coverlet on it, to match the
pillows that were arranged on a loveseat near a tall
window. Gabrielle was too amazed to say a word as she
walked inside. A dressing table mirror caught her reflection, and she tried to get rid of the look of childish
awe on her face. She then noticed a silver brush and
mirror.

"Those are so pretty. May I really use them?" she
said.

"I put them there for you," Flora told her.

Gabrielle looked at her, then picked up the brush,
running a slender finger around the beaded design of
its edge. The surface was etched in a Florentine finish,
and the handle was delicately grooved.

"I've never seen anything like this," Gabrielle said.
"They must be very old."

"Antiques," Flora said. "They've been in my family
for generations."

Gabrielle managed a smile, and thanked Flora for
the gift. It made her feel good that Flora cared enough
to give her something so valuable. She began to run the
brush through her dark hair. Suddenly, her reflection
seemed to waver, to take on a smoky quality. A dizziness overcame her, and the brush dropped to the floor.

"Is something wrong, my dear?"

"I—I don't know," Gabrielle said. "I just felt a little
weird right then."

Flora looked at her watch.

"Well, no wonder! It's dinner time, and you must
be hungry. Come, let's go back to the kitchen."

Gabrielle left the room with her, quickly forgetting
the hairbrush that laid on her rug.

London, October, 1843

Blythe Crest's face was wet with tears as she stared
into her vanity mirror, brushing her long curls. Her
hand moved in a jerking motion, clutching the beaded
silver brush until her knuckles were white. Her husband Calvin had given it to her on their wedding day,
declaring someone so beautiful deserved a beautiful

gift. Recalling the day, Blythe began to cry again. She pulled the brush away from her hair and rubbed the smooth back over her swollen middle.

In her body, a nine-month fetus stirred as if it sensed her melancholy. Blythe set the brush down, then pressed her hands on the moire satin of her buff-colored gown. What was the use of brushing her hair? She hadn't been out of the house since early summer. Although the bell-shaped skirts that were in fashion served to camouflage any change in a body's shape, pregnant ladies were still not expected to be seen in public.

Like freaks and lepers, Blythe thought. But she *did* look strange, with her huge stomach and brown-patched face. Blythe thought being pregnant made her look ugly. Calvin insisted she was the most beautiful woman in London.

But Calvin had been missing for three days. He had said good-bye as usual and had headed to his shop near Baker Street, and he had never returned. Blythe asked the local constable to look for him, but there was no trace at all of her husband.

Feeling cold suddenly, Blythe stood up and crossed the room to be nearer the fire she'd built. A tear rose in her eye to realize it was the first time she'd performed that chore herself. Calvin was always the one who saw to it that the fire kept burning.

It was dark outside, and through an opened shutter Blythe could see the light of a gas lamp playing in a cloud of fog. A dark figure appeared through the mist, approaching her house, smoking a fat, curling pipe. Calvin always loved pipes. . . .

Her heart racing, Blythe hurried towards the door. She stopped just short of it, touching the curls she had so viciously brushed a few moments earlier. Her elation at knowing Calvin was home at last overshadowed the fear and anger she'd felt over the past days.

Someone knocked at the door, and Blythe dropped her arms with a weary sigh. It wasn't Calvin, after all. "Yes?"

"Mrs. Crest?"

"Yes, I am Mrs. Crest."

"It's Constable Wallaby, Mrs. Crest. Might I come in?"

Knitting her brows, Blythe slowly opened the door. A portly man with shaggy Dundreary whiskers and a blue frock coat walked into the house. He had extinguished his pipe, and now he rubbed his nose with it as he shifted back and forth on his small feet.

"Constable, have you found anything?"

"Bad news, I'm afraid," Wallaby said. He glanced at Blythe's stomach, but was not embarrassed by it. The father of twelve children, he knew all about pregnancy. And he could easily have called sixteen-year-old Blythe one of his own.

"Please, tell me directly," she ordered.

"We found your husband," he said in a quiet tone.

"Calvin? Where is he?"

Wallaby shook his head.

"He—he was floating in the Thames, Mrs. Crest. In a bloody awful state, too. We think some animal must have gotten to him."

Blythe's eyes rounded, and she covered her mouth as she backed away. Too shocked to scream, she stumbled towards her bedroom, where she found the silver brush. Holding it to her face, she said:

"Not my Calvin. Please, not him!"

"I'm afraid . . ."

Blythe dropped the brush, squeezing her eyes shut. Wallaby stared, frozen, as the color drained from the young girl's face. She threw her arms around herself and collapsed to the floor.

"My baby," she choked. "Oh, my Lord, the baby!"

Constable Wallaby gazed down at her, his expression suddenly cold. He made no move to help her, although Blythe reached up with a trembling hand to grab his coat. Her eyes were wild, and tears wetted her cheeks.

"Please help me!"

The front door opened suddenly, and a woman

with a large basket entered. She walked into the bedroom, where she stood at the constable's side and watched Blythe with a grim expression on her face. The girl, overcome by the shock of Wallaby's news, had gone into labor.

"The time has come," the woman said to the constable.

Blythe cringed at the sight of her.

"You!" she cried. "Why are you here?"

The woman simply laughed as Blythe tried to pull herself to her feet. She had to run away. She had to get help! This woman was insane! She had been following Blythe ever since the pregnancy began, even lurking outside the house. What could she want?

As the constable lifted her, Blythe screamed and lashed out with all her might. Her fingers caught the fluff of his whiskers, and she pulled hard. But Wallaby didn't even flinch. He carried her to the bed.

"Constable, please," Blythe whimpered. "Please make her go away. She wants to hurt me! She wants my—OH GOD!"

A sharp pain took hold of her body, travelling through her abdomen and into her thighs. She grabbed at the constable, scratching his arm and drawing blood.

"Be still!" the strange woman ordered.

Blythe thought to run away again, but the pain of her sudden labor became too great. She writhed on the bed, screaming, as another contraction pulled at her. She wondered why no one came to her aid. There were so many people on this street. Didn't they hear her?

She suddenly felt her legs being tugged apart, and the feel of scratchy wool at her ankles. To her shock, Blythe realized the woman was tying her ankles to the bed posts!

"NNNNNOOOO!!!!!"

"Silence!"

This had to be a horrible nightmare. Blythe told herself again and again that she would wake up, and that Calvin would be at her side. But the nightmare lasted for hours, and though Blythe screamed until her throat burned no one came to her rescue. Where were all her friends? Where was Calvin?

Delirium made her haad swim, and the room seemed to turn to water. From somewhere far away, a woman said:

"I've got the shoulders."

Seconds later, there were slapping sounds, and the strong cry of a healthy baby. Blythe, panting from the effort of the birth, looked up to see a boy dangling from the woman's fist. The dark curls surrounding his wrinkled face glistened wetly, and he swung himself as if in anger.

"Give him to me," Blythe ordered. "Give me my baby!"

The woman turned and stared at her with pale green eyes, freezing Blythe to her very soul. She cried out, then fell back onto her pillows, unconscious.

The woman carried the baby to the foyer, where she placed him in the large basket. Then, as an afterthought, she grabbed the silver brush and mirror, placing these next to the squawling infant. Hooking it over her arm, she turned to Wallaby.

"You did well," she said. "When she awakens, you will tell her that the baby died. She will remember nothing of me."

The constable nodded his head slowly, his mind in the power of this strange, evil woman. He would obey without question. Blythe would never know that her healthy, normal baby had been kidnapped.

Gabrielle came out of a nightmare with a soft scream, throwing her blankets aside. The room was illuminated by the moon outside her window, and the robe that hung on the back of her door looked like some sort of demon. She pulled her knees up under her chin and rocked herself until her heart slowed down. It had been a strange dream—something to do with the silver brush and a screaming woman. But Gabrielle could not recall any more of it.

"You're just nervous because it's your first night here," she told herself. "You'll be okay."

There was a small clock on the dressing table; it read 1:03. Unable to relax, Gabrielle got out of the bed and walked towards her window, beckoned by the glow of the moon. The yard behind the big house stretched as far as Gabrielle could see, and seemed eerily surrealistic with its light and shadows. An empty animal pen sat next to the barn, and in front of this someone had parked a large tractor. She suddenly heard a strange shuffling noise, like something being dragged over the dirt.

A black shape emerged from behind the tractor. It was a young man, tugging hard at something Gabrielle couldn't see. Curious, she watched him for a moment, just barely able to hear his grunts through the closed window.

Finally, he managed to budge the mysterious object. He pulled it out from behind the tractor and dragged it towards the barn. It was huge, black and cumbersome. Gabrielle couldn't make out exactly what it was, though she could clearly see the impression it left behind in the dirt. She watched, fascinated, her hand twisting the front of her nightgown as if the amulet were still there.

The boy below suddenly stopped, and looked straight up at her window. Gabrielle saw the features of a young man with dark, curly hair. Startled that she had been caught spying, she turned away from the window.

But after a moment, she couldn't resist looking again. The backyard was empty. Gabrielle frowned, and tried to find some evidence of the scene she had just witnessed. But there was nothing. No marks in the dirt, no footprints.

Wearily, she shuffled back to her bed. Tears filled her violet eyes, and for some reason she felt more alone at the moment than ever before.

Five

An ear-piercing shriek jerked Gabrielle from a deep sleep. Her heart pounded as she turned towards the window, only to see the sky was still dark. The noise came again, and this time Gabrielle realized it was a rooster. She pulled her covers over her head and asked softly if the animal knew what time it was.

But a few moments later, she could hear doors opening and footsteps hurrying along the hallway. Running water rushed through the pipes behind her in the wall, electric razors whirred into action, and somewhere a hanger squeaked across a wooden rack. With a groan, Gabrielle lifted herself up and tried to read the clock across the room. Could it really be only 5:15 a.m.? Gabrielle couldn't believe the others were up so early. As for herself, she would sleep for another few hours. . . .

Suddenly, she threw her covers aside and jumped from the bed, hurrying to switch on the light. To her relief, there were no dead animals in her bed, no skull-and-snakes drawn on her mirror. Her first night at Flora's home had passed uneventfully. But as Gabrielle climbed back into bed, she remembered the scene in the backyard. With thoughts of asking Flora about the young man, she fell back asleep.

It was 8:20 when she woke up again, lured from her sleep by the smell of cooking food. Gabrielle climbed from the bed and went to retrieve her robe from the back of the door; it would be a good idea to share breakfast with the others. The more she did to be friendly, the better her chances to stay here would be.

She took the back staircase down to the kitchen, tightening the belt on the worn flannel robe as she walked. Unsure of how to introduce herself, she stood at the threshold of the kitchen for a few minutes. A group of men—the farmhands—sat along the wooden table. Flora, wearing a red and white check apron, was working with a griddle of pancakes. She lifted it up in her bare hand and carried it to the table.

In her bare hand . . .

"Oh!"

Flora turned around, and the farmhands stopped talking.

"Well, good morning," the woman said cheerfully. "Did you sleep well?"

"I—I . . ." Gabrielle did not know what to say. She watched Flora set the griddle down on the stove again and noticed she *was* using a pot holder. She relaxed immediately.

"I slept all right," she said, not moving from the doorway.

The farmhands, some eleven of them, returned her gaze without expression. They all seemed to be older than Flora, and not one resembled the young man with dark curls whom Gabrielle had seen the night before. Gabrielle hoped she would see him later. She wanted to ask him what he had been doing then. Besides, it might be fun to have a friend her own age here.

He must be sleeping late, she thought.

"Let me introduce you," Flora said now as she set a new place at the table. "Everyone, this is Gabrielle."

With that, Flora presented Gabrielle with a string of names, most of which were forgotten by the time she reached the last one. Gabrielle said "hello" and took a seat. To her surprise, the dour expressions at the table suddenly turned to friendly smiles. One of the men— Harold, Gabrielle thought—reached out to shake her hand.

"We're very glad you're here," he said.

"Sure is nice to have a pretty girl like you on Collins Farm," a second man commented.

An obese man with a crew cut slid a plate of flapjacks in her direction.

"Well, go on and eat," he said. "You must be hungry."

Gabrielle attacked the pancakes and found they were delicious. As she was eating, Flora reminded the men they had to get back to work. Gabrielle watched them file out of the kitchen to the backyard. She reached for the platter and refilled her plate.

"I'm glad to see you're a good eater," Flora said. "It's important at a time like this."

"These pancakes are delicious," Gabrielle said. "But I really don't know why I'm so hungry."

"Remember, your body is undergoing many changes," Flora said, sitting across from her. "You'll find a lot of things are different now."

"Flora, did you ever have a baby?" Gabrielle asked. "Do you have any children of your own?"

Flora placed her hands on the tabletop and stared for a few moments at her glittering rings. Gabrielle quickly noticed that none was a wedding band, and she immediately regretted her question.

"No," Flora said in a bitter tone. "No, I have no children."

"I—I'm sorry," Gabrielle said. "I didn't mean to be nosy."

Flora's smile returned, radiant.

"You'll be asking a lot of questions, my dear," she said. "You must feel free to discuss anything with me."

"Do you think I might look around the farm after breakfast?" Gabrielle asked.

"Of course," Flora said. "I'll show you the property after you've dressed."

Wearing a cotton blouse and patched jeans, Gabrielle joined her foster mother at the bottom of the main staircase. The foyer was filled with warming sunlight. Gabrielle paused a moment to look into the living room. In the light of day, even the skull didn't look so menacing.

The grassy front yard rolled down towards a shal-

low creek. Beyond this, two big dogs romped in yet
another field. A low, barbed-wire fence encircled the
land, separating it from the passing road.

"That leads into town," Flora said. "Although I
rarely use it. The farm is equipped with enough provi-
sions to last for six months."

"How far is it?"

If something happens, maybe I could run away. . . .

Flora seemed to be reading her mind when she
said:

"Too far to walk. It's six miles."

She put an arm around Gabrielle's shoulder and
walked down the steps with her. The apple trees that
had seemed silver the night before were now a lovely
white contrast to the deep blue sky. Gabrielle walked
with Flora around the side of the house where Mount
Shasta roses bordered the gray wood. She was admiring
one particular white bloom when, suddenly, something
jumped on top of her head and began pulling her hair.
Gabrielle shrieked in fear and pain.

"Chameron!" Flora snapped. "Leave her alone! It
is not time yet!"

A chattering noise answered the woman, and a
second later Gabrielle saw a small gray monkey jump
into Flora's arms. It turned to look at her, baring its
teeth and twisting the shoulder of Flora's blouse. Gabrielle
shook her head in wonder, a tingling pain running over
her scalp.

"I apologize for Chameron," Flora said. "He's really friendly, but you're a stranger to him. You needn't
worry that he'll hurt you."

"Why did you tell him it isn't time yet?" Gabrielle
asked, keeping her distance.

"I said no such thing," Flora insisted.

"Yes, you did," Gabrielle replied. "Don't you
remember?"

Chameron climbed down Flora's body, leaped for a
rose bush, and made his way toward the front of the
house.

"Oh, I must have meant it wasn't time for him to

eat yet," Flora said at last, nodding her head. "Come, we haven't seen the backyard yet."

It looked bigger now than the night before, when much of it had been hidden in shadow. The barn was a rich red color, with freshly-painted white trim. To its left sat the animal pen, crowded with cattle feeding on field corn. Beyond it, Gabrielle could see another field where some of the farmhands were preparing the land for planting seeds. One corner of the property was edged in evergreen trees, completing a pastoral scene that was so peaceful that Gabrielle began to decide she liked it here.

"You know, I'd like to help with the chores," she said. "I could feed the animals, or clean up, or . . ."

Flora let go of her and placed her hands on her hips.

"No daughter of mine will dirty her hands doing menial labor," she sniffed. "You will be treated as a girl born to quality, and nothing less will be suitable."

Gabrielle felt too awkward to press the matter further. Not because Flora had refused her offer of help (Gabrielle didn't consider working with animals a chore) but because she had called her "daughter." It didn't sound right. Gabrielle wanted to correct Flora, to tell her that she wasn't worthy enough to be so easily accepted. But Flora would find that out soon enough, wouldn't she?

As she walked back to the house, Gabrielle thought of her mother, and couldn't help asking:

"Did my mother come from a good home?"

Flora's smile faded.

"They were nice people," she said. She changed the subject so quickly that Gabrielle hardly noticed. "My dear, those jeans are terribly worn. Don't you have anything else to wear?"

"I have a dress," Gabrielle said. "The one I wore yesterday."

"That old rag?" Flora scoffed. "I can see they didn't take good care of you at Macon Orphanage. Well, we'll just have to go into town to buy you some new clothes!"

Gabrielle's eyes lit up, and she followed Flora back into the house with a smile on her face. Her own room, new clothes—wait until Kerry heard!

After the shopping spree, Gabrielle's closet was filled with clothes more beautiful than any she had ever imagined she would own. There were dresses, jeans, tops, shoes, nightgowns, and a robe. Best of all, they were Gabrielle's alone. She didn't have to share them with anybody.

She thought of the cruel remarks the girls in her dorm used to make, and couldn't help but smile. If only they could see her closet! Suddenly in a very good mood, Gabrielle pulled out a T-shirt with a rainbow on it and a pair of white denim slacks. There were three pairs of regular pants, but the others had wide elastic panels in the front to allow for her pregnancy.

Undressed, wearing only a new pair of panties and a lace-trimmed bra, Gabrielle stood before the mirror and ran her hands over her stomach. Did she feel fatter? What did the baby look like right now? Was it a boy or a girl?

A baby, growing inside of her. A tiny being that was hers alone. Gabrielle wondered if she would ever get used to the idea. For certain, she thought as she dressed, she'd never get used to the bouts of nausea that overcame her. She had been embarrassed in one store when it became necessary to ask where the ladies room was. Well, she thought, once I go to the doctor I might learn what to do about it.

She sighed, and picked up the silver hairbrush. A vague memory of the previous night's dream came to her as she brushed her hair, and Gabrielle felt very uneasy. She set the hairbrush down again and turned to retrieve her new box of stationary from the packages on top of her bed. She sat on top of the mattress and crossed her legs to make a desk, then began writing to Kerry. As she wrote, she forgot her nervousness.

She assured her brother that everything was fine, and that he shouldn't worry. He would really like Flora, and Gabrielle couldn't wait for him to see all the animals—especially a weird little monkey named Chameron. At last, she folded the letter and stuffed it into a pink envelope. She carried it downstairs, where she found Flora knitting in the living room.

"What a lovely outfit," Flora commented. "White certainly brings out the violet in your eyes."

"Thank you," Gabrielle said. "I really like all my new clothes." She waved the envelope. "Do you think I could borrow a stamp?"

"Certainly," Flora said, putting her needles and yarn aside. "I have a few right here in this drawer."

She walked over to a small black desk. Taking the letter from Gabrielle, she put a stamp on it, then set the letter up against a brass paperweight.

"I'll have Roger bring it to town next time he goes," she said.

Gabrielle thanked her, then excused herself and left the room. She decided to take a walk outside, and perhaps even help with the animals. Flora didn't have to know. And as long as it was daylight, she didn't have to worry about hurting one of them.

In the living room, Flora removed the letter from its perch, and held it tightly. She smiled a little to think Gabrielle hadn't noticed the stamp was worth only five cents. With a growl, she ripped it in half, then in half again, and shoved it into the desk drawer.

Six

As she walked past the apple trees, sweet-smelling on the April air, Gabrielle heard a chattering noise. She looked up to see Chameron hanging from a nearby branch, one thin arm stretched upward.

"Hello, monkey," she said. "Are you going to be friendly this time?"

Chameron yowled, scurried down the tree, then raced along the ground to the barn. Gabrielle watched him go, laughing. But just then she noticed someone watching her, half-hidden behind the opened barn door. Gabrielle realized it was the boy she had seen the previous night. She waved to him. But instead of returning her greeting, the boy swung around and hurried away.

"Hey, wait!"

She ran to the barn, catching hold of his arm. He turned quickly, his eyes so filled with terror that Gabrielle immediately let go of him.

"What's your name?" she asked finally.

The dark-haired youth turned to look at the big gray farmhouse. Gabrielle watched him, wondering why he seemed so edgy. He was kind of cute, and seemed somewhere around her age. Hoping to strike up a friendship, Gabrielle said:

"Please tell me your name."

He turned abruptly to her.

"Leave here," he said. "She'll hurt you if you don't!"

"Who will?"

The boy rubbed his arms.

"Going to die soon," he said.

Before Gabrielle could question his strange statement, he turned again and ran away. Gabrielle followed him, but when she rounded the corner of the barn, he was gone. She looked around herself, seeing the other farmhands at work, but no sign of the young boy. Confused, she took a few steps forward, and suddenly fell flat on her face.

None of the farmhands looked her way when she cried out. With a groan at her clumsiness, Gabrielle looked back over her shoulder to see what had tripped her. To her horror, she saw that her legs were thrown over the prone body of a black steer! Scrambling to her feet, she grimaced at the dead animal and wondered why she hadn't seen it before.

"Too busy looking for that guy," she reasoned out loud.

It stared over the dirt with one sightless eye, its tongue hanging from its opened mouth. A faint smell rose from it, indicating it had just begun to decompose. Gabrielle backed away from it, covering her mouth and nose. She'd better tell Flora what she found.

The downstairs rooms of the house were empty. Upstairs she turned down the little hallway. The intricate detail of the door's carved surface scratched her knuckles when she rapped on it, and she stood sucking on them while waiting for Flora to answer.

She heard a woman's voice on the other side of the door. It sounded like Flora, and yet its droning quality was quite unlike the woman's cheerful, rich tone. Gabrielle stood for a moment, listening.

". . . and the child shall be raised in the manner set forth by the Master. And the Master shall have him in his youth. . . ."

The words that followed seemed to be of a foreign tongue, confusing Gabrielle even further. God, this was like something from a movie she'd seen once about witches and all that nonsense. But, in an instant, she caught herself. Why was she eavesdropping like this? What Flora did was none of her business!

"Maybe she's just reading out loud," Gabrielle said, raising her hand to knock again.

"Yes, Gabrielle?"

The voice came from behind her. Gabrielle turned around with a gasp to see Flora there, her jewels glittering under the soft yellow light of the overhead lamp. She clasped her hands in front of her and waited for Gabrielle to reply, a slight smile working on her lips.

"Flora!" Gabrielle cried. "I—I thought you were in your room."

"There is no one in my room, Gabrielle," Flora said. "Now, what is it you wanted me for?"

Gabrielle took a quick glance at the elaborate entrance, then turned back to Flora.

"No, really," she said. "I heard someone in there. Maybe you should check?"

Flora considered this, and then gave a little laugh.

"Oh, of course!" she cried. "It must be one of my workers. Don't you remember I said I was having the room painted?"

"It sounded like a woman," Gabrielle said.

Flora sidled next to Gabrielle and put an arm around her shoulder.

"The wood on that door is thick," she said. "It probably muffled the sound. Now, what did you want to tell me?"

Gabrielle let it drop. Flora was probably right—it was just a painter. She told Flora what she had found behind the barn.

"It was disgusting," she said. "The poor thing was just *lying* there, and no one seemed to care!"

"Show me where the creature is," Flora said as they descended the back staircase. "I'll have Roger and Carl bury it."

Gabrielle hesitated.

"Don't worry," Flora said. "You need only point it out. I don't expect you to go near it again!"

When they walked around the back of the barn, there was nothing there. Gabrielle's brows knitted, and she walked carefully to the spot where the steer had been lying. There wasn't a single indication of the animal's presence, not even a mark in the dirt.

"But it was right here!" Gabrielle cried.

"Perhaps you imagined it," Flora said. "The sun *is* hot today, and in your condition . . ."

Gabrielle stared at the blank patch of ground.

"Wait a minute," she said. "Last night, I went to look out my window because I couldn't sleep. And I saw this guy dragging something big and dark across the yard. This must have been it! *He* must know what happened to the steer!"

"Who?"

Gabrielle looked at her.

"The boy with dark curls," she said. "What's his name? He wouldn't tell me. He acted scared, for some reason."

"I know of no such person," Flora insisted. "Come, my dear, let's go back to the house. You need some rest."

"But the boy . . ."

Flora smiled kindly.

"There isn't anyone here fitting that description," she said. "This was probably your imagination, Gabrielle. It's something you'll have to expect during your pregnancy."

I know what I saw, Gabrielle thought.

"I—I think I would like to rest up before dinner," she said.

"That's a good idea," Flora replied. "You can make it back to the house on your own, can't you?"

"Sure," Gabrielle said.

"I have something I want to discuss with my men," Flora said, turning to walk away.

Gabrielle watched her, wondering if it had to do with the imagined steer. But she let the matter drop and headed into the house. In her room, she dreamt of her mother. Naomi was in a waitress uniform, talking about the amulet. Gabrielle's hand opened and closed repeatedly, grabbing for the necklace that wasn't there.

Kerry's cheeks puffed out round as apples as he blew out the eight candles on his birthday cake. Amy MacClellan, an art teacher who had joined the staff of Macon Orphanage fresh out of college, helped him cut the first piece. The other children at the table watched eagerly as the cake was set on paper plates. They were Kerry's six best friends, and being with them made him very happy. There was just one person missing.

"Hope you made a good wish," Judy Wysatta piped up.

"Don't say what it is," Amy cautioned. "Or it might not come true."

Kerry wished, with all his heart, that Gabrielle

might show up before the day ended. It seemed like an eternity had passed since she left. Kerry had written three letters to her, printed carefully on lined paper, but she hadn't answered one of them. A postcard or a phone call would be enough. Just something to let the little boy know his sister hadn't forgotten him. Just something to ease the eerie feelings he often had that something was wrong with her.

"This cake is sure good stuff," Eric Hollis said, his voice cutting off Kerry's thoughts. "Can I have another piece?"

"Me, too!" a little girl cried, holding out her plate.

Amy laughed and cut two more pieces. She had baked the cake herself, paying for it from her own pocket. Mrs. Macon, she knew, would never have given her the money. Amy had been at the orphanage for only two weeks, but had quickly learned not to cross the old woman. Mrs. Macon probably wouldn't approve of this little gathering, but Amy didn't care. She just wanted the kids to be happy.

"You're real nice," Kerry said. "I only had a birthday cake two other times. Macon-Bacon—I mean Mrs. Macon—says it isn't fair for one to have a party and not everyone."

"Then everyone should have a birthday party," Amy said. She smiled at Kerry's icing-covered face. "You know, I wish I had a little brother just like you."

"I have a sister," Kerry replied. "She doesn't have lots of curly red hair like you do, but she's real pretty. Her name is Gabrielle. But she doesn't live here any more."

"Was she adopted?"

"She went away to Kansas," Kerry said. "I miss her."

Amy patted his head.

"I'm sure she misses you, too," she said. "Look, maybe you'll get together with her?"

Kerry looked up at her, his gray eyes sparkling. "Really?"

Amy had been warned, throughout her training for

this job, never to make promises that couldn't be kept. Bat Kerry's face had such a hopeful look that she couldn't stop herself from saying:

"Sure you will."

At that moment, Mrs. Macon silently appeared in the doorway. She folded her arms and stared at the group of happy children through her thick lenses. A birthday party! When the building was understaffed and money was tight! Well, it figured MacClellan was behind this—the young upstart. Who did she think she was, some kind of patron saint to orphans?

She started into the classroom, but stopped to listen to the rest of the conversation.

"Gabrielle is such a pretty name," Amy said.

"She was real pretty," Judy said. "She even had purple eyes!"

"Purple eyes?"

"Yeah, but she was real sad all the time," Eric put in.

"The big kids said she . . ."

Kerry gave the boy next to him a punch.

"Those were lies, Michael," he said. He looked at Amy. "The big kids always tell lies about my sister."

Mrs. Macon had heard enough. She strode into the room and waved a hand over the array of party things that covered the table.

"What is the meaning of this?"

"Kerry's eighth birthday is today," Amy explained. Quickly, she added: "I paid for it all myself."

As if disappointed to hear this, Mrs. Macon sniffed.

"Oh, very well," she said. She turned to Kerry. "Kerwin, I heard you talking about your sister, didn't I?"

"Yeah?"

"Haven't I told you not to do that, young man?"

Kerry's mouth twisted. "But I don't want to forget about her!"

Mrs. Macon slapped the table, making the children cringe.

"That is no way to answer me!"

"I'm sorry," Kerry said, though he didn't mean it. In his mind, he called her Macon-Bacon, and resisted an urge to stick his tongue out at her.

The old woman waved a hand at the group. "Very well, get on with your party. But be certain to clean up!"

She turned and left the room.

"Boy, she sure is mean," Michael whispered.

"She looks just like a witch," Judy said.

Amy put a hand on Kerry's shoulder.

"Why aren't you allowed to talk about your sister?" she asked.

Kerry shrugged, obviously not wanting to talk about it. Amy respected his feelings, and changed the subject by announcing a game.

Out in the hall, Mrs. Macon glowered. Why did that boy always talk of his sister? One of these days, the wrong people would hear, and she'd find a swarm of people here, the do-gooders and state authorities, asking questions about the girl. They'd want to know why the Hansen children were separated, and why Gabrielle wasn't given medical help. Mrs. Macon had thought her troubles were over when Flora offered to take the girl in, but it seemed Gabrielle was working against her even from all that distance!

Mrs. Macon would never admit the real reason she hated Gabrielle. The truth was, Gabrielle bore a slight resemblance to the woman who had stolen Mr. Macon away. Even though it had happened over thirty years ago, Mrs. Macon still saw his mistress in the face of every beautiful, dark-haired girl. It was a hurtful reminder that Mr. Macon had gotten his mistress pregnant, and had made his wife the laughing stock of the neighborhood by divorcing her. In those days, divorce was a shameful thing, and Mrs. Macon had never gotten over the humiliation.

Well, Kerry would forget Gabrielle soon enough. She had not bothered to write to him yet. Mrs. Macon smiled. Perhaps she thought Kerry had never written to *her*. Neither of them would ever know that the old woman had destroyed all of Kerry's letters.

Seven

Gabrielle had been living with Flora Collins nearly three weeks when she was awakened one night by strange singing, the tune slow and monotonous, like the chanting in a Medieval monastery. It seemed to be coming from outside. Groaning, Gabrielle rolled over and glanced at her clock. Who on *earth* was singing at this hour of the morning? For heaven's sake, she thought, they have chores to get up for in five hours!

"It's awful music, too," she whispered. The off-key quality of the notes made her cringe.

Gabrielle covered her ears, hoping the music would stop. But it was persistent, droning on and on, refusing to let her fall asleep again. Finally, she got out of bed, thinking she would open the window to see where the noise was coming from. Maybe she could yell for them to be quiet? But just as she placed her hands on the sill, it stopped, so abruptly that Gabrielle's heart skipped a beat. She looked out over the dimly lit backyard, but saw no one.

She stood a few minutes, her heart beating rapidly. Had she only imagined the music? Or was it another trick—like the mysterious black steer? Would she wake up tomorrow to find a dead animal in her room?

"No!" Gabrielle said firmly. "I've been here three weeks and everything's been fine. That isn't going to happen again!"

She was about to pull herself away from the window when she noticed something moving in the nearby woods. It seemed to be a human figure, although Gabrielle couldn't be sure because of the distance. It

stopped, crouched low, then bounded across the field.
As it came closer, Gabrielle saw it was the boy with
dark curls. What was he doing here at this time of night
again if he didn't work here?

Gabrielle decided to wake up her foster mother
and report what she had seen. If the kid was a prowler,
Flora should be alerted. Pulling on her robe, Gabrielle
left her room and hurried down the hallway. She knocked
softly at Flora's door, but there was no answer. She
rapped harder the second time, hurting her fingers on
the carvings, but still there was no response.

"Flora?" she called softly. "Flora, are you awake?"

She took hold of the knob and began to turn it.
But, quickly, she jerked her hand away and brought it
to her mouth.

"What about the paint?" she whispered. "Don't
you remember Flora said not to go in there?"

But, she argued with herself, *this is important.
And it's been weeks since the room was painted.*

Still, didn't Flora say just a few days ago that she
was having the room done over because she didn't like
the color? Whatever, it was obvious she didn't want
Gabrielle in there. And if she were there, she would
have answered.

"Maybe she's asleep," Gabrielle thought out loud.
"She really should know about this!"

Gabrielle pounded all the harder on the door, with
no more luck. She was faced with a dilemma: let the
prowler escape, perhaps with something valuable, or
risk getting in trouble for entering the room.

"What am I supposed to do?"

She folded her arms and stared at the door. The
carved decoration was both beautiful and grotesque,
detailed depictions of hunting scenes, complete with
dead rabbits, foxes and deer. Gabrielle thought it was
hideous, and wondered why Flora chose such a strange
door for her room. She had seen a TV show once about
people who performed strange rituals involving dead
animals. Was Flora like that? No, that was crazy. Flora

had been very kind to her, and it was wrong to compare her to the evil people in the movies.

Dead animals...

Suddenly, her thoughts were an amalgam of memories of her other foster homes. She had gotten into trouble so many times over the last two years that it seemed impossible anyone would ever want to take her in. Especially considering the fact that she was going to have a baby! And then Flora came along, asking no questions, completely ready to give her the love she so desperately needed. Gabrielle knew this home was a trial just like the others. She was expected to toe the line, and if she disobeyed Flora's most adamant order she could very easily be thrown out again. She wouldn't be able to go back to the orphanage—she was too old. She'd be on her own, with a baby to care for!

What would Flora do if she caught her? Caught her? That was too strong an expression. Gabrielle wasn't spying or sneaking around where she didn't belong! She only intended to wake Flora up to tell her what she had seen. Flora would thank her, rather than being angry.

Wouldn't she?

"It's the right thing to do," Gabrielle told herself finally. "If she's not in there, I'll leave right away. Before I breathe in too much of the paint fumes!"

Resigned, she held her breath and opened the door, walking carefully into the dark room. It unnerved her; there wasn't a speck of light in here. She felt her way like a blind woman until she came to the bed, then gingerly touched the covers. The bed was empty.

Gabrielle let herself breathe again, and noticed the room smelled more of dampness than of fresh paint. Groping for the light, she switched it on to see a room unlike any other. The bed was covered with a black satin spread, black fabric had been draped over the lampshades, black lace covered the dressing table. There were no feminine decorations in here—no flowers, pictures, or perfume bottles. The windows were hung with heavy black drapes, explaining why the room was so dark.

More surprisingly, the walls showed no indication of having been painted recently. They were papered, in fact, with a pattern of faded roses. Gabrielle moved away from the bed and looked around herself, hardly able to believe what she was seeing. Why had Flora lied to her? Was it possible she wasn't as nice as she seemed?

As Gabrielle turned to leave, she noticed a cradle, half-hidden behind the opened door. In an instant all her earlier doubts faded away. Flora had bought the baby a cradle. She had been hiding it in this room as a surprise for Gabrielle. No wonder the room was off-limits.

It was the most exquisite cradle she had ever seen. It hung freely between two wooden posts that had been inlaid with green and white enamel. The cradle itself was intricately carved with flowers and birds, and draped in buff-colored lace. Carefully, Gabrielle pulled back the embroidered satin coverlet. The matching pillow was delicately trimmed with scalloped edging and had the soft feel of down.

"Oh, how sweet," Gabrielle whispered.

She smiled, and then noticed a book tucked under the pillow. It was a small black one with no more than thirty pages. Forgetting her worries about being caught, she pulled it out and opened it.

She could read only two things: London, and the date, 1843. The remainder of the book was in some foreign language. Gabrielle closed it and placed it under the little pillow again. But as she did so, a hideous black millipede scurried out and ran over her fingers. With a disgusted cry, Gabrielle flipped the coverlet over it and hurried from the room. Her body was chilled by the sudden appearance of so hideous an insect in her baby's cradle; she felt sickened.

"Oh, wonderful," she thought. "Now I'm going to throw up."

She forced herself to calm down. She decided she wouldn't tell Flora. Why spoil the surprise? By the time she reached her own door, she felt much better, and was so relaxed that she wasn't ready for the loud, piercing scream. Gabrielle turned, and in a flash something flew at her from the darkness, scratching and biting.

"Get off me!" Gabrielle screamed, tugging at the ball of fur, teeth and claws that locked around her head. "GET OFF!"

It was Chameron. His tail swung around her neck and tightened, his teeth sunk into one of her ears.

"SSSSTOOOOOPPP!!!!"

Gabrielle had the sudden presence of mind to drop to the floor. She rolled over, trying to force the monkey off of her. Chameron held fast, screeching and chattering. Gabrielle took hold of his two legs—but with his tail it seemed there were three more to grab her.

"HELP! SOMEBODY HELP!"

No one answered. Gabrielle's hand found the monkey's face, and she pushed back on it with all her might. Tiny slivers of pain shot up her arm as Chameron's teeth sunk into her hand.

Gabrielle screamed, tears flowing from her eyes.

"Where is everyone?"

She grabbed Chameron's tail and pulled it, hard. Suddenly, the hall light flashed on, and Chameron jumped away from her. Crying and panting, Gabrielle pulled herself up on her knees and gaped up at Flora. A look of horror came over the woman's face as the two stared at each other. Blood trickled over Gabrielle's eyes, and stained the carpet beneath her hand.

"He—he attacked me," Gabrielle stammered, her voice weak.

"Oh, my dear child!" Flora cried as Chameron hurried away.

She helped Gabrielle to her feet, and without a word more led her to the bathroom. There, she tended to Gabrielle's wounds, stinging her with iodine. But Gabrielle didn't complain. She was too upset to feel any pain.

"I—I don't know why he did it," Gabrielle whispered. "I was just walking along the hallway when he came at me! No one answered when I screamed for help!"

She buried her face in her hands and began to cry again.

"Hush," Flora cooed. "It's all over now. Chameron must have followed one of my men into the house. I'll see to it that the little demon never hurts you again!"

Gabrielle's stomach suddenly jumped, and she turned around to be sick.

"Don't you think I should see the doctor tomorrow?"

Flora straightened, her lips turning down slightly.

"He isn't in town yet," she said. "As I explained to you before, being in so remote an area as this we must rely on city doctors. I imagine though that he'll be coming this way within the next week or two."

"But—but what if Chameron has some disease?"

Gabrielle worried that she hadn't yet seen a doctor; and this attack made it even more urgent.

"I assure you, Chameron is quite healthy," Flora said. "And so are you, my dear! I wouldn't let any harm come to your baby. Don't you know that?"

Gabrielle smiled a little.

"Sure I do," she said, putting her arms around the woman. "I just got scared."

"There's nothing to be afraid of, my dear," her foster mother said, stroking Gabrielle's dark hair and staring at the wall before her. Gabrielle was becoming more and more attached to her. Well, that was good. Flora smiled slightly. It was so good to be trusted so readily. It always made things so much easier. . . .

London, July, 1865

Because the sun was shining for the first time in a week, London's parks were filled with people. Ladies in crinolined skirts strolled with handsome men, nannies pushed wicker prams, children rolled hoops and played leapfrog. But in St. James's Park, near Buckingham Palace, there was one golden-haired little girl of two who made even the sun seem dark. Ermengarde Wilson giggled merrily as she chased a pelican, her hoop skirt swinging, the pink ribbons of her lace caplet flying back over her shoulders. The pelican threw its wings up and flew away, escaping the playful toddler.

"Come here to me, little one," someone called.

Ermie turned around, and looked past the groups of people with wide gray eyes. When she spotted her father, she smiled and hurried towards him. Richard Wilson snatched his little girl up into his arms and smothered her face with kisses.

"It's time to go home, Ermie," Richard said. "Mama will be waiting for us. And I think cook's prepared something lovely for dinner."

Ermengarde chattered on happily, pointing at this and that, playing with her father's bowler hat. Richard grinned at her. What a delightful child she was! She looked exactly like her poor mother, who was confined in her bed these days as the birth of a second child approached.

How Richard loved this child. How he worried about her. His mother had warned him, just before she died, that the child might be in danger. He shivered to remember her sickly face against the huge satin pillows, paled from the toll her illness had taken on her. But Blythe had gripped his hand with a surprising strength, pulling him close because she couldn't speak above a whisper.

"One day, you shall have a child of your own," she choked. "Beware of the woman with cat's eyes! She'll murder the child! You must avoid her at all costs!"

Richard sighed, helping Ermengarde into the coach that waited for them. His mother had been delirious, of course. There had never been any woman with cat's eyes in Richard's life, although Blythe had often spoken of her. He did know, however, that she had lost a baby just two years before his own birth—a son by her first husband. Perhaps her illness had brought that poor little soul to mind. Now Richard glanced at Ermie, who had fallen asleep with her thumb in her mouth. No one had threatened her, and Richard would see to it that no one ever would.

Soon, the carriage arrived at the three-story build-ing that was the Wilson home. No sooner had the coachman opened the door than one of the maids came running out of the house, down the short walk.

"Oh, Mr. Wilson! Thank God you've come home!"

Richard, cradling Ermengarde in his arms, regarded the young girl for a moment, then asked calmly what was wrong.

"It's the missus, sir," the maid wailed, wringing her mob cap in her hands. "The baby's come, and there's been such trouble!"

"Dear God!" Richard cried, bounding into the house. He handed his daughter to another maid. "Why wasn't I contacted? You knew where I could be found!"

The second maid, a heavy-set woman, put a hand on his shoulder.

"It all happened so quickly, sir," she said. "The baby was born in just a half hour's time—there was no chance to send for you!"

Richard hurried up a flight of stairs and burst into the master bedroom. Faith was lying under a mountain of blankets, almost lost in the giant canopy bed. Her pale face was streaked with tears when she turned to look at her husband, and she could not even hold up a hand to beckon him.

"My love, my love," Richard choked, rushing to bury his head near her shoulder. "Had I only known..."

"The baby," Faith whispered.

"Have we a son?" Richard asked, looking up. "Or a daughter?"

Faith did not answer.

"My love, what's wrong?" Richard pressed. "Where's our baby?"

"I'm afraid the baby has died," a gentle voice said.

Richard looked back over his shoulder to see the family doctor. Letting go of Faith, he stood up and walked across the room.

"What are you telling me?"

"It was too early for the birth," the doctor explained. "The child was weak."

Richard shook his head in disbelief. Just a while

ago, he had been so happy. How could this terrible thing be happening?

"What—what was it?"

"A boy," the doctor said. "You had a son, Mr. Wilson."

Numbed, Richard gazed around the room. The knicknacks that had been so carefully placed on the mantel and little tables irked him now, and he resisted an urge to break a bust of Shakespeare that sat close at hand. How could such balderall be permitted when a child had been taken into God's hands?

"I want to see my baby," Richard said finally, straightening himself.

"I'm afraid that isn't possible. I've already sent the body to the undertaker's."

Richard's voice was barely a whisper when he asked:

"You did what?"

"I thought it was best if . . ."

In a flash, Richard had the doctor by the throat, pulling him up close.

"You thought it best!" he screamed. "You thought it best! *I* am the head of this house! I will make the decisions regarding my son. How dare you interfere?"

"He was dead, Richard," the doctor hissed. "Dead! Nothing could have saved him. Would you have had me leave him here, so that your wife would be tormented?"

As a sob escaped his throat, Richard let go.

"How could this have happened?" he asked, tears spilling from his eyes.

"The ways of the Almighty are hard to understand," the doctor said, staring at the broken man before him with an expressionless face.

But it had not been the Almighty who placed the doctor under a spell just as he was walking upstairs to assist Faith in the birth. Something dark and evil had possessed his mind, something that made him tell Faith her perfectly healthy son had been stillborn. Faith, who expected babies to cry at birth, had believed him. Too weak to protest, she had not said a word when he carried the baby downstairs. Sneaking past the servants, the doctor had handed the child to a green-eyed woman who waited behind the house with a wicker basket. Only then did the baby give out a lusty, healthy cry.

Eight

Kerry reached for a black Crayola from the pile of crayons before him. He held it over the blank piece of paper, but he made no attempt to draw a picture. His mind was too full of thoughts about his sister, alternating between fear for her and anger at her. In six weeks, he had written her as many letters, and had yet to get a response. Composing a letter was no easy task for a second grader, who had to print everything in slow, careful letters. Didn't Gabrielle know how hard he tried? Didn't she care?

Suddenly, Kerry's fist tightened around the black crayon, and he began digging it across the paper, oblivious to the happy chatter of the other children. Across the table, his friend Michael looked up at him.

"Hey, you're gonna get in trouble doing that!"

Kerry stuck his tongue out and went on destroying the paper. Tears began to flow from his gray eyes. Suddenly, the other children became aware of his crying, and stopped talking. Kerry, embarrassed, wiped his nose on the cuff of his shirt and returned the crayon to the pile.

"What're you guys starin' at?"

"How come you're crying?" Judy wanted to know.

"I'm not crying!"

Amy MacClellan, noticing the sudden quiet, came over to the table. Kerry pulled the torn paper closer to him and tried to hide it, but as he was doing this he felt Amy's hand on his shoulder. She waved a hand at the other children, and immediately, if reluctantly, they went back to their own drawings. Amy quietly asked Kerry to come out to the hall with her.

In the hallway, she watched him stare down at his sneakers. As each day since his birthday passed, he had grown a little more melancholy and introverted. Amy knew it was because he had yet to hear from his sister. She wondered if the rumors she'd heard about the girl were true. Who could be so mean as to ignore a little boy's letters?

"Got a lot on your mind, huh?" she asked.

Kerry nodded, sniffled loudly, and rubbed the toe of one foot against the back of his other calf.

"I sure wish there was something I could do," Amy said.

Kerry squinted at her.

"On—on my birthday," he said, "you told me I'd see my sister real soon."

"I know," Amy replied, cringing to remember that promise. "I shouldn't have, but it was what you wanted to hear. I wanted you to feel happy."

"I ain't gonna be happy until Gabrielle comes to get me," Kerry said.

Amy thought a moment, and suddenly had an idea. But she kept it to herself, in case it didn't work out. No need to disappoint Kerry again.

"Listen," she said, "go back into the classroom now. I'm going to Mrs. Macon's office for a few minutes."

Kerry's eyes widened.

"Are you gonna ask about my sister?"

"Never mind," Amy said, opening the door. "See you later, okay?"

After Kerry left, Amy walked towards Mrs. Macon's office. She planned to ask if she might take Kerry to visit Gabrielle's foster home. Amy had a car of her own; the two could drive over to Kansas for the weekend. Amy decided she didn't mind giving up her own plans to make a little boy happy.

But then, it meant she'd have to take Kerry over a state line. The director probably wouldn't like that idea, but Amy didn't care. She wasn't afraid of Mrs. Macon.

"You've got nerve for a kid who just graduated college three months ago," Amy told herself. "But look, the most she can say is 'no,' right?"

Amy recalled her first interview with Mrs. Macon. She'd been told in no uncertain terms that an art teacher was the last thing the home needed. But, Mrs. Macon had said, the state wanted to expand the children's curriculum. She couldn't be bothered with interviews, and hired Amy right there on the spot.

"But you should be warned that I stand for no nonsense," Mrs. Macon had cautioned, her owl eyes glowering.

To Amy concern for a little boy was not nonsense. Resolved, she knocked on the office door.

"Mrs. Macon," she said, "I'd like to discuss Kerry Hansen with you."

Mrs. Macon did not look up from her papers. Amy stood with her hands folded in front of her. She looked at an empty chair, but decided to wait until the seat was offered to her.

"What is it?" the woman asked finally. "Is Kerwin in trouble again? His regular teacher reported having him stand in the corner three times yesterday."

Poor kid, Amy thought.

"I think I know the problem," she said. "It's his sister, Gabrielle. He's heartbroken that she hasn't written to him yet."

"I'm not surprised," Mrs. Macon replied. "That girl was wicked. I thank God we've finally seen the last of her."

Amy shook her head. "Why do you say that?"

"We had a good deal of trouble placing Gabrielle," Mrs. Macon explained. "She's got a vicious streak in her. Every time it seemed we found a good home, she would do something horrible."

"Something horrible?" Amy asked, pretending she hadn't heard any of the rumors.

"She was a beast," Mrs. Macon said. "When in a foster home, she would murder the family pet—and would use its blood to draw strange symbols all over the bedroom. Can you blame anyone for wanting to be rid of her?"

Before Amy could answer, she leaned forward.

"Has Kerwin been talking of his sister again?"

"I know he thinks about her a lot," Amy replied. "I feel so sorry for him. I don't know what I'd do if I was separated from my family." She shrugged. "Anyway, I have an idea that might cheer him up a bit. I was thinking about taking my car and driving to . . ."

"Absolutely not," Mrs. Macon interrupted firmly.

"I didn't finish."

"I know what you were going to say," Mrs. Macon said. "And the answer is 'no.' I will not have you driving any of these children over state lines."

I was afraid you'd say that.

"But if you know about it," Amy said out loud, "and if we report to the right people, what harm would there be?"

"The matter is closed," Mrs. Macon said. "Miss MacClellan, you're a very young woman who has a lot to learn about children. I feel it is best for Kerwin to forget his sister."

"I don't see what the big deal is," Amy said. "We'd leave Friday afternoon and come back Sunday night. He wouldn't miss any school."

Mrs. Macon stared at her through her thick lenses.

"Why are you arguing with me?" she asked. She waved a hand. "Leave me alone. I have work to do."

Now she tugged at one of the knobs on her desk, a gesture meant to dismiss the young teacher. But Amy was undaunted, and stood by as the old woman struggled with the drawer. Finally, she came around and offered her assistance.

"I can do it!" Mrs. Macon said, impatiently.

Amy ignored her. Gritting her teeth, she tugged hard, and unexpectedly the drawer pulled clear off its tracks. It flopped down against her leg; papers, rubber bands, pens and the like scattered all over the floor.

"Now look what you've done!"

"I'm sorry," Amy said.

She dropped to her knees to clean up the mess, gathering together a pile of paper scraps. Mrs. Macon suddenly grabbed her hand to stop her, squeezing Amy's wrist so tightly that the younger woman gasped. She looked down at the papers, and quickly realized what had upset Mrs. Macon.

It wasn't just paper—it was the remains of an envelope, scribbled over in childish print. The scrap nearest her held only part of the wording, "IELLE HANSEN," but she could easily guess the rest.

"That's one of Kerry's letters to his sister, isn't it?" Amy asked quietly.

"Nonsense!"

"Yes, it is," Amy said, snatching it up. She pulled out the fragments. "I recognize Kerry's writing. Why is it torn up like this?"

Mrs. Macon stood up, and Amy moved with her. The clutter remained at their feet as they faced each other. Amy knew defying the woman could cost her a job, but she was too annoyed to care.

"Why did you tear up Kerry's letter?" she asked again.

"I won't have you speaking that way to me," Mrs. Macon said. "Get out of my office!"

Amy shook her head.

"Not yet," she said. "You know, I wondered why Gabrielle never answered her brother's letters. She never received them! The little guy trusted you to address them, and instead you destroyed them!"

"Amy MacClellan," Mrs. Macon said, "there are plenty of others who would like your job. Have you forgotten that?"

Amy stared at her, weighing the threat. Much as she disliked Mrs. Macon, she did like working here at the orphanage. And jobs with this kind of pay were few and far between for even college graduates. Despite her anger, she evened out her voice and said:

"Yes, Mrs. Macon. I'm sorry if I caused you any trouble."

I haven't even begun with you, she thought. *When I tell the state board about the letters . . .*

Mrs. Macon's lips were set hard as she watched Amy leave her office. If that girl were to reveal what she'd done, Flora Collins would be infuriated. And then she'd stop sending Mrs. Macon a monthly check to forget Gabrielle ever existed. The director needed that money.

Well, perhaps she should contact Flora. With the woman's help, they could see to it that Amy never interfered again!

Every morning since her arrival at the farm six weeks earlier, Gabrielle walked to the mailbox across the broad field that rolled away from the house. She did this partly because the walk made her feel good, but mostly because she couldn't stop hoping she'd hear from Kerry. After breakfast one May morning, she excused herself and went out as usual. Not for the first time, she asked herself why she bothered. It was obvious that Kerry had forgotten her. Mrs. Macon had finally gotten to him. Why didn't she face facts? But in spite of these doubts she kept returning to the mailbox—just in case.

Rarely used, it was rusted, peppered with tiny holes. The ground beneath it had been soaked with rain so often that the post leaned at a sharp angle, supported precariously by a length of barbed wire fence. It seemed as if the mailbox had long ago given up hope of ever accepting any mail.

But today—miracle of miracles—there *was* something inside. At first, Gabrielle told herself it was probably just a circular from the local Seed n' Feed. She held her breath.

But it wasn't a circular—it was a letter, from Kerry! Too excited to carry it all the way back to the house, she ripped it open. The lined paper was covered with red childish print. Tears welled in Gabrielle's violet eyes, and she had to wipe them away several times before she could attempt to read it. Kerry told her that he missed her—why hadn't she written?

"But I did write to you," Gabrielle protested.

Continuing, Kerry reported everything that had happened in the past weeks—his eighth birthday party, the new art teacher, the times he'd been in trouble. Recalling that her brother had never been a problem for his teachers, Gabrielle began to worry. It was obvious that he needed his sister. She'd asked about his coming to Collins Farm, but Flora always said there was a lot of paper work to be done before he could. Gabrielle would just have to be patient.

She looked back at the letter again, surprised to find adult script at the bottom. Amy MacClellan had written a note explaining that Mrs. Macon had destroyed all of Kerry's previous letters. She apologized for this, and promised she would see to it personally that they got in the mail from now on.

"That bitch," Gabrielle mumbled, seeing Mrs. Macon's ugly face in her mind. She folded the letter and put it into her pocket, looking down at the ground. Poor Kerry! No wonder he never . . .

"Oh!"

There was someone right behind her. She gazed into a pair of gray eyes that were round with fear. Recognizing the boy with dark curls, Gabrielle took a step back and said:

"What are you doing there?"

"You got a letter?"

"It's none of your business," Gabrielle said. "What do you want?"

The boy gave his head a rough shake, like a dog coming from water.

"Go away!" he said. "There's danger here!"

"You're crazy," Gabrielle said, moving around him. She tried to head back to the house, but he took hold of her arm.

"Please, please go away! While you can!"

"Let go of me!"

"I'm your friend," the boy said. "I want to help. If you don't . . ."

He cut himself off. Gabrielle turned to look at what had caught his eye, and spotted her foster mother at the front door. When she returned her eyes to the boy, she saw he had turned completely white. He let go of her, and with a small cry turned and ran away.

Gabrielle hurried back to the house, planning to thank her foster mother for showing up just then. She didn't understand why Flora frightened the boy so much, but that didn't matter. He was getting to be a pest anyway.

Nine

Amy tightened her hands around her steering wheel and leaned forward a little in an effort to see beyond the curtain of rain that poured down over the highway. As the road curved between two mountains, the radio station began to give off more static than music, jumping between her country-western station and some news program. Amy fidgeted with the dial, then finally turned the thing off.

From the corner of her eye, she saw the small figure curled up on the seat next to her. Kerry's black hair was repeatedly stroked by the lights curling over the interstate, turned on to illuminate the road for anyone foolish enough to be driving in weather like this. He mumbled something in his sleep, then turned over on his back, pushing his stuffed raccoon to the car's floor.

They had been on the road several hours, and the

excitement of visiting his sister had exhausted Kerry. The constant swoosh of the windshield wipers had been like a lullabye to put the little boy to sleep. Amy smiled at him, then quickly returned her eyes to the slick road ahead. The rain had subsided a bit, but though the clock in her dashboard said it was only 4:22, the dark thunderclouds above had accelerated the coming of night. Reflections of the taillights of the few cars ahead of her seemed to reach down into the earth, as if the asphalt were made of water.

Amy yawned, suddenly wanting sleep herself. But she kept herself alert by thinking of the most recent meeting she'd had with Mrs. Macon. The old woman had unexpectedly made a complete turnaround towards Amy's idea. Of course she could take Kerry to the farm! Of course it was wrong to keep such loving siblings apart! Mrs. Macon trusted Amy to take care of things in a reliable way. Amy translated her words into "forget the letters I destroyed, and everything will be all right."

"Maybe I'll forget them," Amy said to herself, "and maybe I won't."

She wished there had been time to write to Gabrielle. Kerry had wanted to send a letter to tell his sister the good news, but Mrs. Macon had insisted they had to start on their way as soon as possible. Kerry decided he liked the idea of surprising Gabrielle, and eagerly went to pack his small suitcase. Mrs. Macon told Amy she'd phone ahead to Mrs. Collins, so that their visit wouldn't be a complete surprise.

There was something dark in the road ahead. Amy squinted, trying to discern what it was. A deer? She eased up on the gas pedal, moving her foot towards the brake. She suddenly noticed that all the other cars had turned off the road. She was alone.

The black silhouette was not moving, and although Amy's headlights were shining right at it she still couldn't identify what it was. Not a deer, or any other animal; they would have bolted already. And if there had been an accident, car lights or flares would be visible. . . .

Suddenly, the figure came into view, turning to stare through the windshield.

"What on earth?"

Her words brought Kerry out of his sleep, and he looked up. His eyes widened in horror, for Gabrielle was standing in front of the car!

The little boy's scream was undiscernible from the screeching of the car's brakes.

The tiny seedlings in Gabrielle's garden rustled lightly under the spray from the hose. She moved it back and forth, feeding the thirsty plants, digging her bare toes into the warm spring mud. Flora had given her this little corner of the yard to grow vegetables, and Gabrielle took extra special care of it. It was nice to have something of her own. As she worked the garden she often thought of her baby, and wondered what it would be like to take care of a *human* life.

The magnificent cradle she'd found in Flora's room came to mind, and she tried to picture her baby sleeping peacefully in it. She smiled, wishing she could let Flora know she had discovered the beautiful present. But in all these weeks she had kept it a secret.

In the barn one of the farmhands had a radio playing, and the transition from music to talk cut off Gabrielle's thoughts.

"K-W-P-M . . ." sang a chorus.

"It's 4:30 here in Richfield, and we've got rain in our forecast. . . ."

Gabrielle twisted the nozzle of her hose and began to carry it back to the barn, dragging it like a huge serpent. Halfway across the yard, she suddenly dropped the hose, falling to the ground as a slice of pain tore through her middle.

Inside the house, Flora looked up from a book she was reading at the sound of her foster daughter's scream. A humorless smile spread across her lips.

A blob of rainwater fell on Kerry's upturned face, rudely pulling him from the shelter of unconsciousness.

At first, the little boy didn't realize what had happened, and his young mind didn't register the incongruity of a tree branch poking through the windshield. He stared at it for a long time, uncomprehending. But then, little by little, he began to remember everything. He could hear the sound of the car bounding off the road so clearly that he stiffened, as if reliving that horrible moment.

"Amy?"

His voice was small, far-away sounding.

"Amy, you okay?"

Only the scuttling of the branch overhead answered him.

"Are we in Kansas?" he asked. "I thought I saw my sister. How come she was standing in the road like that?"

He fumbled with the catch of his safety belt, then unlocked it. Slightly dizzy as he knelt on the seat, he pushed down on the branch, hardly feeling the sting of the needles. Amy was flopped sideways against the door. Kerry reached to touch her, seeing that her eyes were opened. She did not respond.

"How come you're starin' like that?" he demanded. "Amy, where's my sister?"

The branch scratched lazily.

Somewhere far away, a car rumbled over the highway.

"Amy?"

An owl hooted.

"Amy, are you okay?" Kerry asked, poking her. "Start the car up so we can go again!"

When she didn't answer, Kerry took hold of her arm and began to shake her. She fell forward, the weight of her body bringing a high screech from the horn. It was then that Kerry saw the blood that covered half her face, seeping from a cut in her forehead. He backed away, letting the branch snap up again.

Just a dream . . .

Kerry grabbed for his raccoon and fixed a stare on the pale red letters of the clock. The second hand had stopped frozen: 4:30.

He'd wake up soon. He'd wake up and they'd be in Kansas, and Gabrielle would be there, and he'd tell her about the scariest dream he'd ever had. . . .

Flora walked upstairs to Gabrielle's room, where the girl slept soundly. Carl had found her outside, unconscious, curled up on the muddy ground. Now Flora walked to the side of her bed and placed a hand on her stomach. She smiled grimly. How ironic that Gabrielle should collapse in pain at the very instant that MacClellan girl was screaming in the face of death!

But Flora didn't care about that MacClellan. She only cared about Gabrielle, and the baby she carried within her.

Night had fallen completely when Gabrielle woke up again. She put her hands on her stomach a few moments and thought about the pain that had overcome her. It had felt as if the walls of her stomach were being yanked inward, a dull yet burning pain unlike any she had ever experienced. Right now, she felt a little light-headed, but the pain was completely gone.

Flora opened her door then and entered with a tray of food, which she proceeded to set up next to Gabrielle's bed.

"I'm not hungry."

"You should eat something," Flora said. "You must get your strength back. You gave us quite a scare, you know!"

Gabrielle stared up at her.

"Is my baby okay?" she asked, panic in her voice. "I don't know what happened to me. I just . . ."

Flora patted her hand.

"Hush," she said. "Your baby is just fine. I had the doctor here, and he examined you thoroughly."

"I don't remember any doctor," Gabrielle said.

"You were unconscious, my dear."

Gabrielle rubbed her eyes. "I wish I had been awake. There were a lot of questions I wanted to ask him. Is he coming back?"

"I'm afraid he was called away on an emergency," Flora said. "It will be a while before he returns to this part of the county. But he assured me you're perfectly fine. He said these things sometimes happen when a girl as young as you becomes pregnant."

Gabrielle turned and fingered the tray beside her, her hunger coming back just a little now that she knew everything was okay.

"Now!" Flora said in a cheerful tone. "I want you to eat every bite of that dinner! I cooked it especially for you."

She helped Gabrielle to sit up, and set the tray across her lap. Suddenly ravenous, Gabrielle eagerly attacked the chicken, honey-drenched biscuits, and salad. She could hardly believe how hungry she was.

"You were so nice to do this," she said. "It's the first time I ever ate in bed, you know."

"If you ever feel too ill to come down to a meal," Flora replied, "just call me and I'll bring you up a tray."

"Thanks," Gabrielle said. She picked up a blueberry turnover. "Kerry would really like this. He's crazy about desserts."

"Is he?"

There was an edge to Flora's voice that Gabrielle didn't hear.

"Oh, yes," she said. "You know, I wish the orphanage would get cracking on those papers. I can't believe it's taking so long for you to be able to adopt Kerry."

"Well," Flora said, patting her hand. "He'll be with us before you know it."

Gabrielle could have no way of knowing that the only attempt at reuniting her with Kerry had been made by Amy MacClellan—and that Amy would never be able to help them again.

Three days after the accident, Kerry sat in Mrs. Macon's office. He stared at a point on the floor where a splinter bent upward, his small legs dangling over the edge of a hard wooden chair. Outside, the yard was filled with children, shouting and laughing. Kerry, usually the most playful child in the home, had no desire to share in their activities. He didn't much want to listen again to Mrs. Macon's questions either.

"Try to remember, Kerry," she pressed. "What caused Mac—Amy to lose control of the car?"

"I was sleeping," Kerry mumbled, sick of hearing the same questions over and over. First the police, then the hospital, now Mrs. Macon. Brother!

"I know you were," Mrs. Macon said. "But this is important. Her family will want to know. Isn't there anything you can tell me?"

Kerry shut his eyes tightly, trying to think. There *was* something, something that had eluded him these past three days. Then, little by little, a picture came to mind. It was something he had seen just before the crash.

"Gabrielle," he said, simply.

"What?"

Kerry looked up at her.

"My sister was in the road," he said. "I remember now. Amy saw her, too, cause she turned the car so she wouldn't hit her."

"You're not making sense," Mrs. Macon snapped. "How could you have seen Gabrielle when you were nowhere near her home?"

Kerry shrugged.

"Well," Mrs. Macon said, "it must have been someone who *looked* like Gabrielle."

"You think so?" Kerry asked. He thought about this a few moments. "Yea—maybe it was! 'Cause my sister wouldn't do something so dumb and then run away."

Listening to him, Mrs. Macon was disgusted to hear how he stood up for Gabrielle. Perhaps she *had* been in the road, perhaps she had tried to murder her brother. Or perhaps Flora had set something up with a look-alike. She *had* promised to deal with Amy, hadn't she?

Suddenly struck with an idea, she took Kerry by the shoulders, and lowered her voice when she said:

"Kerwin, it was evil that made you see your sister."

"Evil?"

"Yes," Mrs. Macon said. "Gabrielle has evil powers, Kerwin. Haven't I always said she was wicked? She can move from place to place in an instant—like a witch!"

"Like they do in scary movies?" Kerry asked, fascinated for the moment.

"Precisely," Mrs. Macon said. "Your sister is hateful. She possesses dark powers beyond your comprehension! She tried to kill you, Kerwin!"

"Aww, you're nuts!" Kerry cried.

Mrs. Macon glowered at him.

"What did you say?"

Kerry sank back into his seat.

"I—I didn't mean it that way, Mrs. Macon," he said. "Really!"

"I'm not 'nuts!'" Mrs. Macon snapped. "Your sister is evil! Evil!"

Kerry stood up now, clenching his small fists.

"My sister isn't bad!" he cried. "She isn't! You just hate her and want me to hate her, too. But I won't!"

He turned and ran from the office.

"I won't! I won't! I WON'T!"

Upstairs in his room, Kerry flopped himself on his bed, the springs beneath his mattress squeaking in protest. He reached out for his stuffed raccoon, but quickly realized it was gone—lost, left in the wrecked car. He began to cry, thinking about his sister, about Mrs. Macon's awful words, about Amy. . . .

"I want my sister!" he wailed.

No one heard him.

Gabrielle was upset when she didn't hear from her brother again. She wondered if Mrs. Macon had been stealing his letters, or if that teacher named Amy MacClellan had left the orphanage. She continued to write to Kerry, hoping that she'd get a response. But none ever came.

Before she realized it, the month of June passed without event. July brought her birthday, but Gabrielle hadn't mentioned it to anyone. Somehow, the idea of celebrating her birthday didn't seem right without Kerry here.

It was nearly ninety degrees that day, but Flora insisted upon serving her hot soup for lunch. Gabrielle sat staring at the bowl, her face tight with worry. Not even a birthday card from Kerry!

"I hope nothing happened to him," she said.

"What was that?" Flora asked.

Gabrielle began to eat.

"I didn't say anything."

Flora smiled warmly, and placed a hand on Gabrielle's shoulder.

"I know exactly what's wrong," she said. "You thought I didn't know what today is, didn't you? Now, you just wait right here. . . ."

She left the kitchen, and returned momentarily with a package wrapped in pink and white. Setting it in front of Gabrielle, she took a step back as her foster daughter gazed at it in wonder. She nodded, and Gabrielle began to unwrap the gift.

"You didn't have to do this," she said.

"Of course I didn't," Flora replied. "But I wanted to. I want to show you how much you mean to me."

Gabrielle wiggled the top off the box and folded back the sheets of tissue paper. Inside, she found a pair of pierced earrings—rubies encircled with diamonds.

"Oh!" she gasped. "They're *gorgeous!*"

"Happy birthday, Gabrielle!"

The young girl stood up and threw her arms around Flora.

"Thank you!"

"I hope they suit you," Flora said.

"They're the most beautiful things I've ever seen," Gabrielle replied, tilting the box so that the jewels caught the summer sun. But in a moment, the elation drained from her face. "Oh, Flora—I don't have pierced ears!"

Flora laughed.

"You can have it done after the baby is born," she said. "But I thought you might like these today. It isn't every day that a girl turns eighteen!"

Gabrielle smiled again. To think she had been worried just a few months ago that she'd be out on the street today! Instead, she was living in a beautiful home, with a foster mother who really loved her. Gabrielle was certain she had never been happier.

"Oh, I want to show these to the others," she said.

"Of course."

Gabrielle left the house and waddled towards the field, where the farmhands labored under the hot sun. They congratulated her, but Gabrielle didn't notice their frowns when she turned away.

"Maybe I should do something to show Flora how much I love her," she said out loud. She spotted a patch of wild roses near the edge of the woods, and decided to gather a bouquet. Suddenly she heard a loud screeching. Instinctively she threw her arms over her head, cringing. But Chameron did not make a move towards her. Gabrielle looked up carefully, and saw the monkey hanging from a nearby branch, anchored by his tail. She continued walking, keeping her eyes on the animal. She realized she hadn't seen Chameron since the attack in the hallway.

"I thought they had gotten rid of you," she said.

Chameron yowled in reply, then swung himself deeper into the woods. Relieved to see him go, Gabrielle bent towards the patch of flowers and continued gathering them.

Suddenly, the roses fell from her hands. She straightened herself, and stared at a rough sketch on a flat rock just a few feet away.

A skull-and-snakes.

"No," she whispered, shaking her head in disbelief. "No, not again!"

She turned and ran as fast as her heavy body would

carry her. Bursting through the kitchen door, she hurried to the living room, where Flora was rearranging the black statues that sat along the mantel. She threw herself into the woman's arms.

"What is it, my dear?" Flora asked, alarm in her voice.

"I—I saw . . ."

Gabrielle cut herself off, for in an instant something had occurred to her. What if it *was* happening again? What if someone found a dead animal near that rock? Chameron, perhaps! She'd be blamed! And then she'd be sent away again!

"Gabrielle?"

The young girl swallowed.

"You won't ever send me away, will you?"

"Why would you ever think such a thing?"

"I—I don't know," Gabrielle said, pulling away to dry her eyes. "I'm sorry. I'm just being silly."

She wouldn't tell Flora about the drawing. Then, perhaps she wouldn't be blamed for it. It was better kept a dark secret.

"Maybe I'll go upstairs and take a nap," she said. "I'm really tired."

"You do look overwrought," Flora said.

Silently, Gabrielle shuffled through the double doors and up the staircase, unaware that Flora was staring at her. Once in her room, she clicked on the gray fan in her window, twisting the white curtains back over their rod. Then she climbed into bed, wishing it were still possible to lay on her stomach. Soon, curled in a fetal position, she was near the threshold of sleep.

But she didn't fall asleep. Suddenly, she bolted upright, wide-awake. Turning to look out at the yard through the blur of the fan's whirling blades, she whispered her thoughts out loud:

"I was never on that part of the farm before today. I'm sure I wasn't!"

That meant someone else had drawn the picture. But who? Who hated her so much to do such a thing?

"I don't know who you are," she whispered angrily.

"But you aren't going to screw things up for me, this time! You aren't going to take away my happiness!"

Ten

"Don't you wanna play monkey-in-the-middle with us?" Judy asked Kerry as he stood watching his friends in the play yard.

"Nope."

"Come on, Kerry," Michael urged. "You never play with us anymore!"

"I don't feel like playing!" Kerry growled.

Eric stuck out his tongue.

"Who needs you anyway?" he said. "Get lost—we don't want any sourpusses around here."

"You go to hell!" Kerry snapped, turning to run away.

He didn't stop until he reached the nearby woods. The run had brought out a layer of perspiration over his skin, staining his sky-blue T-shirt. Turning to glower at his friends, he was disappointed to see they were already back into their game. Kerry took a step towards them, opening his mouth to shout that he wanted to play after all. But he changed his mind again and started to walk into the woods. He didn't feel like playing so much any more. Not since Amy . . .

To cut off that thought, he kicked over a rock, making little bugs scurry off in every direction. Kneeling, Kerry grabbed for a fat worm, and let it slither around his fingers. He wished he could take it back and stick it in Mrs. Macon's desk drawer. That'd show her!

Instead, he let the worm down on the rock. It was then that he noticed something gleaming in the patch of low-growing weeds near his hand. He reached for it, hoping to find a coin. But it was a much greater treasure.

"Hey!" he cried, pulling out a length of chain. "This is Gabrielle's necklace!"

He let the amulet dangle from his hand, watching the silver and gold shimmer. Wouldn't Gabrielle be happy when she heard? He'd write her a letter, and . . .

"Uh-uhh," Kerry said with a sweep of his head. "Macon-Bacon'd just steal it. I'm gonna keep this a secret!"

He made a ball of it and shoved it deep into his pocket. Then, feeling happier than he had in weeks, he ran back to his friends.

"Guess maybe I'll play with you," he said.

"Maybe we don't wanna play with *you*," Eric sneered.

"Shut up, doofus," Michael said. "Come on, Kerry. Let's play red light, green light."

They chose Kerry as "It." All the while he played, Kerry thought of the amulet, and how he would get it to his sister.

Ever since finding the crude skull-and-snakes symbol, Gabrielle had forced herself to be more observant of her surroundings. This time, she would catch the person who had done it—the person who had been following her for two years now, trying to ruin every chance she had for happiness.

In spite of her efforts, she found nothing. As usual, the farmhands were polite but distant. Gabrielle had already ruled them out anyway—none seemed to have the resources to travel into New Mexico just for the sake of making her life miserable. The young boy with dark hair came to mind, and Gabrielle recalled her initial feelings that he was somehow familiar. Could she have seen him before?

"Maybe he was in the orphanage, too," she said out loud as she fished through her dresser drawer for a nightgown. The lightweight fabric fluttered in the breeze of the fan as she pulled it out. It had been another gift from Flora—just one more thing to endear Gabrielle to her new mother. She undressed and slipped the gown over her head.

"Maybe he hates me, for some reason," she went on. "But what could I have done? I don't even know the guy!"

Climbing into bed, she pulled the cotton sheet up to her chin and reached to turn off the light. The lulling noise of the fan soothed her; the haunting questions drained away. As her body relaxed, Gabrielle placed her hands on her stomach, as if to caress the seven-month fetus within her.

"Don't worry, sweetheart," she whispered. "Mommy'll never let anything happen to you."

The end of the sentence was caught somewhere in Gabrielle's subconscious as she fell fast asleep. As the hours passed, the fan blew the coverlet off her, and iced her body with a chilling breeze. Gabrielle shivered, waking herself up. She sat up groggily and reached towards the floor for her covers. But as she did so, a sharp pain ripped down her lower back. It was as if her pelvis had been disconnected from her spine. Gabrielle tightened herself into a ball.

The pain was like fire within her, making her body tremble as she lay on the bed. She had felt like this only once before—on that day when she had been working in her garden. The doctor had said she was all right, Flora had told her, but right now Gabrielle could not recall her foster mother's reassurance. When the pain finally subsided, she was covered with sweat. Pulling herself from the bed, she tucked her feet into a pair of slippers and put on her robe. Maybe Flora could give her something.

Fearful that another attack would overcome her, Gabrielle inched down the hall towards Flora's room. There was a small point of heat within her, just waiting to flare up again. Gabrielle prayed her foster mother would be able to help. When she reached the carved door, she raised a trembling hand and knocked as hard as she could. There was no answer.

"Flora?"

She was answered by a humming silence. Exhausted, chilled, and in pain, she shuffled back to the main hallway. The banister of the front staircase supported her as she made her way downstairs. She looked for Flora in her study, but she wasn't there—nor was she anywhere else in the house. Gabrielle considered for a moment waking up one of the farmhands. But as she turned to leave the kitchen, faint music reached her ears. Gabrielle limped towards the back door and looked out at the yard, still and wet after the rainstorm. No one was back there.

Gabrielle listened, realizing it was the same chanting she had heard before. Maybe someone was playing a radio? Desperate to find Flora, Gabrielle opened the back door and stepped out into the humid September night.

She headed first to the barn, but heard only the sounds of animals. Tracking the music's source to the nearby woods, Gabrielle headed in that direction. Flora would be displeased at the mess she was making of her new gown and slippers, Gabrielle thought, but under the circumstances she would have to understand.

The music grew louder, beckoning to her. She was too intent on finding Flora to worry about the darkness, or her fear of wild animals. She noticed a light shining between the distant trees.

At last, the trees thinned to reveal a clearing lit so brightly that Gabrielle had to cover her eyes. The bizarre chanting became louder, encircling her head, burning her ears. Hidden by the undergrowth, she carefully pulled her hands away. When her eyes finally adjusted to the light, what Gabrielle saw caused them to go round in terror.

She stood frozen, staring at the group of figures gathered in the clearing, unable to believe what they were doing. Suddenly, her baby began to punch and kick, as if sensing her fear. Feeling him, Gabrielle wrenched herself around and began to run back to the house. Sharp stones sent dull pain up through her bare feet, but in spite of the pain and in spite of the baby's punching, she did not stop, even when splinters slid into her palms as she tripped up the back steps. Sobbing, Gabrielle pulled herself to her feet and made her way to the upstairs bathroom.

She knelt before the toilet, feeling nauseous, but as yet unable to be sick. The room spinned around her, her vision was blurred by her tears.

I must have been dreaming!

But she knew it was no dream. Something had been going on in those woods—something dark and evil.

"No!" Gabrielle choked. "I imagined that! It wasn't . . ."

She suddenly vomited as if to release the nightmare she had just witnessed. Finally, her heart pounding, her skin chilled with perspiration, Gabrielle collapsed on the bathroom floor. There was a full-length mirror on the back of the door, catching the reflection of her pale skin and dark-rimmed eyes. Her hair was in a complete disarray, like that of a madwoman.

"But I'm not mad," Gabrielle whispered to the image. "I know what I saw."

In the safety of the locked bathroom, Gabrielle tried to make sense of the ugly scene she had witnessed. Visions of it came back to her as clearly as if she were still hiding in the woods.

Hooded figures circled around a woman who knelt on the ground. The old-fashioned gown she wore must have been pretty once, but now it was faded and stained. The woman's hairstyle looked like ones Gabrielle had seen in her history books. It hung in limp, straw-like tendrils, tied back with a faded ribbon and brown-edged flowers.

The woman rocked back and forth, holding something in her arms, stroking it. And though she had been bathed in the shadows created by the hooded figures, Gabrielle could not deny who the woman was.

Flora.

And in her lap she cradled the skeletal remains of an infant.

"Nnnnooo. . . ."

Gabrielle covered her face as she groaned. But still the image stayed with her, ugly and horrible. And real . . .

You have to run away, Gabrielle, her thoughts commanded. *You have to get out of here!*

She lied to you! She isn't sweet and kind, like she made you believe!

"It's just a dream! Just a dream. . . ."

No, it happened. You're not crazy! You know what you saw! Flora is insane. That baby skeleton—she might have murdered that child! She may be planning to murder yours!

"There must be some explanation!"

No explanation. She's going to hurt you! Just the way that boy said she would.

"Where will I go! I haven't got any money, and my baby is coming soon, and . . ."

Gabrielle grabbed the rim of the sink over her head and pulled herself up.

"Yes, yes," she choked. "I've got to get out of here. There is something wrong with Flora. I can't risk letting her hurt my baby!"

She leaned against the door, meeting her reflection eye to eye, seeing a face that seemed to belong to a stranger. Slowly, she opened the door and walked out to the hall. The wall offered support as she limped to her bedroom.

She hurt all over. Not from pain but from the sting of betrayal. Why had Flora acted so sweetly these past months? What dark secret had she been hiding? Gabrielle thought about the cradle she'd found in Flora's room. *Who was the baby in her arms?*

Finally, Gabrielle opened the door to her room. She was exhausted, and the bed looked so inviting that she couldn't help gazing at it.

"Get out your suitcase and get packing," she told herself.

But a few minutes of rest wouldn't hurt. . . .

"She's going to come back soon," Gabrielle said. "You've got to leave *now!*"

She couldn't help herself. Her legs were weak, her head was swimming. If she rested for just a few moments, she would have enough strength to face the unknown world beyond the farm's borders.

Just a few minutes...

Eleven

Kerry bolted upright, wakened from a nightmare by the sound of his own gasp. In the nightmare, he had seen Gabrielle reaching out to him, needing his help. But he hadn't been able to get to her.

"What's the matter?" his friend, Michael, whispered from the next bed.

"Nothing," Kerry said. "Go bacta sleep."

Michael groaned and turned over on his stomach. Kerry sat up in the darkness, keeping his eyes opened so that he wouldn't see the image of his sister in his mind's eye. He tried to tell himself it was just a stupid dream, but still he couldn't stop shaking. Gabrielle was in trouble, he decided. And she needed him!

Carefully, Kerry turned and placed his feet on the floor. Under his bed there was a small trunk containing his belongings—clothes, a little money he'd earned from odd jobs, and the baby toys that had been with him when he first came to the orphanage. Moving as quietly as he could, the little boy pulled the chest out, bringing a soft whisper from the floor.

"What're you doing?" Michael demanded, pulling himself up on an elbow.

"None of your business," Kerry hissed.

Michael was too curious to take that for an answer. In a moment, his face peered over the rim of Kerry's bed. He watched in silence as his friend fished through the trunk for clothes, hastily pulling them on.

"You're gonna run away?" Michael asked, in both fear and admiration.

"If you don't shut up, you're gonna wake up the whole room," Kerry replied, wriggling his feet into a pair of socks. As he pulled on his sneakers and tied the laces, he said, "I ain't running away. I'm just gonna go find my sister."

"What if Mrs. Macon finds out?"

Kerry reached up and grabbed the collar of his pajama top.

"She ain't gonna find out, is she?"

"I won't tell," Michael promised.

Kerry let go. Standing, he removed the case from his pillow and filled it with a few things he wanted to bring. Then he arranged the pillow to look like a body under the blanket. Michael stood across from him, watching Kerry in amazement. He thought his friend was crazy, and decided he didn't want to be around when he got caught.

Kerry, without a word, turned and slipped from the room. The hallway seemed longer than usual, every doorway a trap from which the enemy—any adult—might spring. But Kerry wasn't afraid. He felt in the pocket of his jeans for the amulet, and tightened his fist around it as his sister used to do. With a sudden burst of adrenalin, he broke into a run. His sneakers made no sound on the tiles, and only his own soft panting interrupted the stillness.

Reaching a wide staircase, he slowed himself, keeping close to the wall. But as he moved off the bottom step, he noticed a light under Mrs. Macon's office door. What was she doing up at three-thirty in the morning?

"Oh, brother," Kerry whispered, pushing himself even closer to the wall.

He slid along it, keeping his eyes on her office. If he could just make it to the kitchen around the next hallway, he could get out through the service entrance. He'd be in Kansas before anyone knew he was gone!

Just as he reached the connecting hallway, he heard the office door squeak open. His heart gave a quick jerk, but his small legs moved swiftly, and he disappeared into the shadows.

"Who's there?" Mrs. Macon called.

Kerry pushed through the cafeteria door, racing between two rows of lunch tables. Chairs that had been turned upside down on their tops looked like skeletons, but the little boy didn't give himself time to think about the strange silhouettes. He reached the kitchen door, pressing his hands against the cold metal. It was heavier than he expected, and it took all his strength to push it open. At last the door gave way, and he found himself in the darkened kitchen.

The door at the other end of the cafeteria squeaked open at the exact moment.

"I know someone's in here! Answer me!"

You ain't gonna catch me, Owl-eyes!

Kerry hurried to the service door, wanting only to be on the other side of it.

It was locked.

And Mrs. Macon was getting closer . . .

With a gasp, Kerry opened the door under the sink and crawled inside. He wrapped his arms around his knees and listened to the sound of Mrs. Macon's footsteps. Disinfectant, drain opener, and a fresh spraying of Raid assaulted his nose; he wanted to sneeze. He held his breath.

"I thought I saw someone run in here," Mrs. Macon said to herself. She sighed. "It's late and I'm tired."

She left the kitchen. When Kerry heard the door at the far end of the cafeteria open and close, he let a small sneeze escape. Then he scrambled out of his hiding place, twisting the pillow case to fit it under his arm. He knew it was no use to try the door again, and turned around to inspect the window over the sink. Kerry hoisted himself up onto the counter and reached out to unlock it. The latch held fast, despite all his efforts, and in a moment Kerry knew why.

The window had been painted recently, and was stuck shut.

"Now what am I gonna do?"

He sat there with his feet dangling over the edge, the pillow case bundled on his lap. He couldn't get out any other way—since Mrs. Macon was up she'd probably catch him. But he had to leave tonight! Tears fought to fill his eyes, but he gritted his teeth to stop them.

And then he saw a way out. The metal door was fixed with an air vent at its bottom, held in place with only four screws. Just big enough for a kid his size to squeeze through. Kerry leapt from the counter, his sneakers thudding loudly, and hurried to it. Using a bottle opener like a screwdriver, he managed to loosen all four bolts. He removed the vent cover and placed it softly on the floor, letting in a rush of cool night air. First, he pushed his sack through the opening. Then he worked on getting his upper body past the square hole, stretching his arms forward like a diver. It was easy for him, being small-framed, and soon he was kneeling on the gritty sidewalk that ran along the outside of the cafeteria.

"007 couldn't have done that!" he whispered proudly, thinking of his favorite movie hero.

Scrambling to his feet, he raced towards the woods, his body like a small animal's under the silver moon.

Flora pulled a tray of homebaked muffins from the oven. After lining a basket with a blue napkin, she put them in one at a time, placing the largest on the bottom so that it would last until Gabrielle came downstairs. It was the little things that endeared people to each other, she thought.

"Has anyone seen Gabrielle this morning?" she asked as she placed the basket on the table.

The farmhands shook their heads.

"Didn't see her," Harold said.

"She's usually up by now," Flora said worriedly. She snapped a ringed hand at the men. "You may start eating. I'll be down momentarily."

Flora climbed the back staircase, playing with one of her bracelets. In her mind, she counted the weeks until the infant's birth. Weeks, not months. It hardly seemed possible.

Without knocking, she entered Gabrielle's room to find the girl lying on her side, her knees tucked up into her stomach. Gabrielle stared at her dressing table, her hair fluttering in the breeze of the window fan. She didn't turn around.

"What is it, my dear?"

Don't call me "my dear," you liar!

Gabrielle said nothing.

"Are you ill?"

Flora touched her forehead, and frowned when Gabrielle cringed away from her. The girl had no fever, but she was sickly pale. Flora decided she wouldn't take chances with her health. She stood up and went to turn the fan down. Gabrielle stared at her, wanting to scream but too terrified to make a sound.

"It's all right," Flora cooed, turning to her again. Her voice was sweet as always, though now Gabrielle was certain she could hear the underlying bile in it. She hated herself for having been so trusting. "I'll bring something up for you later."

She bent to kiss Gabrielle's forehead, but the young girl turned away from her. With a grim expression, Flora straightened herself and started to walk from the room. It was then that she noticed Gabrielle's robe, thrown over the back of a chair.

There was mud on it. Flora paused, noticing the slippers that flopped against the chair leg. Mud streaked their soles.

Gabrielle had been outside last night.

She must have seen something.

"Sleep for now," Flora said, hiding her rage. "I'll return later."

After the door closed and Flora's footsteps retreated down the hall, Gabrielle pulled herself from the bed. Somehow, her weight seemed greater today than before, and she had to take little steps at first to keep her balance. Seven and a half months, she thought. It seemed as if a lifetime had passed since that night with Keith Brody. Funny how she had never given him a thought until this moment. But it was a short-lived memory; Gabrielle had more important things on her mind.

She had decided against carrying a suitcase, since it would draw too much attention to her. Instead, she would dress in several layers. It was going to be hot today—she could tell that by the chirping of the crickets outside—but she'd only have to wear extra layers until she reached the town's bus station.

She went to her closet first, pulling out a handful of maternity tops and one pair of jeans. There was a mirror built into the closet door, and as she closed it, she faced the reflection of her foster mother's grim face.

"Flora!" she cried, turning. "I . . . I . . ."

"I see you're feeling better," Flora said. She held out a china cup. "I brought you some tea."

Gabrielle held the shirts in front of her like a protective wall.

"N-no," she stammered. "I don't want any tea."

Flora smiled, and in that smile Gabrielle saw all the evil of the previous night. Before she could speak, two farmhands burst into the room and grabbed her arms, twisting them back painfully.

"Let me go! Flora, why . . ."

"Fool!" Flora cried. "You were outside last night! Why did you leave this house?"

"I came out to look for you," Gabrielle said. "I was sick! Please tell these guys to let me go!"

There was silence.

"Flora," Gabrielle said carefully. "Flora, what's going on here?"

"Silence!" Flora commanded. The gentle tone was gone. The loving glow of her green eyes had turned dark and ugly. "You must be taught your place here!"

"My place?" Gabrielle echoed. "My place? I thought I was your foster daughter. I thought you loved me!"

Flora sneered at her, regarding Gabrielle's tears with disdain. She signalled to the farmhands.

"Take her to the bed."

"NNNNOOO!!!!"

Ignoring Gabrielle's screams, the two did as they were told. She was no match for them, and they effortlessly pinned her arms and legs to the mattress. Gabrielle felt something hard and cold slide against her lips, and twisted her head from side to side to resist. Flora grabbed her hair and thrust her head back. Suddenly, Gabrielle was no longer able to scream. Flora began to pour warm liquid down her throat. Gabrielle tasted tea—and something else. Something slightly bitter.

Everything went black.

"She's in my power now," Flora said, staring at the unconscious figure. "Take that thing from her mouth and tie her wrists to the headboard."

Quickly, silently, the farmhands obeyed. Gabrielle's arms were limp as they were pulled up, her fingers making little jerking motions as the cords were tied around her wrists. Flora leaned down and placed her hands on the girl's stomach, feeling the slight movements of the unborn child. She smiled.

"Soon, a new cycle will begin," she whispered.

The men looked up to see her eyes virtually glowing. They exchanged glances, then slipped quietly from the room, suddenly afraid of her.

Kerry's pillowcase bumped against his leg as he walked, flopping lazily from his tired hand. He yawned, looking through the morning haze at the road that stretched up into the distant mountains. It seemed as if days had passed since he left the grounds of the orphanage, though it was less than five hours behind him. In that time, Kerry had gotten two rides, but otherwise had seen nobody. Right now, he was completely exhausted. His feet were sore, he was tired and hungry, and it was getting hot.

"You sure were stupid, Kerry Hansen," he said, his

voice mellow in the still, heavy air. "Right there in a kitchen and you forgot to bring something to eat!"

Well, somebody had to come along pretty soon. It'd been quite a while since the last ride—with two young girls who giggled a lot and fussed over him. There had been a funny smell in that car, something Kerry was too young to recognize as marijuana. He was glad to get out of it. He wondered what James Bond would do. Kerry had seen every movie featuring 007, and thinking of the secret agent's exciting adventures made him feel a little stronger. Rescuing his sister was just one of those episodes, wasn't it?

At last, he heard the sound his ears had been perked for—a rumbling motor. Turning, he saw a pick-up truck, and thrust out his thumb to flag it down. He was greeted by a middle-aged man in overalls, with a face so red it seemed the desert sun had colored it to match the mountainside. Kerry pulled himself into the front seat, dropping the pillowcase to his feet.

"Where're you goin'?" he was asked.

"To see my sister," Kerry said eagerly. "She lives in Kansas."

"Kansas, huh? Mighty long way from here."

The pickup started to roll again.

"I guess so," Kerry said. "But I gotta get there. My sister is waiting for me."

"Your parents know you're out here?"

"Haven't got any parents," Kerry said. "Just my sister."

No parents, the driver thought. *I'll just bet!*

"Shoot, I suppose I could drive you to Kansas then."

Kerry thanked him and turned to look out the window, wriggling his feet to ease the pain he felt under his soles. Boy, was this luck? The driver was going all the way to Kansas. He'd be with Gabrielle in no time!

A few miles later, the truck took a sharp U-turn, bumping over the rocky banks of the road. To Kerry's amazement, they were headed in the opposite direction!

"Hey, why did you turn around?" he demanded. "This ain't the way to Kansas!"

"Darn right," the driver said. "I'm gonna get the sheriff after you!"

Twelve

It was warm in the room. The air was heavy, wrapping around Gabrielle's body like a shroud, seeping through her every pore to heat the blood in her veins. She opened her eyes, looking straight above her, seeing only darkness. She couldn't really feel her body, as if her spirit had risen from it to float in the void. There were no thoughts, no recollections that her name was Gabrielle, that she was a prisoner on a Kansas farm, that her body sheltered a tiny life. There was only an awareness of warmth and floating.

She closed her eyes again. Now voices poked holes in the emptiness, far-away voices.

"The Master's will shall be done," a woman said.

"The girl can't fight you now," a man answered.

"She looks the way her mother did eighteen years ago," the woman said. "Just the way Naomi looked."

Naomi . . .

A spark of remembrance illuminated a point in the darkness. Gabrielle stared at the light, watching it grow, seeing nothing else. Flora stood at her bedside with Roger, one of the farmhands, but Gabrielle was not aware of them.

"Is she waking?"

Flora shook her head. "See how she stares? She's watching something."

"I wonder what?"

"It matters little," Flora said. "Come, there are things we must do."

She turned and left the room, Roger at her side. Somewhere in the darkness, Gabrielle heard the door shut, and her body jumped a little in reaction. But still she watched the point of light, watching it grow like an opening curtain, until a picture of a kitchen appeared before her. Bright light bounced off rows of hanging pots and across a length of polished countertop. Gabrielle could barely make out the speckled tile floor and smooth metal cabinets. In the midst of all this stood a little girl with long dark braids. She was Gabrielle as a child.

The younger Gabrielle rocked her baby brother's cradle as her counterpart watched from eight years in the future. She had a worried look on her pretty little face, and seemed relieved when the double doors leading into the kitchen swung open. Naomi Hansen entered, and said something the comatose Gabrielle could not hear.

Suddenly, she became one with her younger self.

"The Pampers are in the left-most cupboard," Naomi was saying. "On the bottom."

Gabrielle crossed the room to fetch the diapers for her mother. As she was bending to pull them out, the amulet she wore fell from her neck, dropping with a soft ping to the floor. In a flash, Naomi grabbed her, shaking her roughly.

"Didn't I tell you not to take that off? Didn't I say bad things would happen if you did?"

In the bed where she lay at Flora's house, Gabrielle whimpered and tried to struggle away from the cords that shackled her wrists.

"It just fell off, Mommy!"

The scene blurred, like water running over a photograph, and Gabrielle found herself staring into darkness again. Within a few seconds, a new picture formed. Bodies.

Bodies lying on the floor of the diner in pools of blood. There was blood everywhere Gabrielle looked.

Staining the floor and the furniture. And little pieces of half-chewed food . . .

"Mommy?"

Naomi stood with her back to her daughter. Gabrielle reached for her, needing her comfort. Naomi did not turn.

Someone screamed.

In her bed at Flora's house, Gabrielle twisted her head back and forth.

Something was floating towards her from the far end of the kitchen. It moved slowly, about six feet off the ground, a black glob.

It was a dead rat. Like the one on her dresser at the Brody's house. With blood dripping from its throat.

Gabrielle screamed, a scream that was carried eight years into the future, filling the upstairs of Flora's house. No one paid attention to her.

Kerry grabbed handfuls of hay from the floor and threw them with all his might, venting his anger at having been caught in his attempt to run away. He was sitting inside a dark, cold barn, waiting for the sheriff to arrive to take him back to the orphanage. The driver of the pickup had taken him back to a ranch, where he dragged the screaming, kicking little boy to the barn for safekeeping—"until the sheriff gets here."

Kerry stood up and shuffled over to the wide doors, dry hay crunching under his sneakers. Peeking through a crack in the wood, he saw that the yard outside was filled with busy ranch hands. Any attempt to get past them would be futile. But Kerry hadn't given up yet. Somehow, he'd get out of this. James Bond would have some sort of secret weapon to help him escape. Kerry wished he had a secret weapon.

Plunking himself down on a splintery ladder, he placed his chin in his hands and watched the door. A moment later, the darkness broke apart and sunlight shone into the barn. The rancher stood in the opened doorway, hands on his hips, shaking his head. Kerry scowled at him.

"Sheriff's real busy right now," he said. "But you stay there and he'll come get you soon's he can!"

Kerry said nothing.

"And," the rancher went on, "since you're so stubborn 'bout tellin' me who your daddy is, you can just wait here until he does come!"

"I ain't got any parents," Kerry insisted.

The rancher turned and left, pulling the doors shut and locking them from the outside. Kerry stayed on the ladder, wondering what he should do next. But his young mind was too exhausted by the events of the day to begin making plans. He yawned, rubbed his eyes, and fell fast asleep.

When he woke up again, it was even darker than before, and he knew that night had fallen. Wondering why the sheriff hadn't come yet, he got up and went to look out the crack between the two doors. He tried to open one, and remembered it was locked.

He felt a little scared, and wanted to cry.

"Aww, don't be a baby," he told himself. "007 wouldn't be scared! Now—what would he do if he was stuck like this?"

Sure, Kerry thought. 007 wouldn't sit around. He'd be looking for an escape. The only way out seemed to be a window up in the hayloft, but even if he could get to it he'd probably hurt himself climbing to the ground.

"Maybe I'd better try," he said out loud.

He started up the ladder, holding his breath. He was nearly to the top when he suddenly noticed something that hadn't been visible to him from the floor. Behind stacks of hay sat a door, a passageway leading to another section of the barn. Encouraged, Kerry scrambled down the ladder and crawled over the hay. He wanted to push his way through the door, but instead stopped and listened, in case anyone was there.

But he only heard the snorting of an animal. He turned the knob slowly and entered another room. It was a stable; four horses stood quietly in a row of stalls. Beyond them, a door to the outside gaped wide open.

"Great!" Kerry whispered.

He went to the door, keeping very close to a wall hung with riding equipment, and looked out. The backyard was empty, and only one light was on in the nearby house. Kerry could make out silhouettes, figures that seemed to be seated around a table. If they were busy with dinner, he could make his escape unnoticed.

The sound of a horse's whinny made him gasp and turn. He was alone—no one had snuck up behind him. He gazed longingly at the horses, wishing he knew how to ride. But none of them was saddled, and he certainly wasn't strong enough to do that anyway.

Then he saw something he could use—a bicycle! The Schwinn, an ancient model with pedal brakes, sat forgotten and rusting against the wall. It was covered with cobwebs, but Kerry didn't mind about spiders. He pulled it carefully away from the wall and rolled it back and forth. The tires were still full of air, although the seat was a little loose and the frame was bent.

He wheeled the bicycle out into the yard, keeping his eyes on the house for any movement. He didn't dare mount it until he was behind the barn and out of sight.

Fortunately, this bicycle had once been used by someone about his size, and he had no trouble reaching the pedals. He started pumping, bringing a satisfying squeak from the long-unused wheels. Boy, never mind those fancy sports cars in all the secret agent movies he'd seen; this was all he needed.

The bicycle rattled across the field, but Kerry was able to keep it steady. He soon reached the road he had been hitching on when the rancher caught him. Now the going was much smoother, and in no time he passed the spot where he'd accepted the ride. He kept going until his legs were too tired, then dismounted the bike, and walked it beside him.

When a car passed him on the road, he ducked behind some pine trees. Kerry didn't know that the rancher had gone to the barn to bring him something for dinner, and was infuriated to find his prisoner had somehow escaped. He was determined to find him before he got very far. The rancher didn't want to have to admit to the sheriff that he'd let a little kid escape.

Gabrielle heard voices in the room. She stirred a bit, but did not have the strength to open her eyes. A soft moan escaped her lips, like the pitiful cry of a child caught in a nightmare.

"She's waking," a man said.

"No, the spell is too strong," a woman replied. *Flora*. Gabrielle recognized the woman's voice and went cold.

"It's been days," Roger commented. "Is the infant safe?"

Flora glared at him.

"Do you think I'm a fool?" she demanded. "I would do nothing to endanger its life! It is promised to the Master!"

The Master . . .

The word echoed over and over in Gabrielle's mind, but the young girl could not ask who the "Master" might be.

When Kerry arrived in a small desert village, he saw by a huge clock on the town hall's facade that it was nearly eight o'clock. He'd been alternately walking and riding for the past hour, and was famished. A hamburger stand beckoned him, and he parked his bike in the shadows alongside it.

He ordered two hamburgers and a chocolate shake, and carried the tray to a blue Formica table. The place was decorated with plants, separating each table from the next and providing some sense of privacy. Kerry gobbled down the first burger and drank half the shake, easing his hunger pangs. He finished the rest of the meal at a more leisurely pace.

Just as he was slurping up the last of the shake, he saw a familiar figure walk in through the glass doors. The rancher! Hidden behind the foliage, Kerry kept his eyes on the red-faced man as he walked towards the counter. Then, carefully, he climbed from his chair and hurried for the door marked "Rest Rooms," which led to a short hallway. Keeping the door opened a crack, he looked beyond a cactus to see the man speaking to the counter girl. She looked over at the table Kerry had left and shook her head.

"Musta been here a while ago then," the rancher said.

Kerry bit his lip and watched him go, waiting until he saw the lights of the pickup pull back and turn away. Only then did he leave his hiding place, scurrying towards the door.

"Hey, wait!"

Kerry stopped in his tracks.

"Don't be afraid," the counter girl called. "Just come over here and talk to me."

Sheepishly, Kerry did as he was told. The girl was leaning over the counter, her forearms resting on its smooth surface.

"Listen, kid," she said, "no matter what kind of licking your daddy gives you, it won't be so bad as what's out there if you run away. Now, he seemed like a nice man, so why don't you go home to him?"

Kerry simply nodded his head without a word, then turned and hurried from the building. He wanted to tell the girl that man wasn't his daddy, but he really didn't have the time to waste. When he got outside, he pulled his bicycle from its hiding place and sped off. Silently, he thanked the girl for not giving him away.

Soon, the little boy grew too tired to pedal. Seeing an empty playground, he took refuge for the night underneath a small grandstand. When the morning sun coaxed him awake, he felt full of energy, and headed straight to his bike to continue his journey.

"I wonder how far it is now?" he asked himself, lifting the bike from the sandy ground. Well, at least he was on the right road—he knew the highway he'd been following led straight into Kansas.

He walked his bike to a water fountain, and took a long drink of warmish water. Kerry rode for some time before stopping in yet another small town. By the clock in the gas station, Kerry saw it was well past noon, and became angry with himself for having slept so late. Still, he was hungry, and had to take the time to eat something before going on. Lunch was put together by purchasing a jar of peanut butter and a box of crackers. Kerry sat himself down on a curb and scooped out globs of Skippy until he was satisfied. Then, as he was tucking the remaining food in his pillow case, something caught his attention.

It was a Pepsi truck, pulling up alongside the general store. A broad-shouldered man jumped out, walking around to the back. The proprietor of the store came out at that moment, and gave the delivery man a friendly greeting.

"Long haul ahead, Bill?"

The back door of the truck slid up noisily.

"Going clear through to Kansas today," came the reply.

Kansas! Kerry wished he could get a ride in that big truck. But he didn't dare make an attempt to hitch a ride. Not if it might get him in trouble again, like yesterday! Disappointed, he started to mount the rickety old bike again.

But then something happened to change his mind. The driver wheeled a handcart stacked with bottles down a ramp and into the store, followed by the owner. They left the truck unattended! *What a chance*, Kerry thought. *I can sneak inside the truck, just like James Bond would do!* Quickly, Kerry wheeled his bike behind a patch of cactus and hid it. Then he raced into the back of the truck.

Bottles and cans jutted up from crates tinkling softly as he brushed by them. Kerry's small body was easily hidden behind the stacks, and there he scrunched himself up tight, not daring to breathe until the door had been closed and the truck started to move again.

What luck, he thought. *And this time, I will get to Gabrielle!*

Flora entered Gabrielle's room late in the afternoon and placed her hands on the girl's stomach. She felt the baby give a sharp kick, as if in response to the touch of cold hands. Gabrielle did not stir. The time had come, Flora decided, to release the spell. Gabrielle would be too weak by now to attempt running away. Flora's cold fingers began to make strange patterns on her forehead. After a few minutes, there was a flutter under Gabrielle's eyelids. Soon, the young girl was staring blankly at her.

"You will feel better," Flora stated. "Then, I will get you something to eat."

She turned to stride from the room. Gabrielle heard the door open and shut, but nothing registered in her tortured mind. Weakened by the days she'd spent under Flora's spell, she was unable to even think clearly.

Then, little by little, awareness crept back. Bewilderment turned to fear when she saw how her wrists were bound. And then that fear turned to anger as memories of what had happened came back to her. She had seen something horrible in the woods (she wouldn't let herself think of that), and Flora had been furious about it.

By the time the woman came back to her room with a tray of food, Gabrielle was famished. It had been days since she last ate, and though she didn't want to cooperate with Flora at all she accepted the spoonfuls of food that were shovelled into her mouth. But she remained silent, glaring at Flora with hurt eyes.

At last, Flora stood up to leave the room, taking the tray from Gabrielle's lap. Gabrielle watched her, full of questions and yet too afraid to voice them. Then, as Flora opened her door, she somehow had the feeling she'd better ask now, before it was too late. She blurted out the woman's name.

"Flora!"

Flora turned.

"Yes, my dear?"

Gabrielle stiffened at the sound of "my dear."

"What—what do you want from me?" she stammered, her voice small.

Flora stared at her for a long time, then said in a soft voice:

"Your baby."

Thirteen

Because he was so close to the front of the truck, Kerry could overhear everything the driver was saying on his radio. He listened carefully for the names of towns, and recognized a few from his earlier trip with Amy. Finally, he heard what he had been waiting for: Bill was pulling into the town where Gabrielle was staying!

Kerry pulled himself tightly against the wall of the truck as the back door slid open. The pink light of dusk shone inside, blocked by the driver's burly frame. Kerry watched his silhouette, shadowed on the ceiling, not moving until it was gone and the sound of the handcart's wheels faded away. Then he scrambled to his feet and hurried out to the parking lot. After being cooped up in the back of the truck for hours, Kerry found the cool air invigorating. Now—how would he find Gabrielle's home?

He had made a decision while sitting behind the stacks of soda containers. Much as he wanted to go right to Gabrielle, he thought better of it. Mrs. Macon had probably called Flora by now, and someone might even be waiting to take him back to the orphanage. No, he would wait until it was really late before making any attempt to get his sister. Then he'd sneak into the house somehow, and find her.

So, what to do now? The answer came quickly: a small movie theater about a block away. He fished through his pillowcase and gathered up enough money to buy a ticket. Then, deciding he was hungry after the long truck ride, he purchased a hot dog and chocolate milk at the counter. In the midst of a Bugs Bunny cartoon, he left his seat to buy a big container of popcorn.

By the time the movie was over, a little more than two hours later, half the bucket was still full and Kerry's stomach felt ready to burst. He held on to it as he entered the lobby, and noticed it was about ten o'clock. To a little boy whose curfews had always been before nine, it seemed incredibly late. He decided it was okay to try to sneak onto the farm now. Outside, he saw a group of teenagers piling into a huge, muralled van, talking animatedly about the film they'd just seen. Kerry ran up to them.

"Hi," he said.

One of the girls giggled, and a boy with sandy hair said:

"What do you want, kid?"

"Um, my sister forgot to pick me up," Kerry lied, "and I wanna go home. Could you take me?"

The boy heaved his shoulders. "I guess so—hop in."

Kerry, relieved that it was so easy this time, gave him Flora's address. Barely ten minutes later, he was let off in front of a gloomy-looking patch of land.

"That's it back there," the driver said. "I used to deliver papers here a long time ago. But I didn't know anyone was living there now."

"We just moved in," Kerry said, thinking quickly. "Thanks for the ride!"

He jumped down onto the road bank, feeling mud squish under his sneakers. As the van pulled away, he turned to look at the house, a black silhouette against the purplish sky. Resting his hand on top of a rusty, dilapidated mailbox, Kerry whispered:

"Creepy old place!"

Something that had made the mailbox its home crawled out over his hand. Kerry shook it away impatiently and pushed open the gate. In the stillness of the night it made an ear-piercing shriek. Kerry held his breath. But none of the house lights went on, no dogs started barking, no gunshots were fired. Finally, he started to run, keeping his eyes on the house.

Kerry wasn't usually afraid of the dark. But this was the kind of dark where you couldn't see what was following you until it had you by the throat. The mooing of cows sounded like ghostly moaning, the chirp of crickets like the maniacal laugh of an escaped lunatic. . . .

With a gasp, Kerry dove behind the thick trunk of an apple tree. He sat there until his breathing calmed, and suddenly heard someone singing. Straining to listen, he tilted his head in one direction, then the other. It was coming from the woodlands across the field. A group of voices now. He shivered.

"Dumb time to go singing," he said.

Maybe that was why the house was so dark. Maybe they were all having a party outside. Weird!

Well, if that was the case, then it meant the house was empty. Kerry could just sneak inside, find Gabrielle's room, and hide there until his sister found him. He stood up and walked around the back of the house, surprised to find the kitchen door had been left unlocked. Kerry glanced over his shoulder, then pushed through the door into the dark kitchen. When his eyes adjusted to the light, he crossed the room and entered a hallway.

He found the back staircase and eased his way up it, keeping his ears open for any sudden noises. The upstairs seemed deserted, a series of similar doors leading to bedrooms that looked exactly alike. Peering through the keyholes, Kerry tried to find something that belonged to his sister, some hint that a room was hers. There was nothing. When he came to the branch hall, he mouthed the word "wow" at the sight of the carved door. He stood for a moment gaping at it, reaching out to touch the carved wood. But he stopped his hand a half inch away, suddenly afraid. Somehow, it gave him the creeps.

Quickly, he hurried from the hall and continued

his search down the main hall. All at once he heard soft weeping, coming from a door just beyond the bath. Kerry twisted his lips. That was Gabrielle! He'd heard her cry often enough to know. But just to be double sure, he bent down and looked through the keyhole.

Someone who looked like Gabrielle was lying in a big bed, her wrists tied to the headboard. But Kerry could hardly believe this was his sister. Her usually pretty eyes were trimmed with red, her face was as pale as a ghost's and sunken-looking. Forcing himself to see that this was indeed Gabrielle, Kerry stamped his foot in anger. What was going on here?

Without further hesitation, he pushed open the door. Gabrielle turned in his direction, expecting that Flora had returned to torment her. When she saw Kerry, she cringed, pulling her knees up. This was an illusion, wasn't it? A cruel joke, or a product of her own tired mind. In a moment, it would vanish.

Kerry had often wondered how the reunion with his sister would be. He'd finally decided he'd probably run up to her, throw his arms around her, and laugh with joy. But instead, he kept his distance as he said quietly:

"Gabrielle, you got really fat."

Then he raced across the room and jumped up onto the bed. Feeling the warmth of his body, Gabrielle dared to believe he was really here. She relaxed enough to lean her face on the soft nest of his black hair. He *was* real! No apparition could duplicate the flashes of violet she saw now in his gray eyes.

"How come you're all tied up like this?"

"Just—just get these things off me," Gabrielle choked.

Kerry started to work on the cords, and in a few minutes had managed to unfasten them. Immediately, Gabrielle threw her arms around him and hugged him tightly.

"This is a crazy place, Gabrielle," Kerry said. "We've gotta get out of here!"

Gabrielle looked towards her window, hearing the sound of chanting.

"They'll be back soon," she said.

Kerry jumped from the bed.

"Then come on," he said. "Get your things and we'll run away!"

He helped his sister from her bed and towards her closet. With his arms around her, he was more aware of her round middle, and wanted to ask about it. But there was no time for that right now. Moving as if in a trance, Gabrielle pulled her suitcase down and filled it with her clothes, packing the silver brush and mirror and the ruby-and-diamond earrings last of all. If they needed money, she might be able to pawn them.

"Hurry!" Kerry urged.

Despite his encouragement, the doubts Gabrielle had still hovered over her. None of this seemed real. Her brother was rescuing her? An eight-year-old?

Too many questions, not enough time . . .

The hallway and stairs were dark and cold. The big kitchen, where Gabrielle had once felt so loved and welcome, now seemed hateful. She couldn't cross it fast enough, fearing that any hesitation might prove this really was a dream. Kerry spotted a small black purse on the counter and snatched it up, tucking it under his shirt. A few moments later, as they touched the bottom step of the porch, they heard voices.

Flora was coming back!

Gabrielle caught her breath, but Kerry had the sense to pull her down behind the adjacent bushes. They huddled there, waiting in heart-pounding silence. Kerry could feel his sister trembling, or was that him?

She's going to catch us, Gabrielle thought frantically as tears rose in her eyes.

Inside her, the baby answered the thump of her heart with quick little jabs. Gabrielle rubbed a hand over her stomach and silently told it to be still. She bit her lip and pressed closer to Kerry as two farmhands climbed up the steps and into the kitchen. Carl appeared next, dragging something long and dark in his fat hand. Gabrielle remembered the black robes at the ceremony.

Suddenly, she heard a loud scream. To her horror, Chameron was hanging from the porch light, yowling and waving a skinny arm in their direction!

Oh, God, I'm dead....

At that moment, her heart seemed to stop. Chameron went on screeching, prompting Carl to yell at him. Then Gabrielle saw something fly at the monkey's small head. With a final screech, Chameron jumped down and ran off in the opposite direction. Gabrielle turned to Kerry, and caught his wrist in time to stop him from throwing another stone. She shook her head, her eyes wide with fear. But Carl hadn't noticed what caused the monkey's retreat.

Now the others returned, one by one, or in pairs. Soon, Gabrielle saw Flora walking across the field, her arms around the young boy with dark curls. She kissed him, then sent him away from her. A few moments later she came up the back steps, walking stiffly. It was not until she was inside that Gabrielle dared to breathe. When the porch light clicked off, she stood up.

"Let's get the hell out of here," she whispered to Kerry.

They moved as swiftly as possible, slowed by the fact that Gabrielle was carrying so much extra weight. Kerry kept looking back at the house, expecting to see a light go on when it was discovered Gabrielle was missing. But that didn't happen, and eventually they reached the road that led into town.

Some time later, they were given a ride by a young couple headed to a local diner for a late snack. They were left off in front of the bus station, a small building situated in the middle of a brightly lit parking lot. Gabrielle felt as if the lights were shining directly on her, as if to point her out to Flora's men.

"Don't stand there," Kerry said, pulling her into the depot.

Before the young couple had picked them up, he'd removed the wallet from Flora's purse, and tossed the purse into an empty field. Now he opened the wallet to find it stuffed full of bills. Gabrielle watched him with a blank expression as he counted the treasure.

"Gabrielle, there's over four hundred dollars here!" he gasped. "Boy, that Flora must really be rich!"

Gabrielle said nothing.

"Well, let's go," Kerry said, with as much authority as an eight-year-old could muster. "Don't you worry, Gabrielle. I'll get you away from that crazy woman!"

He put a serious expression on his face and sauntered over to the ticket booth. Standing on tiptoes, he asked:

"When's the next bus?"

"Where're you going?"

Kerry frowned, falling back on his heels. *Where was he going?* All this money could get them pretty far, couldn't it? All the way to Colorado. No—Utah! The idea struck him when he saw a poster nearby advertising Arches National Monument. Sure, he knew that place. They'd read about it in school. He squinted, reading the name of the nearest town to the site.

"Got anything for Moab?"

"Somethin's heading into Utah in about twenty minutes," the ticket seller said in a weary tone. "It passes along 70, which is as close to Moab as I can get you unless you wait for morning."

"I'll take two tickets on that bus, then," Kerry said.

The seller told Kerry the price, and drummed his fingers impatiently as the little boy counted out the bills. He didn't stop to ask what a child that age was doing in a lonely bus terminal at this late hour. It wasn't his concern what other people's kids did.

Kerry paid for two tickets and brought them to Gabrielle, beaming with pride that he had succeeded in making such an important transaction. She didn't even smile.

"We gotta wait twenty minutes," he said, plunking down on the cracked red plastic seat beside her.

Gabrielle's blank expression turned to one of terror.

"Twenty minutes! Kerry, they could be here in that time!"

"And Mrs. Macon coulda caught me when I ran away," Kerry pointed out. "But she didn't, and Flora ain't gonna catch you! So, take it easy!"

Though Kerry insisted everything was going to be fine, Gabrielle couldn't yet believe him. All this had to end at any moment. She would hear that evil voice, and then the farmhands would grab her. . . .

Kerry watched her in silence, wanting to ask so many questions but somehow afraid to break into her private thoughts. He didn't think about being scared, but it did worry him that Gabrielle looked so deathly ill.

Maybe he could buy her a candy bar in the vending machine, to cheer her up. He reached into his pocket for some change, but instead his fingers felt the smooth disc of the amulet. He'd forgotten all about that!

"Gabrielle, look!" he cried, pulling it out.

Gabrielle stared at the silver and gold pendant a few moments, then snatched it from her brother. Pulling it over her head, she squeezed it tightly and closed her eyes as her mother's words came back to haunt her:

Bad things will happen if you take it off, Gabrielle!

"Oh, Mommy," she whispered. "You were right!"

Kerry touched her arm.

"Gabrielle, Mommy isn't here," he said.

She blinked at him. "Kerry, where did you find this?"

"In the woods by the orphanage," Kerry said. He looked up towards the doors.

"There's the bus, Gabrielle. Let's go!"

Holding her amulet in one hand and her valise in the other, Gabrielle waddled out towards the bus. Kerry handed the driver his tickets, then chose a seat towards the back.

A few minutes later, they passed a sign indicating the boundary of the town. Reading it, Gabrielle dropped her head and began to cry tears of relief. Maybe, just maybe, this wasn't a dream after all.

Fourteen

"Please don't cry, Gabrielle," Kerry pleaded. He knelt on the seat beside his sister's, one leg tucked underneath him, his hands pressed on the vinyl armrest. "We got away. Those crazy people will never catch us now!"

Gabrielle couldn't answer. She sat staring at her stomach, tears on her cheeks. The baby was still now. Gabrielle rubbed the front of her smock as if to caress it.

The bus was nearly empty at this hour, but the heavy smell of discarded food and stale cigarettes indicated it had been crowded earlier on. Kerry was glad they were alone, with no one to ask questions.

"I wonder when I'll ever learn," Gabrielle said. "You can't trust anyone, Kerry. Everyone wants to hurt you."

"I don't want to hurt you, Gabrielle."

Gabrielle ran the backs of her hands across her eyes.

"I can't believe I fell for it again," she said. "I can't believe I was stupid enough to think someone would want to adopt me."

She curled her hand into a fist and pounded the armrest.

"There were so many clues," she said. "That weird guy with dark hair tried to warn me about her. But I wouldn't listen. . . ."

"Gabrielle?"

She turned to Kerry. There was a moment of silence, and then the two put their arms around each other. Though it had been months since she last saw her brother, Gabrielle could tell his love for her was as strong as ever. She still had him, if nothing else.

"Flora seemed so nice," she said, gazing out at the passing scenery. "She couldn't do enough for me, Kerry. But that was because she wanted something."

"What was that?"

"She wanted my baby," Gabrielle said, simply. A vision of the pitiful little skeleton Flora had been cradling came to mind, but Gabrielle pushed it away.

"How come?"

Gabrielle kissed the top of his head.

"I don't know, Kerry," she admitted. "None of this makes sense to me."

"Well, you don't have to worry anymore," Kerry said, sitting back. "We've got a lot of money, and we can go really far. Heck, when this ride is over we'll be far away from that kook!"

"It's going to take about eighteen hours," Gabrielle guessed. "Flora's going to have started looking for me long before we reach Utah."

"Don't think about her," Kerry suggested. "She'll never find us, and no one will stop us. It'll be just great, Gabrielle. Really!" He took his sister's hand. "Anyway, we'll live together like we're supposed to do," he went on.

"Oh, Kerry," Gabrielle sighed. "You're so brave for such a little kid. How did you ever make it all the way to Flora's? It was so dangerous!"

"Aww," Kerry said with a shrug. "I just kept thinking of all those James Bond movies I've seen. 007 could've done it easy, too."

Gabrielle put her arm around him again. She only wished she could be as sure as he was.

Ida Macon shuddered when she heard a familiar voice on the other end of the phone line. She had expected to hear from Flora Collins when she discovered Kerry Hansen was missing. But, fearful of the woman's anger (and more fearful the checks would be stopped), she had not contacted her with the news. Now, Flora was in a rage.

"Fool!" she hissed. "Why didn't you call me as soon as you knew the boy had run away? I could have stopped him—but he's already left here with Gabrielle!"

"I—I thought the police would find him on the road," Mrs. Macon said tremulously. It unnerved her that she, usually so strong, was so easily frightened by a voice on the phone.

"You thought!" Flora echoed. "Imbecile! Dolt!"

"How dare you..."

"Be silent!"

Ida Macon's lips hardened, but she quieted herself. *Think of the checks....*

"What do you want me to do?"

"Have you access to all the boy's papers?"

Mrs. Macon confirmed this.

"I want them destroyed," Flora said. "Every one of them—whether in print or on a computer. Can you do that?"

"Yes," Mrs. Macon said.

"Good," Flora said, and Mrs. Macon heard a soft sigh. "Burn them, and when you have finished, call me back."

"Why should I do this?"

"There is something in it for you," Flora coaxed. "Some—oh, some small payment. Say, twenty thousand?"

"I'll do it," Mrs. Macon replied firmly.

She hung up the phone and went to the records office. While there, she told the secretaries that Kerry had been placed permanently, and that they wouldn't be hearing from him again. But she needed to go over his records to be certain everything was in order.

She carried them to her private bathroom, where she set them on fire, dropping the ashes into the toilet. Within half an hour she returned a call to Flora.

"When do I get my money?"

"Never."

Mrs. Macon turned to look out her window at the children playing in the yard.

"What do you mean, 'never'?"

"You'll have no use for it," Flora said. "Mrs. Macon, don't you feel rather strange right now?"

"N-no." But there was a slight chest pain.

"Goodbye, Mrs. Macon," Flora sing-songed.

Mrs. Macon stood listening to the buzzing receiver, numbed all over but for a strange pain that travelled across her chest and arms. Then the receiver dropped to the floor. . . .

When they found her, several hours later, her death was attributed to heart failure.

Flora set the cradle in her room in motion and watched it rock lazily. She smiled, satisfied. Now, with records of both Hansens destroyed, and with the death of the only person who knew of her connection to them, nothing could stop her from bringing Gabrielle back again.

And she would. She knew she'd eventually find the girl. Gabrielle thought she was safe, but Flora's influence extended far beyond the little Kansas farm. Only a handful of people realized just how many followers of the "Master" there were. Professionals, blue-collar workers, clergy. . . .

Yes, many had tried to escape, but the Master's will was always done.

On the Atlantic, May, 1924

The wind blowing across the surface of the ocean caught the fringe on Virna Stossel's dress and tickled her bare arms with it. She stood on the deck of the *Gaiety,* a luxury liner bound for New York, holding her infant son in her arms. The air was brisk, the sun was shining brightly. She smiled at her husband.

"Happy?" he asked.

She nodded. Donald stood beside her, dressed in a navy blue jacket and white linen pants, looking just like one of the crew.

"Isn't it wonderful?" she asked. "Just a few hours ago, we were in England, and now we're heading for the States!"

She looked back at the ocean again, concentrating on the sunlit ripples that stretched toward a deep blue horizon.

"To think you'll be teaching there," she said. "At a university. It's so prestigious, Don!"

"Not to mention profitable," her husband replied. "Darling, I'm going to make you so happy. We'll have a flat in the city and a cottage on Long Island—and we'll see every inch of America!"

He ran a gentle finger along the face of the baby in Virna's arms.

"Little Jackie will be so happy," he said.

"I know I am," Virna told him.

She kissed her husband warmly. She *was* happy, not the least bit sad about leaving her homeland. Don and Jackie were the only family she had—her mother had died before she became pregnant and she hadn't seen her father since her parents' divorce many years earlier. She probably wouldn't have missed her mother anyway. Louisa hadn't been an easy person to live with. She was an extremely introverted woman who was much too protective of her daughter. Virna had felt stifled by her right up to her wedding day. And it wasn't until then that she learned the reason for Louisa's behavior.

"I cherish you, Virna," she had said, looking pale and timid as she sat on the edge of her daughter's bed. "You were a gift from God, given to me after my first baby was taken."

She had squeezed the young woman's hand so tightly that Virna had winced.

"When your first son is born," Louisa went on, "he will be in danger. It's a curse, Virna. A curse that was placed on our family long ago. My first-born son was stolen from me at birth. Your grandmother also lost her first son, and her mother, too. Never the daughters— only the sons."

"Mother, that was coincidence," Virna had insisted. "And in those days, many babies died. But we're so much more careful now. Our doctors are so much more skilled!"

Louisa had shaken her head adamantly.

"No, there was nothing wrong with those babies," she said. "My son was healthy! Something evil befell him, and the others!"

She had taken her daughter's shoulders.

"There is a woman who appears each time," she said. "You must avoid her! She is tall, with green eyes like those of a cat. And she was there every time a baby disappeared!"

The feel of Don's arm around her waist interrupted Virna's thoughts.

"Is something wrong, darling?"

Virna shook her head.

"Not at all," she said. "I was just thinking of that story my mother told me. You know, about the curse that was supposed to have been put on all first-born males in this family?"

Don's lips sided over in a teasing smile.

"Jackie looks just fine to me," he said. "You mustn't think of the things your mother said."

"I don't," Virna assured him. "I know it's ridiculous. Just think, if that woman she spoke of was still around, she'd have to be nearly one hundred years old!"

"Assuming she did exist. You know, mothers mourning the loss of a child are not always the most emotionally stable people," Don pointed out. He glanced at his pocket watch. "Let's get ready for dinner now. I'm terribly hungry and don't want to talk about family curses!"

"Not a word more," Virna promised.

Dinner was a pleasant affair. The sparkle of candlelight, the bottles of champagne put Virna in a romantic mood, and when she started giggling loudly, Don decided it was time to bring her back to their room. Virna leaned heavily on her husband's arm as they walked down the hallway, laughing about nothing in particular.

As Virna collapsed on their bunk, Don prepared a

bottle the babysitter had been ready to give Jackie before they arrived.

When he turned around, Virna had already wriggled out of her sequined gown, and was lying on the bed in a black satin teddy. Her bobbed hair fell over heavily made up eyes, and her lipstick was smudged. She had a look of provocative innocence that Don could not resist. He quickly worked himself out of his tuxedo and climbed in next to her. As they made love, they didn't even notice as the ship started to pitch and roll.

Later. Don was awakened by someone yelling at the door. He sat up slowly, hearing the sound of a wailing siren. Virna, moaning, turned over and rubbed her eyes.

"Anybody in there?"

"What's wrong?" Don answered.

"Ship's sinking!" came the reply. "Up on deck, quick!"

Footsteps pounded away down the hall. Virna scrambled for her lingerie, dressing quickly.

"Donald, what's the trouble?"

"I don't know," Don said, pulling their life jackets out from under the bunk. "Get this on Jackie, will you? Come on, then, quickly!"

Virna jerked a dress over her head and slipped her feet into a pair of pumps. The commotion had wakened her baby; Jackie screamed and kicked so much that she was unable to get the life jacket on him. Don took it from her and did it himself, ordering her to get her own on.

"Donald, I'm frightened!"

Don, usually quick to comfort her, merely handed the wailing baby to Virna and grabbed her by the wrist. As he pulled the cabin door open, an ankle-deep rush of water sped into the room. Don held fast to his wife to help her keep her balance. In the hall, other passengers were wading towards the stairs, screaming and pushing, staggering like drunks as the ship tossed and pitched.

Suddenly, something came crashing down on Virna's

head. Don felt her hand slip through his, and turned to
see her fall. He grabbed for the baby, then with his free
arm tried to help his wife. But he couldn't get enough
traction on the wet floor to manage it.

"Someone help me here!"

None of the others paid attention.

"Please, she'll drown!"

A hand touched his arm, and he turned to see an
attractive woman of about thirty-five. Her green eyes
were full of pity.

"Let me hold the child for you," she said.

Don started to give her Jackie, but suddenly snatched
him back. Somehow, he didn't feel right about this
stranger.

"No, I . . ."

"Give me the child," the woman said, with such
icy firmness that Don could not resist obeying.

A moment later, he felt something cold and thin
and painful in his chest. His eyes widened in shock as
the woman turned and ran down the hall with his son.
Unable to cry out, Don looked down at his half-buttoned
shirt. There was blood all over him. Blood that dripped
down a knife protruding over the armhole of his life
vest. He collapsed next to his wife; in moments the
water around him had darkened to a deep, rich crimson.

"Poor thing," someone in the life raft said, adjusting
a blanket over the woman beside her. "Keeps talking
about a husband and baby."

"I hear she was found wanderin' around the upper
deck in quite a tizzy," an old woman replied. She
patted Virna's hand, but there was no reaction in the
vacant eyes. "You're quite safe now, love. Nothing to
worry about."

Virna shuddered, chilled to the bone. "Where's my
baby?"

The others in the boat exchanged glances.

"Her husband and child musta gone down with the
ship."

"Wait a bloody moment," the old woman replied.

"There are other lifeboats, you know. She'll find them."

But Virna Stossel would never see Donald or Jackie again.

Fifteen

Flora was smiling, bending down with her lips pursed to kiss Gabrielle's cheek, her green eyes bright. And suddenly the eyes flashed, and the lips curled into a grimace of anger. Flora was angry. Flora wanted to hurt her.

She was holding a knife.

"Give me the baby, Gabrielle. Give me the baby!"

"I will take what is mine!"

Metal flashed as the knife plunged downward, somehow feeling like the brush of a feather. Blood dotted the air.

"The Master wills it!"

Blood, everywhere . . .

NNNNNOOOO!!!!!

The scream in Gabrielle's nightmare was no more than a sharp gasp as she woke to find herself on the bus. Trembling, her mouth dry, she glanced around herself as if expecting to see Flora standing over her with a knife. But there was no one there except for Kerry, who slept curled up in his seat with his head against the window ledge, sunlight bathing his skin.

Once she had convinced herself it was only a dream, Gabrielle stood up and hobbled on unsteady legs to the lavatory at the back of the bus. In the hours since they boarded, the bus had picked up more passengers, and Gabrielle kept her eyes straight ahead to ignore their stares. When she returned to her seat, Kerry had awakened.

"Are we almost there?" he asked.

"I think so," Gabrielle said.

Kerry turned to look out the window, watching the barren Utah countryside. Thoughts of Flora started to crowd Gabrielle's mind, but she forced them away, falling once more into a deep, dreamless sleep.

When they finally reached their destination, Gabrielle was so queasy from the long ride that she spent twenty minutes getting sick in the ladies' room. When she reentered the depot's waiting area, Kerry handed her a fistful of brochures.

"Some of them have places to stay," he said.

Gabrielle sat down wearily and opened one, reading it. After going through the entire pile, she shook her head at Kerry.

"These places are expensive," she said. "We can't afford them!"

"But we have a lot of money," Kerry protested.

Gabrielle shushed him, looking around at the others in the station. No one paid attention to them.

"Four hundred dollars won't go very far," she said. She wriggled on the wooden bench. "Well, we've got to find some place to spend the night. I'm tired and I'm sick and I don't want to look very far."

But it was nearly sundown before they found a motor hotel they could afford. Tucked behind a gas station and next to a grocery, it would have received no better than a half star rating had any critic bothered to notice it. But the rates were low, and Gabrielle was easily able to pay for two weeks' stay. She soon learned why.

"Hey, Gabrielle!" Kerry yelled from the bathroom. "There's somethin' crawling in the sink!"

Gabrielle had collapsed on the bed, onto a spread that reeked of too much Clorox. She grimaced.

"Get rid of it," she said. "And don't bring it in here. Throw it out the window!"

She rolled from her side to her back and ran her

hands through her hair. It felt greasy, and she decided she'd take a shower before going to bed. Then she asked herself what was the use, since no one would be seeing her. She didn't dare contemplate leaving this room. Not when Flora or her men could be lurking out there.

It was still too hard to believe she wasn't sleeping in Flora's house, with her wrists painfully bound. Gabrielle held her hands up and studied the welts underneath them. She didn't look up when Kerry entered the room again, crawling onto the bed to sit Indian-style.

"We showed them, didn't we?" he said triumphantly. "Old Macon-Bacon and old Flora won't ever find us again!"

They'll find us, Gabrielle thought as she stared at her wrists.

"Gabrielle, can we go to Arches?" Kerry asked. "It's a real neat place I read about in school. And it said on the poster at the bus station that they go there a coupla times a week."

"Sure," Gabrielle said. "Sure, we'll go to Arches."

Kerry bounced up and down a little, grinning.

"You're my best friend in the whole world, Gabrielle," Kerry said.

"Thanks," Gabrielle said. "Kerry, don't bounce like that. It hurts me."

Kerry frowned. "The baby hurts you?"

"Oh, no," Gabrielle said. "Not the baby. I guess it was just the long bus trip. I'm really tired, Kerry. I want to take a—oh!"

"What happened?"

Gabrielle took his hand and placed it on her stomach; the baby gave a second hard kick.

"Neat!" he cried. "Make him do it again!"

"I can't," Gabrielle said. "He kicks a lot, but only when he wants to."

The baby's movement launched Kerry on a spree of questions that he had been unable to ask the previous night. What did it look like? What did it feel like?

When was the baby coming? Was it a boy or a girl? On
and on . . .

Gabrielle answered each question patiently, reliving
the wonder she'd first felt about her pregnancy through
her eight-year-old brother. And when he had exhausted
his questions, she gave him a smile that stretched from
ear to ear.

"I love you, Kerry," she said.

"Me, too," Kerry said.

"And we'll go to Arches as soon as I feel better. I
promise."

But a week went by, then another, and in spite of
Kerry's cajoling, Gabrielle still wouldn't leave the motel
room. She even had Kerry pay for another week, rather
than do it herself. She spent her time in bed, praying,
worrying, and hoping. Gabrielle, weakened by her
ordeal, slept most of the day. When she was awake, she
would often burst into tears. The worry of her baby's
arrival was overshadowed only by the thought of Flora
Collins catching up with her. Kerry didn't understand
why she kept thinking about the woman, but was as
patient as he could be. He did their shopping at a local
grocery, and they ate in the room every night. But
eventually, the prison-like atmosphere got to him. One
morning, in protest, Kerry brought home a bagful of
junk food.

"Where's the quart of milk I asked you to get?"
Gabrielle demanded, pulling a bag of Cheetos from the
sack. "What's all this garbage?"

"Gotta do something exciting," Kerry said. "I'm
really bored, Gabrielle! I want to go outside!"

"We can't!"

"Yes, we can!" Kerry cried. "Flora isn't here, is
she? She ain't coming! Not now!"

Gabrielle closed her eyes.

"I'm sorry," she said. "This is hard for you, too,
isn't it? I'm sorry to keep you in here like this."

"Then let's go to Arches National Monument today," Kerry pleaded. "You promised, Gabrielle!"

She nodded. The little boy had been so good these past weeks, so grown-up. Didn't he deserve a reward?

What was she afraid of, anyway? After two weeks, Flora must have given up on her. Maybe the woman wasn't so powerful after all. Maybe it had been drugs, or hypnosis, that had pulled Gabrielle under her spell. Besides, she had better start getting used to going out. She'd have to find a doctor pretty quickly, in time for the baby. And then she'd have to get a job of some sort to support them all. It was now or never. . . .

Even Gabrielle had to admit Arches was more fascinating a place than any book could depict. Eerie formations of entrada sandstone rose up towards the sky, the result of millions of years of erosion. The area was quiet but for the sweeping wind, and terribly lonely despite the other members of the tour group who whispered in wonder.

"Look at that," Kerry said, pointing.

Gabrielle followed the line from his finger. At the top of a wind-etched trapezoid sat an egg-shaped boulder so deftly carved by the wind that it resembled a face.

"It looks like a Martian," Kerry said.

"This whole place reminds me of another planet," Gabrielle said, feeling chilled by the passive barrenness around her. She felt exposed here, anyone could see her. She wanted to leave. But Kerry was so delighted by it all that she couldn't help picking up on his enthusiasm. There were formations that resembled pipe organs and rocket ships and even one that looked like an Egyptian queen. Gabrielle's favorite was the delicate arch, an impossibly beautiful formation that seemed to resemble a stone rainbow. Beyond it, she was able to see snow-capped mountains.

"Those are the La Sal Mountains," the guide told her. She turned to the others. "Now, as your itinerary says, we'll stay until after dark so that you can see the sunset. We'll be heading for the Fiery Furnace now, and afterwards we'll enjoy a picnic dinner."

The Fiery Furnace was a section of the park that glowed red as the sun came down, hence its name. Gabrielle heard cameras click around her, and smiled when Kerry couldn't stop making sounds of amazement.

At last, the group headed back to the bus. They were taken to a picnic area, where everyone was treated to a campfire and a meal of hot dogs, roasted potatoes, and soda.

"This is great," Kerry said. "Better than eating in that dumb motel!"

"Shh," Gabrielle hissed. "Kerry, I don't want anyone to know we're staying in a motel. We're hiding out, remember?"

Kerry, knowing she was right, nodded. Then he accepted another hot dog from the tour guide, ducking his eyes from her smile.

"You're brother and sister, aren't you?" the guide asked. She sat down beside Gabrielle. "I can tell by your dark hair and light skin."

"Yes, we are," Gabrielle said.

"My name's Judy," the guide said, holding out a thin arm, darkly tanned from a summer of outdoor work. Gabrielle shook Judy's hand and said her name was Virginia.

"I couldn't help noticing that necklace you're wearing," Judy said. "It's so pretty, so unusual. Can I ask where you got it?"

Gabrielle eyed her suspiciously. She took hold of the amulet.

"Why do you want to know?"

Judy shrugged. "Just curious."

"It's—it's a gift," Gabrielle said. "From my mother. I never take it off."

"I don't blame you," Judy said. "It must be worth a fortune, with that gold and silver."

Gabrielle nodded, still unsure why the guide would be so interested in her amulet. Unknown to her, she was being watched by someone hidden behind a nearby boulder. Someone who had more interest in the amulet than as a piece of jewelry. . . .

No one paid much attention to the man who wedged himself into a phone booth outside the monument. He dialed a long distance number, and when he heard a woman's voice, said:

"I've found her."

After a pause, the woman replied:

"Don't let her out of your sight. I will come for her. . . ."

"I'm beat," Kerry said, falling back on the bed. "We sure had a nice day, didn't we?"

"It was wonderful," Gabrielle said. "I've never seen anything like that place."

And nothing happened . . .

"Well, I'm going to bed," Kerry announced, untying his sneakers.

He was barely undressed and under the covers before he was sound asleep. Exhausted, her legs throbbing from so much exercise, Gabrielle sank into the mattress and breathed deeply, relaxing. Soon, she too was asleep.

Some time in the night, she was awakened by the sound of frantic scuttling underneath the bed. Gabrielle listened to it for a few moments, staring through the darkness. It went on, working over the wooden floor, accompanied now by hoarse breathing.

Mice?

She decided to wake up Kerry, hoping she could persuade him to chase the rodent out the door. Shivering, she turned on her side and gave her brother a slight nudge. He didn't move.

"Kerry?"

His arm felt funny—hard and cold. Gabrielle could barely make out his silhouette in the dark. There was something strange about him. Something wrong . . .

She switched on the light as the scratching became more intense.

It wasn't Kerry in the bed beside her. It was a skeleton, dressed in Kerry's pajamas, its mouth gaping open.

It wasn't until she saw a snake running through the eye sockets and out the mouth that Gabrielle screamed.

"KEEEERRRRREEEEEE!!!"

People appeared out of nowhere. People dressed in black robes surrounded her bed, reaching out, yet not touching her. She heard familiar voices—Harold, Carl, Roger, the others.

"Leave me alone!" Gabrielle screamed.

"We've come to take you home, Gabrielle!"

"We miss you!"

"Flora waits for you!"

"Flora loves you!"

Gabrielle closed her eyes and covered her ears. But still their words tormented her.

"Come home, Gabrielle. Come home with us!"

"Noooo. . . ."

She felt someone pulling her into a sitting position, tight hands around her arms. She tried to resist, but was too weak.

"Come, Gabrielle."

"Leave me alone," Gabrielle sobbed, still not opening her eyes. "Please, go away!"

Suddenly, the pressure on her arms ceased, and she fell back hard on her pillow. Someone screamed, so loudly that she was forced to open her eyes. She saw one of the farmhands holding his wrist roaring as if in great pain.

"The amulet!" he screamed. "The amulet burned me!"

Gabrielle looked down at the gold and silver disc, resting crookedly against the front of her nightgown. Then she gazed through tears at the figures around her bed.

"Take off that amulet!"

"Take it off!"

Instead, Gabrielle held it up and pointed it at them, her eyes wild.

"NO!"

This time, it was a shout of anger, not of fear.

"No, I will not take it off! Leave me alone, all of you! Leave me alone!"

She was answered by a series of screams that seemed to rise from the very depths of hell itself. High-pitched, deep-toned, melancholy voices blended to surround her head, making her dizzy, creating a rush of wind that forced her eyes to shut.

When it was over, she heard a small voice.

"Gabrielle?"

Kerry!

She turned over to see her brother hoisted up on his elbow, his hair smoothed down over his forehead. Not a skeleton, but her brother—alive!

"Oh, Kerry!" she sobbed, throwing her arms around him.

"I heard you yell," Kerry said. "Did you have a bad dream?"

A dream. Of course—that was it. Just a dream. The girl named Judy had made her think so much of the amulet that she dreamt Flora's men were here to steal it from her.

"Yes," she said wearily. "It was horrible, too. But I'm all right now. Go back to sleep, Kerry."

But she couldn't fall asleep.

Somehow, the dream seemed too horribly vivid.

Sixteen

When Gabrielle awoke the next morning, Kerry was already up and sitting on the edge of the bed, watching a Bugs Bunny cartoon. Hearing her stir, he turned around and said:

"Hi, Gabrielle. What're we gonna do today?"

Gabrielle pushed her head back into her pillow and groaned.

"I'd like to sleep," she said.

"Awww, come on," Kerry whined. "You slept all night—except when you had that bad dream. And it's beautiful outside."

Gabrielle pulled herself up into a sitting position.

"You've already been out?" she asked. "What time is it?"

"About ten," Kerry said. "So, what're we gonna do?"

Gabrielle got out of bed and shuffled towards the bathroom, not answering him. She took a long hot shower, trying to ease the strange dull pain she was feeling all over her muscles. She picked up the amulet, glistening with sheets of water, and looked at her reflection in it. In the dream, the farmhands had tried to get her to take it off. *Why?* She remembered now that it had burned one of them. Did that mean they couldn't touch her as long as she was wearing it?

"Why are you trying to make sense of a nightmare?" she asked herself. "That's all it was—a nightmare. How could those men have gotten in here? How could they have disappeared?"

And the skeleton . . .

She turned off the shower.

"Listen to you," she said. "Why are you so afraid all the time? You're hundreds of miles from that crazy woman, in a place where she would never think to look for you. Forget about her. Whatever happened on the farm is over now!"

She wouldn't sit around all day, brooding over her dark dream, worrying about Flora. Kerry wanted to do something, and they would. Gabrielle wrapped a towel around her long black hair, then dressed. When she entered the bedroom, she said:

"Let's ask the guy at the desk if there're any other tours today."

Kerry jumped from the bed and clicked off the TV, ready to leave at that moment.

"Let me get my hair dry first," Gabrielle said.

"Well, hurry up!" Kerry replied. "I want to go somewhere."

Somewhere turned out to be Capitol Reef, a hundred-mile-long land barrier forged of shale and sandstone. There was a bus going there with the same company that had visited Arches the previous day, and though the ride was to take two and a half hours, Gabrielle didn't hesitate to join the group. It was the only available tour, and she didn't want to go back to the motel room now.

Today, the guide wasn't Judy, but a middle-aged man who sat in the front seat of the bus without speaking. He turned and caught Gabrielle's eyes, smiling at her. She ducked her head, but still had the feeling he was looking at her.

Don't start worrying again, Gabrielle, she told herself. *He's just being a flirt.*

Finally, the man turned his head away, prompting Gabrielle to breathe a sigh of relief. She didn't like being watched like that, for whatever reason!

When they reached the entrance of the park, everyone followed the guide into a building marked "Visitor's Center." Because it was September, the summer tourists had thinned out, and Gabrielle saw only a few people in the lobby. The guide held up his hands and beckoned everyone around him.

"My name's Joe," he said. "We're going to be using the bus through some of this trip, but a good deal of hiking will be done, too. Remember, this is treacherous land, and it's very easy to get lost. If you do wander from the group, stay put, and we'll come get you." He looked at his clipboard. "Now, the first thing on the agenda is the Scenic Drive. If you'll follow me . . ."

Holding Kerry's hand, Gabrielle headed back out to the bus. As she was passing the guide's seat, he touched her arm and said:

"If you feel tired at all, please let me know. I'll be glad to help you."

"Thank you," Gabrielle said with a straight face.

But she caught herself and smiled. "Thanks. I'll be fine."

During the short drive, Joe explained about the millions of years of evolution it had taken to carve the Reef, and as the bus stopped he began to talk of man's existence in the area. Kerry leaned forward and took in every word about the Fremont Indians.

"They lived here some one thousand years ago," Joe said, "and left drawings in the stone which we call 'petroglyphs.'"

He led everyone from the bus and walked with them to the site. Kerry ran ahead to get a closer look, excited by the crude depictions of people and animals. He looked behind himself and asked:

"What does it mean?"

"Nobody knows," Joe answered. "It might be a hunting scene, because of the animals. Or it might have religious significance."

Kerry looked back at the sketches.

"I just think they're nice pictures," he decided.

Gabrielle watched Joe nod. He made her uneasy, and yet there was no reason for it. She chided herself for thinking that way. The whole idea of coming all this way was to be happy, and yet she was fretting as much as if she were still back in the motel room!

The group returned to their small bus, and continued with the sightseeing. In order to keep herself from becoming overly paranoid, Gabrielle concentrated on her surroundings. Capitol Reef is a contradiction, thick with willow trees and cottonwood along the Fremont River, as foreboding and barren as a distant planet in its more arid sections. Kerry marvelled at the fact that some trees did grow in the dry area—Utah juniper and pinyon pine. He chased an elusive chipmunk until it disappeared into a crack along one of the rocky terraces.

"Please don't chase the animals," a woman in the group said. "This is *their* home, not ours."

Joe reached out to pat Kerry's head.

"Oh, it's all right," he said. "He's just being a kid."

Despite the slight smile on the man's face, despite

Kerry's bright eyes as he looked up at the guide, Gabrielle felt her stomach sour. She had seen something that justified her previous doubts about the man. He was wearing a ring.

A ring in the shape of a skull, with a snake twisting through it.

Quickly, she turned away to hide the fear in her eyes. Her heart pounded as she climbed on the bus again, but she faked a smile for Joe.

Don't let him know what you saw, and maybe you can escape....

She leaned over her armrest to whisper to Kerry.

"Listen, we can have more fun if we go on our own," she said. "Want to split apart from the group?"

"We're not supposeta."

"Just for a little while," Gabrielle coaxed. "Look, the tour is almost over. You don't want to go home yet, do you?"

Kerry shook his head.

"Then stick with me."

As the bus pulled into the parking lot that marked the area of Capitol Gorge, Gabrielle told herself Joe (if that was his name) would never be able to follow her without making a scene. That would give her a little leeway at least. When they got off the bus, she pulled Kerry back and waited until the group was some distance away. Then she mingled for a few minutes with another tour group, and when she saw what path Joe took she chose a different one. Soon, the two had wandered far off from the other tourists; it seemed they were lost in their own world.

"Gosh, it's really quiet here," Kerry whispered, as a soft wind tousled his black hair.

"And peaceful," Gabrielle agreed. She yawned. "It's making me sleepy, Kerry."

"Don't get tired again," Kerry implored. "I wanna look around."

"We will," Gabrielle promised. "I just want to rest a few minutes."

She looked around herself, squinting in the late

afternoon sun, and saw a cave in the distance. Kerry followed her gaze until he also saw it.

"Neat," he said. "Let's see what's inside!"

His voice echoed off the stone cliffs, prompting Gabrielle to hush him. The two walked to the cave, a pocket of cold darkness in the midst of the warm, sunny park. Kerry, unafraid, bounded straight inside.

"I don't see a thing," he called.

"Don't go too far back," Gabrielle cautioned. "It might be dangerous."

Kerry returned to her.

"Maybe there's animals?"

"Could be," Gabrielle said.

It isn't animals I'm worried about, she thought.

"Kerry," she said, "I'm really tired. I'm going to rest in here for just a little while, and then we'll explore, okay?"

"Aww, having a baby is so boring," Kerry pouted. "All you do is sleep!"

"I'm sorry," Gabrielle said. "Now, listen. You stay right here in this cave until I wake up, okay?"

Kerry shuffled, looking down at his sneakers.

"Oh, okay!"

Grateful to know he really wouldn't leave, Gabrielle settled herself on the dry ground and closed her eyes. Let that guy Joe look all he wanted. He'd never find her in here!

After a long day in the sun, Gabrielle was more than tired. She was so exhausted that she fell fast asleep in the middle of her thoughts. Kerry, still full of energy, decided to explore the cave. In spite of his sister's warnings, he headed far towards its back. He soon found a small passageway, and like most kids his age could not resist checking it out.

At that same moment, the tour guide was contacting Flora to tell her that Gabrielle had somehow eluded them again.

In another section of the park, a Frenchman named Andre Paget leaned over the steering wheel of his jeep and squinted at the sky above the Reef. His experience as an outdoorsman made him adept at reading weather signals, and the message he was getting now said "rain." Altostratus clouds swept over the sun as if painted by a quick brushstroke, heralds of a storm that would probably come within twelve hours.

It amazed him how quickly the weather could change in this area. But that was one of the things he loved about the American Southwest: it was full of surprises. More than this, he liked the fact that he could be all by himself here. After presiding most of the year as co-chairman of the board for one of Europe's largest sporting goods companies—a position inherited along with his brother from his late father, Andre felt he deserved all the vacation time he could get. Henri, his older brother, could handle things well enough at the Paris offices. Andre didn't intend to return home for quite a few months, planning to stay with his sister in San Francisco. But, he thought, he wasn't due to arrive in California until the end of the week. Right now he'd just enjoy the mountains.

Utah was a world away from his native Paris, not just in miles, but in its very spirit. Paris was elegant, beautiful, breathtaking—well, all the songwriters had yet to describe it fully. But the beauty was manmade, and so very young compared to the monuments Nature had sculpted here over the past several million years.

Andre sighed, starting up the engine again. Having obtained a camping permit, he planned to spend the night in the back country, where no tourists came. He felt happy, and began to sing a French tune. It was good to be only twenty-eight, already "filthy rich"—as his American friends would say—and free from all worries.

Kerry wished he had a flashlight. He felt his way along the walls of the passage, trying to get back to the entrance. It was like walking through a maze, and more than once he hit a dead end. He tried calling to Gabrielle, but it was useless. His little voice wouldn't carry that far.

"I only meant to look a little bit," he said out loud.

But he'd taken a wrong turn, and now he couldn't get back. He yelled again, then broke into a coughing fit. It was so *cold* in here!

Gabrielle stretched herself out of a deep sleep, feeling surprisingly refreshed despite the strange bed she'd chosen. She rubbed her eyes and struggled to her feet. The chilly air woke her completely. Night had fallen, and the temperature had dropped considerably.

"Oh, God," she sighed. "I didn't mean to doze off for so long."

She turned to peer through the darkness.

"Kerry?"

No answer.

"Kerry, are you asleep?"

She inched her way forward, her hands swimming through the air like a blind person's. Finally, her eyes adjusted to the dim light, and she saw her brother wasn't there. She returned to the entrance of the cave. The moonlight shone brightly over the rocky terrain, but Kerry was nowhere in sight.

"I can't believe he just wandered off," she whispered.

She thought about Joe, and suddenly the night grew colder.

She didn't dare yell for her brother. What if they were waiting for her out there in the dark? Carefully, she walked along the pathway that cut in front of the cave. The wind was blowing strongly now, throwing her hair into her eyes and making it difficult for her to walk. She steadied herself against the side of a cliff and stopped to look around.

"Kerry?"

No answer again. She moved forward, at last coming to a long dried-up stream. Thinking Kerry might have followed it, perhaps chasing an animal, she walked down its center, holding her arms out to either side to balance her large stomach. Her legs felt heavier now than ever before, and she was angry with her brother for making her walk like this.

Anger at Kerry helped hide her fears.

Suddenly, she heard something that made her stop dead. Chanting. The very same chanting she had heard on Collins Farm. She turned to run back to the cave, but moved no further than a few yards when she slammed into a darkly-robed figure. Gabrielle screamed and backed away, losing her balance. She fell heavily onto the dry sand as they descended upon her.

"Gabrielle, we found you!"

Such a friendly voice . . .

"We miss you, Gabrielle!"

"Why do you run away from us? We're your friends!"

Gabrielle scurried backward, realizing this was no dream.

"NNNNNOOOOOO!!!!"

"If you give us the amulet, we can . . ."

The amulet! She remembered now that they were afraid of the amulet.

"GO AWAY!"

She rolled over onto her side, curling herself into a tight ball. The hard rim of the amulet cut into her palm, but she felt strength emanating from it, and breathed hard to steady herself. They couldn't hurt her as long as she was wearing it. They couldn't touch her.

Suddenly, she realized the night had gone silent. The chanting and the torment had stopped, and all she could hear was the steady howl of the wind. Slowly, she looked up. The dark figures were gone.

But there was someone else there. Someone bending over a large animal with a big head and broad frame. A cow? Now, that was crazy, in a place like this. It was probably a deer that looked bigger because of the shadows.

Shivering, Gabrielle pulled herself up to her feet and started to move away. But the figure turned, as slowly as if moving through water, cupping a pair of bejewelled hands before her face. Something dripped from her fingers, something thick and dark in the moonlight. Blood.

Flora drank from her hands, then glared at Gabrielle with her cat's eyes.

She began to laugh.

Seventeen

Andre stirred the pan of *poulet sauté* that sat on
the portable stove he'd set up outside his tent. Sauted
chicken à la freeze-dry, he thought with a laugh. A far
cry from anything he'd ever had in Paris. But after the
difficult task of erecting his tent and setting up camp for
the night, it smelled as delicious as any gourmet meal.

He felt the wind rise up again, and hoped he'd be
able to enjoy his dinner outside before the rain started.
Finally, he pulled the skillet from the stove and dished
it into a metal plate. Sitting on a flat rock, he ate his
dinner while watching the clouds roll over the night
sky.

He heard something in the distance, something
like a woman's scream. Curious, Andre listened, but
the sound did not repeat itself. He shook his head and
decided it must have been the wind. It had a way of
changing its identity as it ran through the gaps and
twists of the Reef.

Flora took a step towards Gabrielle. Though the
moon was now caught behind a string of clouds, Gabrielle
could still see the glistening of her eyes, like a hunter
studying its prey. She backed away.

"My dear," Flora said, "what an awful place to have
your baby!"

"What are you doing here?" Gabrielle demanded.

Flora smiled. "Why, I've come to take you home.
Wouldn't you rather have your baby in a warm, dry
bed?"

"So you can take him from me?" Gabrielle accused, wiping tears from her eyes. "Mrs. Collins, why don't you leave me alone?"

"I will have what I came for!" Flora hissed.

She moved towards Gabrielle in a quick motion, making the young girl turn and run. But it was difficult to carry her extra bulk on such uneven terrain, and she stumbled forward with a scream. Cold hands grabbed at her, pulling her to her feet. Gabrielle struggled to free herself.

"Fool!" Flora cried. "You'll never escape me now! The Master will have what he demands, and the new cycle will begin!"

"What Master?" Gabrielle cried. "What cycle? What are you talking about?"

"Be silent!"

Flora reached for her, trying to touch her stomach. But as Gabrielle wrenched her body to one side, the amulet swung forward and hit the woman on the wrist. A sizzling noise reached Gabrielle's ears, followed by Flora's scream.

The amulet had burned her.

"Remove that at once!"

Gabrielle shook her head defiantly.

Suddenly, a sharp tug pulled at her stomach muscles. She held her breath until it passed, then opened her eyes to look at Flora.

"What are you doing to me?"

Flora said nothing.

She had something in her hand, something that glistened even in the darkness. Gabrielle screamed when she saw the knife. Almost in answer to her cry, there was a sudden clap of thunder, and the sky opened up to let down a rush of water. Gabrielle and the others were soaked in a matter of seconds. Lightning cracked through the sky, finding its way to the knife Flora held. Watching Flora shiver under its impact, the men screamed and ran off, certain this was some sign from above. Flora regained herself, but realized she could not deal with Gabrielle alone. And she didn't want the baby harmed. "I will get you!" she cried, leaving Gabrielle standing alone in the rain.

It took her a moment to realize she had somehow been spared again. Awkwardly, she hurried along the bank of the stream bed, her tears of relief mixing with the rain wetting her cheeks. She tried to head back to the cave, hoping Kerry had returned. Moving towards a trio of pinyon pines, she struggled to see beyond the sheets of rain, walking unsteadily on the sticky sand.

A hand shot out of the darkness, grabbing her arm, pulling her up the embankment.

"NNNNOOOO!!!!!"

Kerry sniffled, and ran the back of his wrist across his nose. He had no idea how long he'd been lost in the cave, but now he was feeling tired and sore and hungry. His throat hurt terribly from screaming for help.

"Gabrielle, where are you?" he whimpered.

The tunnel was about three feet wide, and filled with dank, thick air. Kerry yawned, his body's effort to take in more oxygen, and leaned against the slimy side. Something furry brushed his cheek.

Bats.

Kerry pulled away with a groan, and heard a squeak and fluttering of wings. They seemed to stop a short distance ahead, then to turn right. He thought of all the horror movies he'd seen and then tried to forget them. Shuddering, Kerry began to walk again. He found a turn a few yards away, and followed it, wishing he had a bat's power to navigate through the dark.

But the air was fresher all of a sudden, and he could hear a steady drumming sound in the distance.

Rain?

He began to run towards its source, praying he had not taken another wrong turn.

Gabrielle heard someone shouting to her through the driving rain, words she did not recognize. She continued to struggle, fearing some sort of wicked spell was being cast on her. Hadn't the chanting been in a foreign language?

She was pulled into what seemed to be a tent, and found herself looking beyond the light of a lantern at a blue-eyed young man. He rubbed his wet brown hair with a rugged hand and looked around for a blanket.

"I heard screams," Andre Paget said in English, wrapping the blanket around Gabrielle. "I thought it was a trapped animal."

"Let me out of here," Gabrielle ordered through chattering teeth.

"I can't," Andre replied. "Don't you see how it's raining? If I hadn't pulled you from that stream bed, you might have drowned. A flash flood could occur at any moment!"

Gabrielle pulled the blanket from her shoulders and ran for the tent flap. But suddenly, the tugging pain took her again, and she doubled over. Andre hurried to put his arm around her, helping her down to the floor.

"You are in pain," he said. "Please, do not try to move!"

Gabrielle's eyes rounded.

"Don't hurt me, please," she said.

"Why would I hurt you?" Andre demanded.

Gabrielle squeezed her eyes shut and began to pray, even as Andre laid a blanket over her. *Make this end, please make this end* . . . .

"*Pauvre*," Andre clucked. "Such a strange place for you to be!"

He sat back on his heels and studied her, amazed she would be wandering through such dangerous territory in her condition. Had she run away from something? Or was she lost? Whatever, he could tell she was terribly frightened, and in pain. He adjusted the blanket.

"Don't worry," he said. "The storm will pass quickly, and then we'll find your family."

Gabrielle opened her eyes.

"You're going to take me back to Flora, aren't you?"

"Who is Flora? I know of no such person."

Gabrielle didn't believe him. It was just too much of a coincidence that he had set up camp here, like some guardian angel sent from heaven to help her. She pulled herself up on her elbow.

"You have to let me go," she said. "My brother is lost out there!"

"It's impossible to find him," Andre said matter-of-factly, "until after the rain stops. Do you want some coffee?"

He turned and reached for a Thermos.

"I made it earlier," he said, pouring some into the plastic top, "but it's still hot."

"I don't want any," Gabrielle said. "Help me up, will you? You have no right to keep me in here! I have to find my brother!"

Andre put the cup in her hands and raised them to her mouth.

"*Nom de Dieu,*" he swore. "You want to die, don't you?"

"You want to kill me!"

Andre rolled his eyes upward and groaned.

"Drink that coffee," he ordered, in such a way that Gabrielle obeyed him.

Somehow, though she didn't usually drink coffee, the warm aroma rising from the cup was too soothing to resist. She sipped carefully, testing for any other taste, but found none. The room didn't go blurry, and she didn't feel odd. She finished it.

"Do you feel better?"

"Yes," Gabrielle replied. "But my brother . . ."

"Forget your brother," Andre said. "There is nothing you can do for him now."

Gabrielle felt cold at the sound of his words. Had Flora's people hurt Kerry? Was this man trying to keep her from her brother on purpose? The coffee had seemed all right, but what if it wasn't? What if there was a delayed reaction?

What if this man was one of the farm hands, in disguise?

She remembered the amulet now, and held it

forward. If he was one of Flora's men, he couldn't hide his fear of it, could he?

"Would you like to look at my necklace?" she asked.

Andre frowned at her.

"A moment ago," he said, "you were accusing me of wanting to kill you. And now you're showing me a piece of jewelry?"

Gabrielle held it higher, turning it so that the gold and silver caught in the lantern light, tempting him. Andre took it and turned it over.

It didn't affect him.

"A simple piece," he said. "I could buy thousands of the same. But why do you show it to me?"

Gabrielle closed her eyes and heaved her shoulders. He wasn't one of Flora's men after all.

"I'm sorry," she said. "It's just . . ."

Once again, the pain came; she fell to her side with her arms wrapped tightly around her.

"Is it the baby?"

Gabrielle breathed hard, then relaxed.

"No," she said. "It isn't due for three weeks."

"Well, that's a good thing," Andre replied. "But you're in pain. After the storm is ended, I'll look for your brother, and he can get you to a doctor."

Gabrielle looked up at him.

"He's only eight."

"Eight!" Andre cried. "I thought you were talking about an older man!"

Gabrielle shook her head.

"He's just a little boy," she said.

She heard an abrupt silence outside the tent as the rain came to a halt. Andre stood up.

"Don't move," he said. "I will bring the little one back as soon as I find him."

He buttoned the front of his wool mackinaw, smiling at the pretty girl who laid on the floor of his tent.

Look at me, Andre thought as he walked outside. *I travel thousands of miles to be alone, and I find trouble the first night I am here. Not just a woman, but a pregnant woman! And now, instead of sleeping in my warm, dry tent, I am searching these slippery rocks for a little boy!*

"Ahh," he sighed, "but at least she is a pretty woman. I wonder why she has come to such a place, alone? What kind of husband would let such a beautiful wife be endangered?"

He spotted a shadow a few yards away, and walked more quickly. But it moved out of his way, the soft clapping of hooves telling him it was only a deer. He searched the area for half an hour, and was about to give up when he heard a strange whimpering sound. Like a child crying...

"Little boy?" he called.

He found Kerry at the mouth of the dark cave, huddled on the wet ground. Kerry looked up at him with a tear-stained face, bits of dirt and pebbles stuck in his tousled hair. He set his lips hard and glared at Andre.

"My name is Andre," the Frenchman said softly. "Your sister is back in my tent, and I've come to take you to her."

Kerry jumped to his feet.

"What's she doing there? Is she okay?"

"Yes, of course," Andre insisted. "If you come with me, I'd..."

He tried to take the little boy's hand, but Kerry shrugged away from him distrustingly. Andre led the way back to his tent, and when he entered he found that Gabrielle had fallen asleep. Kerry sat down beside her and took her hand.

"Don't waken her," Andre said. "She is hurting, and needs to sleep."

Kerry wouldn't let go of his sister's hand.

"I got lost," he said, not looking up. "There was a secret passageway in the cave, and I went inside. I couldn't get out!"

"What were you doing in a cave?" Andre asked.

"Gabrielle wanted to take a nap."

"A nap?"

Kerry shrugged.

"She gets tired a lot."

Andre saw him shiver, and took off his jacket to wrap around his shoulders. Kerry seemed half-drowned in the thing, but he stopped trembling after a few moments. Andre wanted to ask him about his sister, but to his surprise Kerry started talking on his own. The little boy had kept his feelings bottled up for too long.

"Me and Gabrielle ran away," he said. "There's this crazy lady who wants to take Gabrielle's baby away. Anyway, we got on a bus and drove for a real long time, and went to Arches National Monument."

He glanced at Andre.

"Arches is a neat place."

Andre smiled. "I know."

"Anyway, we came here today on a tour," Kerry went on. "Then my sister said we'd have more fun if we didn't stick with the group. But I guess I goofed everything up getting lost like I did."

"But aren't you with anyone else?"

"No. We don't have anyone else but ourselves."

Andre shifted his legs and tried another question.

"Why are you running away?"

That was the wrong question. Kerry suddenly clammed up, and concentrated on rubbing his sister's arm in a gentle motion. Suddenly, Gabrielle's face twisted, and she moaned as if in pain.

"What's wrong?" Kerry asked with alarm.

"Perhaps it is too cold," Andre said, worry in his tone. "I'll give her another blanket."

As he laid it over her, he thought how glad he'd be when morning came. There was no use in trying to take her to the ranger's station now, when the roadways were too dark to follow. No, Andre thought with a sigh, he had to be responsible for the young girl's welfare until the light of morning.

"*Merde*," Andre whispered, watching Gabrielle toss and turn under her blankets. "What do I do with her?"

He had a bandana knotted around one of his belt loops, and he unfastened it to wipe the sweat from

Gabrielle's forehead. Next to her, in Andre's sleeping bag, Kerry slept soundly. It had been two hours since he first brought Gabrielle here, and it was becoming more and more obvious that she was in labor. If only morning wasn't such a long way off!

Half an hour later, Gabrielle woke up, and let Andre hold her. The pains were coming more frequently now, and as they came she dug her fingers into the muscles of his arms.

"*Chéri*," Andre whispered. "When morning comes, we will get help for you."

But when the sun rose, Gabrielle was in such pain that Andre couldn't think either of leaving her to get help or moving her to his jeep. Kerry, huddled in Andre's sleeping bag, watched her with big eyes.

"How come she looks so white?"

"I think the baby is going to come," Andre said. "Kerry, would you wait outside for me? If you see anyone, have them get help for us as quickly as possible!"

Kerry, relieved to get away, did as he was told. Gabrielle squeezed Andre's hand tightly, watching the tent flap fall shut.

"I know, *pauvre*," Andre said. "But, didn't your doctor teach you a special way to breathe to lessen the pain? I saw this in a movie once, and . . ."

Gabrielle laughed, almost maniacally. Doctor? There hadn't been any doctor. Only Flora. Dear sweet smiling Flora, who wanted her baby.

She cried out again. Andre glanced at his watch, timing the contractions. He tried to help Gabrielle into a kneeling position, clucking at her in French. But the pain was too much for the young girl, and she fell unconscious again.

Andre brushed her hair from her face. Why hadn't anyone come? Surely a ranger should be riding through this area! But it was desolate here, and it was still very early. Watching Gabrielle, Andre wondered if anyone would believe this was happening to him. The chairman of Paget International, camping out in the Southwest of the United States, delivering a baby? Ah, well, his father had always praised his sense of responsibility, his ability to take charge in difficult situations. That was why he was an equal partner in the business with his older brother. Andre only wished the old man was alive to hear about this.

Gabrielle cried out again, and lapsed into unconsciousness.

Hearing screams, Kerry raced into the tent. He stopped short, wide-eyed; he saw Andre holding a tiny, slick-skinned little body. The baby looked funny.

Gabrielle was lost somewhere in limbo. She began to scream at the sight of her baby, seeing something that looked like a little ghost.

"*Chérie*, it's all right!" Andre cried.

But she blacked out again.

Andre looked at Kerry.

"It's only a caul," he said, brushing it away. "Babies are sometimes born with them. Quickly, now, take that undershirt there and bring it to me!"

Kerry scrambled to obey him, his back turned as Andre continued to work. Gently, the Frenchman wrapped the shirt around the wailing little boy.

"You have a nephew," he said.

Forgetting his initial fears, Kerry came up to Andre and started to skip back and forth.

"Let me see! Let me see!"

He sat on the floor beside Andre, grinning broadly when the baby was placed in his lap. Andre, rubbing his eyes, stood up and said:

"I'm going to get the jeep ready. Your sister needs to be taken to a hospital."

He left the tent. Gabrielle shivered in a dreamless sleep. Kerry stared in fascination at the tiny new life he held in his arms.

Eighteen

In a waiting room chair outside the small hospital's obstetrics ward, Kerry swivelled back and forth, staring up at the brightly lit ceiling. He didn't hear the chair's loud squeaking, or Andre's request that he quiet down. All he could think of was Gabrielle. Why hadn't the doctor come out yet?

Wasn't she okay?

Andre watched the little boy. When he'd brought Gabrielle to the ranger's station, he had thought his involvement with them was over. But then the ambulance arrived, and the attendants refused to take Kerry as a passenger. What was Andre to do, when the little boy looked up at him with those big gray eyes and begged for a ride to the hospital? He was no ogre—of course he said he'd take the kid. So now here he was, sitting in a hospital waiting room rather than hiking through the Reef.

"Kerry," he said. "I'm going to find the doctor. I'll be right back."

The squeaking stopped and the room was silent as Kerry tilted the chair forward.

"Can I come?"

"I don't know if . . ."

"She's my sister!"

Unable to argue with that logic, Andre beckoned him. Together, they walked to the nurses' station, where they were told they'd be able to speak to a doctor shortly. Soon, a dark-skinned man came up to them.

"I'm Dr. Frazer," he said, extending a hand to Andre. "You are the husband?"

Andre had been expecting to hear that question, and he was ready for it. He said "yes." Kerry looked up at him with knitted brows, wondering why he should tell such a lie. But Andre gave him a look that told him to be quiet, and together they walked into the doctor's office.

"How is she?" Andre asked, taking a seat across the wide desk.

"She needs rest more than anything," Dr. Frazer replied. "Mr. Hansen, how did your wife come to have a baby in such a terrible place? Didn't she realize how close she was to term?"

"Perhaps we miscalculated," Andre said. "The baby wasn't due for a month, and when we left for this trip she felt just fine."

The doctor considered this.

"You took a chance," he said.

"I'm well aware of that," Andre said. "But you must realize we planned this trip many, many months ago. My wife insisted we keep it, and . . ."

Kerry interrupted with a question of his own.

"So, when's Gabrielle gonna be able to leave this place?"

The doctor looked at him blankly, and Andre quickly explained that Kerry was his brother-in-law.

"He accompanied us on the trip," the Frenchman said. "He is my wife's only blood relative."

"I see," Dr. Frazer mumbled. "Well, young man, it may be a few days before she can go. You see, she's very weak."

"What about the baby?" Andre asked.

"Now *he's* a robust little fellow," the doctor said. "Weighs seven pounds eleven ounces, has all his fingers and toes. He eats well, and sleeps well, too. You have a fine son, Mr. Hansen."

Andre smiled. A son, eh? Wouldn't his brother and sister laugh at that one! Andre loved children, but the thought of having one of his own was just too far-fetched.

"*Merci*," he said, smiling. "Now, when may I see the—my wife?"

"She's sleeping at the moment," Dr. Frazer said. "Why don't you go down to the cafeteria for now and have a bite to eat?"

Kerry and Andre did just that. Over tuna sandwiches and Nehis, they talked about Gabrielle and the previous night.

"Were you frightened?" Andre asked.

Kerry shook his head. "Heck, no. I thought it was neat!"

Andre smiled, knowing this was a lie. But he played along and said Kerry was a brave little boy. That wasn't far from the truth, he thought, considering all the child had been through. Andre wondered what the rest of his story might be, but before he could say anything Kerry piped another question of his own.

"Andre, why did you say you were Gabrielle's husband?"

"I thought it might have looked strange," Andre said, "my coming here with two young people I don't know. It was easier to lie—to say we were related—than to do a lot of explaining."

That was good enough for Kerry.

"So, whadda we do now?"

"I know what I would like to do," Andre said, opening a bag of pretzels. "I'd like to return to the mountains and continue my camping expedition before I must fly to San Francisco." He handed the bag to Kerry. "But I've gotten myself very involved, haven't I? I really can't leave now without these doctors sending the police after me for being a deserting husband."

Kerry started to lick the salt off a pretzel.

"What's in San Francisco?"

"My sister, Emilie," Andre replied. "I planned to visit her at the end of the week."

"That's pretty far away, isn't it?" Kerry asked, reaching for another pretzel.

Andre nodded.

"Can we go with you?"

"What?"

"I said, can we go with you?" Kerry repeated. "That crazy lady is gonna come back again. I know it! But if we're so far away maybe she won't find us."

"Little boy," Andre said, "you spoke earlier of this—how did you say—crazy lady. Who is she?"

"Her name's Flora," Kerry answered. "See, she adopted Gabrielle last spring. She didn't want me though. Said there wasn't enough room for me. But I missed Gabrielle so much I ran away, and when I found her they had her all tied up to this big bed."

"You . . . ran away?"

"From the . . ." Kerry cut himself off, then heaved his shoulders. "Oh! You're gonna find out anyway. I ran away from an orphanage. See, I just wanted to visit Gabrielle. I was gonna go back, really! But then Gabrielle was in big trouble so we ran away together."

"And what about Flora?" Andre pressed. "Why has Gabrielle run from her?"

"Gabrielle says it's cause she wants her baby," Kerry answered. "Flora's the one who tied Gabrielle to that bed."

He knelt up on his chair and leaned across the table.

"Can't we go to San Francisco with you?" he implored. "We won't bother you after we get there, honest! We lived by ourselves these whole coupla weeks!"

His pleas had taken on a high-pitched tone, making others in the cafeteria turn their heads. To hush him, Andre pressed his hands on the boy's shoulders and pushed him down until he was sitting again. In a quiet tone, he said:

"I can't bring you to San Francisco. If I were caught with you, someone would accuse me of kidnapping."

"Nobody's gonna catch us," Kerry said. "And if they did, we would pretend we didn't know each other!"

Andre rubbed his eyes. He really should call the police about this, but wasn't in the mood for all the questions they'd ask. Being a foreigner, he was afraid he wouldn't be treated as kindly as a native American—let alone as a native of Utah. He'd heard about these backwoods police stations, and was happy to keep out of them.

"Look," he said. "Since my camping trip is interrupted, I will stay with you until your sister can leave here. But then I am going on my way. I can't become any more involved than I am."

"Okay," Kerry sighed, realizing this was better than nothing. "I'm finished eating, Andre. Can we go see Gabrielle now?"

She was sitting up in her bed, staring at the i.v. bottle that hung upside down next to her, dripping something yellowy-white into her veins. When she saw Kerry, she smiled weakly. Kerry gave her a hug and sat on the edge of the bed.

"Boy, am I glad to see you," he said. "They made me wait and wait, Gabrielle."

"I was sleeping," his sister replied.

"You okay?"

"I guess so," Gabrielle said, looking up at the bottle again. "This stuff is supposed to be nourishing, but I don't think it's working. I'm really hungry."

She saw Andre now and smiled a little for him.

"I understand that I have you to thank for bringing my son into the world," she said.

"You did most of the work," Andre replied.

In the safety of the hospital room, with the pain of her ordeal behind her, she thought she could see kindness in his handsome face, and that made her relax. His eyes smiled at her now, sparkling blue eyes. His brown hair was parted slightly off the middle, and feathery bangs brushed his eyebrows. His skin was tanned, rough-hewned by the hours he loved to spend outdoors.

She laughed a little. Being worn out was making her sentimental, wasn't it?

"What's so funny?" Kerry asked.

"Nothing," Gabrielle said quickly. "Andre, I don't

know how to thank you. If it hadn't been for your help..."

Andre cut her off. "There's no need for that. I was simply there."

Gabrielle looked down at the amulet that hung around her neck.

"Well, I decided something," she said. "I'm naming my son Jared Andre." She looked up again. "Is that all right?"

Andre beamed. "I'm flattered, *chéri!*"

"Andre's a real nice guy," Kerry said. "Know what, Gabrielle? He's gonna stay with us while you're here. That Flora lady won't be able to touch us with Andre around."

Gabrielle's serene expression turned to one of fear. She'd been too weak and tired to think of Flora. Kerry's innocent statement brought reality back to her, and she felt a slight trembling wash under her skin. Jared was alone at this moment. He might be in danger!

"Bring my baby to me," she said. "I want to be with my baby!"

"I'll find the nurse," Andre offered.

Maybe Flora followed us here. Maybe she's taking Jared right now!

As Andre left the room, Kerry asked:

"What's the matter with you?"

Without answering, Gabrielle brought her hand to her lips as if to hide their trembling. She cried softly, watching the door, praying the nurse would come back immediately.

But maybe Jared was already gone....

The door opened, and Gabrielle tensed. But a second later, a tall, big-boned nurse walked to the bed with a tiny blue bundle in her arms. She smiled warmly at Gabrielle and laid the baby next to her. Jared was sleeping soundly, soft breaths coming from the pink bud of his mouth.

"You see?" Andre said. "The baby is fine."

"He's a darling boy, too," the nurse, Dora Smythe, put in.

"Thank you," Gabrielle said softly, running a finger around the softness of Jared's face. She looked at the nurse.

"Would you see to it that no one is allowed near him without my permission?" she asked.

"Certainly," Dora said, straightening her already stiff shoulders. "What makes you think we would?"

Jared stirred in his sleep, revealing a tiny arm with an ID bracelet around it. Gabrielle began to fidget with it.

"A woman might come here claiming to be related to me," she said. "She might say she's my mother, but she isn't. My mother is dead—except for my brother here, I have no relatives. Do you understand?"

Dora nodded. "I can assure you the baby is quite safe here."

Dora and Andre exchanged glances as Gabrielle yawned. Then the woman bent down and lifted Jared. Gabrielle looked alarmed, but the nurse told her all was well, and left.

At that moment, Dr. Frazer entered, and dismissed Kerry and Andre from the room. A while later, he returned to the hall where they were waiting.

"She looks much better," he reported. "But Mr. Hansen, you must be exhausted. Have you made arrangements for a place to stay?"

"I was hoping to remain here in the hospital," Andre replied. "So I can be near my wife. Is that possible?"

He kept his eyes fixed on the doctor's as he pushed something towards him. Dr. Frazer's eyes widened to see it—a crisp hundred dollar bill.

"Yes—yes, of course we have a room," Dr. Frazer said, quickly. "Under the circumstances . . ."

"*Merci*," Andre said. "And if possible, I would prefer a room near my wife's."

"There's one down the hall that isn't being used," the doctor said. "It's far enough from the others to give them privacy, but I think you'll like it."

Andre and Kerry were led to the room, furnished

in a cold, standard style with two adjustable beds, a suspended TV set, and some metal tables. There was a private bathroom and a closet. When the doctor left, Kerry jumped on a bed and started examining the buttons at its headboard.

"What're these for?"

"To call the nurse," Andre explained. "I have to get my things from the jeep, Kerry. You can wait here until I return, can't you?"

"Sure," Kerry said. "How do you turn on the TV?"

Andre looked around for a switch, then turned on the set. After finding a program Kerry was satisfied with, he left the room and headed for the elevator. When he returned, laden with his backpack, he rode the elevator back up to the obstetrics ward. He didn't pay much attention to the green-eyed woman who stood beside him, twisting one of several gold bangles at her wrist.

Kerry was kneeling on the bed when he entered the room.

"This moves all over the place," he said.

"Wonderful," Andre replied. With all his money, his sole source of entertainment was to be an automatic bed? He wished he could go out tonight, but he'd made a promise. Andre always kept his promises. Still, it was early.

"Look," he said. "I see a nice park across the street. Want to take a walk there?"

Kerry shook his head.

"Unh-uh," he said. "I'm not leaving Gabrielle for a minute."

"Well, perhaps I'll go by my . . ."

"No!" Kerry cried, jumping from the bed to run to him. "You promised you'd stay right here! If you don't, maybe that crazy Flora will come and . . ."

He looked ready to burst into tears.

"*Ça va!*" Andre cried. "I'll stay!"

Kerry blinked away his tears and gave the Frenchman a hug. Curling his lips as he looked out the window, Andre patted Kerry's head. He could see himself al-

ready becoming too involved with these young people.
Oh, well. In a few days he'd be off again, and could
forget them.

"You're the only friend we've got," Kerry said.
"You're real nice, and you're strong, and . . ."

"That's enough," Andre said. "You make me into
some kind of saint."

"But you're helping us," Kerry said. "No one else
would."

Andre gazed down at him.

"You're really afraid of this Flora, aren't you?"

Kerry nodded his head slightly.

"Don't think about her," Andre said. "If she tries to
hurt any of you, she'll have to answer to me."

He yawned just then, and realized he hadn't gotten
much sleep since the previous night. Too busy bringing
Jared Andre into the world. Well, maybe he'd better
take a nap rather than going out. He was suddenly very,
very tired . . .

Kerry waited until he heard soft snoring, then left
the room. The corridor was silent now, except for the
occasional ringing of a call bell. He hoped Gabrielle
wasn't sleeping. On his way to her room, he stopped in
front of the nursery window. But blinds had been
drawn, and try as he might, he couldn't catch a glimpse
of his new nephew. A nurse was entering the room now.
Kerry waited for her to ask what he was doing there,
but she only glanced at him, then went about her work.
Kerry grimaced at her back. She had the scariest green
eyes he'd ever seen. He left the nursery.

He opened the door to Gabrielle's room and said:
"You awake?"

She turned and smiled.

"Hi, Kerry. I don't think you're supposed to be
here."

"Tough," Kerry replied, coming to sit on the bed.
"I tried to see Jared, but they got these shades pulled
down."

"Oh, that's to let the babies get more sleep,"
Gabrielle replied. "But I wish I could see my son again,

right now." She looked up at the i.v. bottle. "I wish I could keep him in this room."

"Well, at least we got Andre here," Kerry said.

"I can't believe he . . ."

The sound of a baby crying silenced her. Could that be Jared? He sounded so frightened!

"Kerry, help me up!" Gabrielle cried. "I have to make sure that isn't my baby!"

Kerry looked at the tube in her arm.

"What about that thing?"

Without hesitation, Gabrielle pulled it out and climbed from the bed as drops of the liquid stained the sheets.

"Gabrielle, that was crazy!"

But Gabrielle had already entered the hallway and was rushing down to the nursery. With Kerry at her heels, she burst into the room, to find a petite, blonde-haired nurse trying to comfort her son.

"I knew it was Jared!" she cried. "Give him to me!"

"Now, now," the blonde nurse said. "You shouldn't be here. Why don't you go back to bed while I . . ."

"Look," Gabrielle said angrily, "no one is supposed to touch my baby except Nurse Smythe or Dr. Frazer. Who the hell said you could . . ."

The blonde woman turned her head abruptly towards the back entrance of the room. A look of anger came over her face, and in that look Gabrielle saw something vaguely familiar. The flashing of the green eyes . . .

She put Jared down and hurried out of the room as Dora Smythe entered.

"What is this?" she demanded.

Gabrielle met her eyes. "Some other nurse was handling my baby. I thought I made it clear that that wasn't supposed to happen!"

Dora looked genuinely confused.

"I told my staff what you requested," she said. "I'll see to it that this doesn't happen again."

"Good," Gabrielle said, relaxing. She looked down

at her still wailing baby. "Oh, it's all right, sweetheart! Mommy's here!"

Without asking permission, she lifted the tiny bundle in her arms and carried him to a rocking chair that sat nearby. Dora said a few quiet words to Kerry, telling him he wasn't allowed in here. Reluctantly, he left, but waited directly outside the door.

Gabrielle cooed and whispered at her son, rocking him gently until he had calmed down. Seeing the placid scene, the nurse smiled and busied herself checking the other infants in the room. Suddenly, a room buzzer sounded, forcing her to leave Gabrielle alone.

As her arm grew tired, Gabrielle switched Jared to the other. When the blanket moved, she noticed a red stain on his little cotton undershirt. She pulled at the Velcro fastenings.

Her scream set off a chain reaction of bawling in the other babies, and brought Kerry running back into the room.

"What happened?"

"She's here!" Gabrielle cried. "She's here and she hurt my baby!"

As Kerry looked at Jared's tiny bare chest, a look of horror came over his face. Someone had drawn a picture on the baby's skin—a red picture of a skull with a snake running through it!

"Yuk!"

"Kerry, help me!"

The little boy skipped back and forth in indecision, then finally chose to get Andre. He ran off down the hall, and in a few moments returned with the groggy Frenchman. But it took only a glance at Jared for Andre to become fully alert.

"*Mon Dieu*," he said. "Gabrielle, give the baby to me. I'll find out what this means!"

"I know what it means," Gabrielle snapped. "Flora is here and she almost had my baby! If I hadn't heard him cry . . ."

She bent her head forward as tears rushed from her eyes.

"Please, *chéri*," Andre said. She let him take the baby, and he stormed to the nurses' station, where Dora was busy with a phone call.

"Oh, my Lord, what happened?" she asked, putting the receiver down to take Jared. "What sick person..."

"You tell me that," Andre said. "My wife is terrified half out of her mind now. I want to know who did this!"

The nurse shook her head, running a finger over the design.

"It comes right off," she said. She pulled a tissue from a flowery box and wiped it away. "I'll take him for a bath, and..."

"Never mind a bath!" Andre said angrily. "I want the person who did this, *now!*"

Trying to help, Kerry pulled himself on tiptoes and said:

"There was a lady in the nursery before we came in."

"The other nurse?"

Kerry nodded. "She was holding Jared."

"What did she look like?" Dora asked.

"She was real short and she had blonde hair," Kerry answered.

Dora thought about this.

"There is no one in my staff fitting that description," she said. She glanced at Andre. "I'm going to call the police."

"You do that," Andre said. "Please give me the— give me my son. I will take him back to his mother now."

One of the other nurses had brought a reluctant Gabrielle to her room. She was busy putting the i.v. back in when Andre entered with Jared and Kerry.

"He's all right," Andre said, after the nurse left. "The picture wiped off easily."

He placed Jared in his mother's arms.

"I thought it was—was blood," Gabrielle said. "I thought she had hurt him."

"No, no *chéri*," Andre said. "No one has hurt your baby. And no one will!"

"Oh, God . . ." Gabrielle whispered.

Suddenly, she was in Andre's arms, sobbing. Kerry came to her and put a hand on her back, an angry look on his little face. Why were people always trying to hurt his sister?

"Ahh, *chéri*," Andre whispered, stroking her hair. "Nothing will happen more tonight. You are safe now."

"She wants my baby!"

Andre hushed her again, rocking her, suddenly feeling very protective of a girl he had known only a few hours.

At the nurse's station, the head nurse was trying desperately to make the sheriff understand her. But all she got over the phone was static. Planning to try another phone down the hall, she hung up and turned around. A woman was there, staring at her.

Dora Smythe didn't have time to scream before the knife was plunged into her chest.

Nineteen

Deep in the night, baby Jared stirred in his sleep, turning his head towards the sound of the nursery door clicking open. Down the hall, his mother slept soundly, sedated by Dr. Frazer. Uncle Kerry and Andre were also sound asleep.

The obstetrics ward was very, very quiet.

Flora Collins smiled as she walked across the room, her nurse's uniform seeming to glow in the soft light. *At last*, she thought, *I will have what I want!*

What did it matter if Gabrielle suspected she was here? The girl was too heavily drugged to interfere.

Flora laughed humorlessly, grateful for the wonders of modern medicine. A few drops of this or that and you were asleep for the night.

She went to stand over the crib, studying the sleeping baby with unloving eyes. He was a strong, healthy child, with a slight blush to his cheeks and thick black lashes. In truth, he was more beautiful than any baby Flora had ever seen. The Master would be pleased to take him when he grew up. . . .

Slowly, she reached into the crib, sliding her hands under the small body. But all of a sudden she pulled her hand to her mouth as a burning pain shot through her palm. Stifling a cry, Flora looked at the red welt on her skin. She'd been burned!

Now she saw it—the amulet, shining gold and silver. Flora glared at the thing. The triangle, pointed upward, represented Good. Its equilateral shape stood for the entity that was most hateful to her—the Holy Trinity. And the golden circle surrounding it had the power to banish evil spirits.

Flora felt weak, and turned quickly from the sight. It took only a few moments for her to realize she had not lost yet—this meant Gabrielle was unprotected! All she had to do was bring the girl out of her sleep and force her to remove the amulet!

But first it would be best to deal with that Frenchman and the little brat, Gabrielle's brother. . . .

At the nurse's station, Martha Norwich went through the papers that were scattered on the desk, trying to find a note from the head nurse. Dora Smythe hadn't been in earlier when she came to take over the night shift, but Martha had gone straight into making rounds and hardly noticed. Now, she wondered why Dora had taken off without a word, leaving such a mess. It wasn't like her at all!

She took a look at the admission book and found a new name there: Gabrielle Hansen. Her eyebrows went up to read that the woman had given birth to a son somewhere out in the mountains.

Martha decided she couldn't wait for Dora to return in the morning so she could learn the entire story.

Andre woke to the feeling of something being tightened around his arm. He blinked, mumbled something in French, and looked up into a pair of cold green eyes. A woman in a nurse's uniform held up a hypodermic needle, spraying liquid into the air.

"It's time for your medicine, Mr. Hansen."

"My name is Paget," Andre protested. "I'm not a patient here."

"Oh, now, now!" the woman scolded. "Mustn't give nursie a hard time! This won't hurt but a little bit!"

Slowly, the woman bent towards him, her eyes concentrating on the vein that bulged in the crook of his arm. Andre, too stunned for the moment to protest, watched her with wide eyes. This was a mistake!

"Don't you understand?" he asked. "I'm not a . . ."

He felt the point of the needle touch his arm, and jerked it away. But it dug into his flesh, stinging him.

"You fool! I missed the vein!"

Andre roared in protest, knocking the hypo from the nurse's hand.

"Leave me alone!" he cried. "What kind of insanity is this?"

A string of French swear words filled the room, accompanied by the woman's shouts of anger. She lifted a heavy lamp from the nightstand, and with a loud, animal-like roar she threw it with all her might. It missed Andre's head by a few inches, putting a crack in the plaster wall.

"Who are you?" Andre demanded. "What do you want?"

"You've interfered with my plans!" Flora screamed. "You must die!"

She lunged at him, a knife coming from no where to slash at his throat. But Andre, a sportsman well-trained in the art of self-defense, easily parried the motion. The woman hit the floor with a sharp thud, and was silent.

Andre, breathing heavily, looked down at the prone form.

"*Mon Dieu,*" he whispered.

He had to get out of here. Crossing the room to Kerry's bed, he shook the little boy gently, but could not wake him. He saw a spot of blood on the child's arm, and understood. She had managed to get to him first.

Gently, he bent to lift Kerry into his arms. He never saw Flora rising, walking slowly towards him, lifting a piece of the shattered lamp over her head. She brought it down hard, and laughed as he fell unconscious to the floor.

Andre breathed heavily, feeling pain all over his body, but mostly at the back of his head. Slowly, he pulled himself to his feet, rubbing his scalp. His fingers touched thick, warm blood.

She had hit him over the head. He looked around himself. Kerry was still curled up in his bed. And Gabrielle?

Not wasting a moment, Andre opened the closet and pulled a bowie knife from his knapsack then he left the room and felt his way dizzily along the white corridor. He paused near the nurse's station, waiting until he was certain the woman there wouldn't see him. Then he rushed to Gabrielle's room.

When he burst through the door, he found Gabrielle kneeling on the bed, her hospital gown twisted around her pale legs. She held her arms straight out, balancing Jared on the palms of her hands. The nurse, the woman who had tried to kill Andre, turned with a hiss at the sound of the door opening. Gabrielle stared at her, but did not react.

"GABRIELLE!"

"How dare you?" Flora cried.

"What are you doing to her?" Andre demanded. "Leave her alone!"

"Be gone from here!"

It was a deep-throated voice, almost masculine,

that came from Flora's mouth. Her eyes seemed to glow, but Andre was too angered to be frightened. He stood his ground, feeling in his pocket for the bowie knife.

"Let her alone," he ordered in a firm voice.

"No!" Flora snapped. "The Master wills this! And the Master wills that you should die!"

She lunged at him, her long nails aimed at his throat. In a flash, Andre pulled out the knife. Flora backed away from him, surprise covering her face. She had run into the sharp blade.

Doubled over, she choked:

"Fool! You'll pay for this!"

Andre said nothing, watching a circle of blood at her stomach grow bigger and bigger. Blood mixed with saliva dripped from her mouth. But still, somehow, she had the strength to turn and run from the room.

At the sound of the door slamming, Gabrielle screamed, the spell broken. Andre moved quickly to catch Jared. He placed a knee up on the bed and took Gabrielle into his arms.

"It's all right now," he said.

"Flora?" Gabrielle whimpered. "Flora was here?"

"Yes—yes, she was," Andre said. "But she's gone now. And we must leave this place at once!"

"She almost had my baby!"

"Please!" Andre cried. "You must be strong! Get dressed!"

Though she was sickened and horrified at what had almost happened, Gabrielle had sense enough to realize Andre was right. As he held Jared, she climbed from the bed and went to find her clothes. She fumbled with the straps of her sandals, her hands shaking visibly.

"Hurry!"

"Andre," she said softly. "Where is she? Where is Flora?"

"She's gone. She can't hurt you now," Andre said. He wouldn't explain further. When Gabrielle was completely dressed he took her arm and started to lead her from the room. She pulled away.

"Wait!"

Gabrielle ran to the bed and grabbed the amulet, putting it around her neck. Then she followed Andre to Kerry's room. The drug Flora had given Kerry had yet to wear off, and he refused to wake up despite a strong shaking from Andre. Finally, the Frenchman gathered him up into his arms. Holding his backpack with the other, he led Gabrielle out.

"We'll take the service elevator," he said. "No one will see us."

As they rounded a hallway, a nurse came from one of the rooms. They ducked back and waited in silence until she was gone, then hurried to the elevator. It amazed Andre that no one in the fairly busy lobby even looked at them as they crossed it to a nearby hallway. Too busy with their own problems, he decided, as the four headed towards the back entrance.

Soon, they were in the jeep, Kerry stretched across the camping equipment that filled its back. Andre revved the motor and turned the vehicle out of the parking lot. He managed a friendly smile for the attendant, who hardly noticed him.

"There is a map in here somewhere," Andre said with a flick of his hand. "Under the seat perhaps. It will tell us where to find the nearest airport."

"Airport?"

"We're going to San Francisco," Andre said.

"I don't . . ."

"Please, find the map!"

Gabrielle obeyed quickly, and found several. She shuffled through until one for Utah appeared, then opened it, keeping one arm tightly around Jared.

"Here's an airport," she said. "But it's almost a hundred miles away."

"It will have to do," Andre said. "What road is it on?"

"We'll pass it on this one," Gabrielle said.

"Good."

He stared straight ahead at the road.

Gabrielle looked down at Jared, sleeping peacefully in her arms. Bits and pieces of the last fifteen minutes came to her like the remnants of a dream. She vaguely remembered Flora bringing her to the nursery, then making her take Jared back to her room. She could almost hear Flora speaking to her now. Something about removing the amulet...

She shuddered.

"Andre?"

"Hmm?"

"What happened back there?"

"I don't know."

"What happened to make Flora leave?"

"I—I stabbed her," Andre said, finding no gentle way to say so. "She ran into my knife. She ran off bleeding."

"Andre!"

"*Chéri*," Andre said, speeding off an exit ramp onto the main highway, "I think you'd better explain this to me."

"No," came the barely whispered reply. "You've been so kind, but you're in trouble enough already. You can just leave my brother and me at the airport, and..."

Andre glanced at her, then back to the dark road.

"Let me say something. When that woman ran from your room, there was blood in her mouth. Do you know what that means? It means she may not live. Probably won't."

"Oh, God..."

"So I am involved very deeply, don't you see?" Andre said. "If that woman dies, I am a murderer."

"But it was self-defense!" Gabrielle protested.

"And who would believe that?"

"Well, I was a witness," Gabrielle said. "And a doctor might have seen how Kerry's been drugged! And Nurse Smythe—she saw the drawing on Jared's body."

"Would you want to go to the police?"

"N-no," Gabrielle said. The police would ask too many questions, and in the end they'd take Kerry away from her. And maybe even Jared! "No, I don't want to go to the police. But don't you think the hospital will put two and two together? They find a dead woman, and we've mysteriously disappeared?"

"And how would they know where to find us?" Andre asked. "They know me as Mr. Hansen, not as Andre Paget."

"But they know my name!"

"Flora ran from your room," Andre said. "Wherever she ends up, no one could suspect that you left the hospital in your condition to commit such a crime. In fact, they may not make a connection at all. We showed up—'out of the blue,' as you Americans say—at the hospital one day, and left in the same way." He changed lanes at a higher speed than necessary. "They'll probably just think we were avoiding paying the bill. What I want to know is what your involvement with Flora is. Now that I am part of it, I have a right to know!"

Gabrielle breathed deeply, and began to tell Andre her story. He listened in amazement to reports of midnight rituals, of dark-robed figures, and of a young boy with dark curls who had tried to warn Gabrielle of the danger. She told him of her adoption by Flora, and how a small dead animal had been found in the homes she'd been in previous to that one.

"I think it was set up," Gabrielle said. "Flora arranged to make me look like a monster so that the orphanage would be glad to be rid of me. And then she thought I'd be so grateful for her kindness that I'd see through the lies." Gabrielle rubbed her eyes. "She was right."

"It wasn't your fault," Andre said. "I saw the woman only a few moments, and could see that she would frighten anyone. What sort of evil is in her?"

"I don't know."

Andre reached across the seat and put a hand on Gabrielle's shoulder, squeezing it. Then he pointed to a sign up ahead.

"See, the airport is coming up," he said. "And I think your brother is waking, Gabrielle—it would be best if he knew nothing of this."

"Of course," Gabrielle said.

Kerry groaned loudly, saying something about his aching head. He sat up and looked around at the back of the jeep, as it pulled into the airport parking lot.

"Where're we?"

"The airport," Gabrielle said. "How do you feel?"

"Yukky," Kerry said. "My head hurts."

"We'll go inside and have some hot chocolate and coffee," Andre suggested. "But first let's get these things out of here."

He helped Kerry from the back, then went around to open the door for Gabrielle. It was nearly eleven P.M., and a flight had just come in from Oklahoma City. Gabrielle and Kerry found seats in the crowded waiting room, weaving through a throng of passengers waiting for their baggage. Andre went to the ticket counter. He didn't come back to Gabrielle and Kerry for a half hour.

"There is a flight at seven-thirty in the morning," Andre said. "I have three tickets."

"I can't believe you're doing all this for us," Gabrielle said, "when you don't even know us."

"I know you now, don't I?" Andre asked.

In truth, he had considered getting them tickets to some other state, then he wouldn't have to worry about them. But his good sense got the better of him. If they were caught as runaways, no doubt they'd tell of what he'd done to Flora. No, it was better to keep them with him, as much of a nuisance as it would be. He was certain anyway that his sister would be willing to take them in.

"What do we do now?" Gabrielle asked.

"Spend the night in a motel," Andre said.

Gabrielle and Kerry followed him back to the car. After Kerry climbed in the back, Gabrielle put her hand on her new friend's arm and said softly:

"How do you feel right now?"

"I'm cold, all over," Andre said. "I am thinking of nothing but tomorrow."

"I don't want to think of anything at all," Gabrielle replied, opening her door.

*　　*　　*

Even as they were boarding the flight to San Francisco, Dr. Frazer was taking Dora Smythe to task for having let Gabrielle and the others leave.

"Don't you realize how weak that child was?"

"But sir," Dora said. "No one can be held in a hospital against his wishes. Mrs. Hansen wanted to leave, so how could I not let her?"

"You should have advised against it!"

"Don't you think I tried?"

Dr. Frazer made an impatient gesture.

"Well, they're gone now," he said.

He turned and walked away to begin his rounds. The face staring at him resembled Dora Smythe, but it was Flora Collins who possessed the dead woman's body. She began to laugh.

Gabrielle thinks the Frenchman killed me, she thought. *Well, let her think that! Let her think she is safe!*

Twenty

In the bustling San Francisco International Airport, Andre, Gabrielle and Kerry stood waiting for Andre's luggage, watching the carousel go around and around. Jared slept soundly in Gabrielle's arms. Some of the people nearby smiled to see such a tiny baby, but Gabrielle kept her eyes lowered and ignored them. She had spent the entire flight thinking of Flora, and what might happen to Andre for what he had done. She was afraid to look anyone in the eye, afraid to see a familiar face that would tell her the woman knew where she was and had come to get her.

"When we get my things," Andre said, "I am going to call my sister."

"What are you going to tell her about us?" Gabrielle asked.

"That you are friends," Andre said simply. "Ah! There they are. Now, look—" he grabbed one suitcase, flung it behind himself, then reached for the other before it got too far away "—while I am calling her I want you to go into that little shop over there and buy yourself some new clothes. You must be tired of wearing that ensemble."

He pulled some money from his pocket and pressed it into Gabrielle's hands, then strode off towards the telephones before Gabrielle could say a word. At that moment, she decided that Emilie must be a saint if she was half as kind as her brother.

She seemed as much when she finally arrived. Emilie Paulsen was a petite woman, standing no more than five feet tall, with very short red hair and smiling blue eyes. She called to her brother in a high-pitched French accent and raced to throw her arms around him. She kissed both his cheeks as she stood on tiptoe, then backed away, still holding his hands.

"It's so good you've come early," she said. "I am sure Barry will be delighted to see you."

Andre turned to the Hansens.

"Emilie," he said, "I would like you to meet new friends of mine. This is Gabrielle Hansen, and her brother, Kerry. We—we met in Utah."

Gabrielle could read a message to Emilie in his eyes: *don't ask questions*. Emilie nodded, then grinned at the two.

"*Bienvenue!*" she said, offering her hand. "I'm happy to have you as my guests. And who is this?"

She smiled into the folds of Jared's blanket, seeing a tiny pink face.

"My son," Gabrielle replied. "Jared Andre Hansen. I used your brother's name for his middle name because Andre . . ."

The Frenchman cut her off.

"It's a long drive to Emilie's house," he said. "I think we should be going, don't you?"

After the wide open spaces of the Southwest, San Francisco seemed like another world. It was congested, overrun with traffic, and impossibly hilly. But Gabrielle was certain she had never seen a more beautiful city. Houses lining the steep hills were carefully painted in an array of gay colors.

"How pretty!" Gabrielle cried. "I never thought Frisco was like this."

Emilie held up a small hand. "Oh, no! You must never call this city 'Frisco.' The people here don't like that. It is *San* Francisco."

Andre laughed, then turned to point out his window. "Look at that, Kerry," he said. "There's a trolley down that hill."

Kerry scrambled around to see it.

"Can we ride on one?"

"*Mon petit*," Emilie said, "you will ride on so many that you will be tired of them!"

Kerry gave his head an emphatic shake and watched the trolley climb the hill. The traffic light changed again, and Emilie continued on her way. Soon they arrived at a pretty street of Victorian houses. Emilie asked Kerry to guess which one was hers.

He peered out the window, studying each facade, then started to bounce up and down.

"I know! I know! It's that one!"

"*Oui!*" Emilie cried. "How did you know?"

She pulled into a driveway.

"'Cause that's the flag of France painted at the top," Kerry said.

"You're very smart," Emilie said. "Now! Come inside and I'll make lunch. You must be hungry."

Kerry studied the sky blue house as Andre pulled his luggage from the trunk. Ten stone steps led up to the entrance, a white door directly in line with a white scallop-trimmed bay window. A white railing separated it from a matching upper floor. The bottom level held the garage. Around the roof there were more scallops, these painted dark blue.

The interior of the house matched Emilie's personality. It was breezy and cheerful, with simple lines and pastel colors. The pictures on the walls were of flowers and kittens and old French nightclub acts. There were statues of clowns all along the white mantel.

No skulls, Gabrielle thought.

"Kerry," Emilie said, "would you like to play with our TV games? I can show you how."

She led him into a den, where she set up the television for "Space Invaders." Kerry took a control box from the glass coffee table and started playing with it.

"Boy, this is better than that dumb old hospital!"

"Hospital?"

"Uh—why don't you show Gabrielle her room?" Andre interrupted. "Perhaps the baby needs to be changed, or..."

"I understand," Emilie said. She put her arm around Gabrielle's waist and let her up a narrow staircase. "Our bedrooms are on this level. I hope you don't mind, but you'll have to share with your brother. Barry—my husband—will bring a cot down from the attic when he comes home tonight."

Gabrielle stood in the doorway of the green-and-white room, rocking Jared. It seemed she was on the threshold of a garden; she couldn't help smiling.

"It's so cheerful in here," she said.

"And you can see the Bay from your window," Emilie pointed out.

Gabrielle went to it, and watched a boat glide by on the distant water. She spotted a bridge and wondered if it was the Golden Gate. But instead of asking, she turned and said:

"Thank you so much for letting us stay here, Emilie."

"You are in trouble, no?"

Gabrielle looked down at her baby's face, thinking. Should she tell Emilie? No—why involve another person? Andre was in enough trouble already without Emilie being hurt too. She was much too sweet for that!

"I think my baby is waking up," she said, a reply

that told Emilie she didn't wish to discuss her problems. "I'll be downstairs again after I've nursed and changed him."

"Of course," Emilie said. "I will leave you to your privacy."

She left the room, thinking she would ask Andre for a full explanation later that night.

Cradling Jared, Gabrielle sat on the window seat and let the sun warm her. She prayed that San Francisco would be a safe haven for her. She didn't know that someone was contacting Flora at that very moment, someone who had seen Gabrielle enter Emilie's house.

They met Barry Paulsen at dinner that night. He was a bear of a man with a deep, soft voice. His sandy hair was cut short, and he had a slight mustache. The jeans and T-shirt he had changed into before dinner showed off large shoulders and a flat stomach.

"I used to have a shirt like that," Kerry said. "Except it was for the Dallas Cowboys, not the Forty-niners."

"We'll get you a Forty-niners shirt," Barry said.

During dinner, Gabrielle and Kerry learned that Barry was a private investigator, a fact that alarmed Kerry.

"You're a cop?"

"I was one," Barry said. "But I didn't like it very much."

"What kind of 'vestigating do you do?"

"Oh, to see if husbands are cheating on their wives, or . . ."

"Barry!" Emilie cried. "That is no way to speak to a little boy!"

"Sorry," Barry said. "I'm not used to having kids in this house. But, as Em said, any friend of Andre's is welcome here."

Kerry relaxed a little. Barry wasn't a cop, and that meant he wouldn't be telling anyone they were here. At least he didn't have to worry about being sent back to the orphanage! Barry didn't ask the Hansens any questions about themselves, sensing they wouldn't answer anyway. But even so, Gabrielle took Andre aside after dinner.

"Are you going to tell them what happened?"

"I've thought of a story," Andre whispered. "I am going to tell them I became ill on my camping trip, and you helped me. They will understand I owe you a favor."

"But what if they ask where we're from?" Gabrielle pressed. "What if they want to know about our family, or . . ."

"Emilie and Barry won't ask such questions," Andre reassured her. "They trust my judgment. I wouldn't worry."

"You seem so certain of all this," Gabrielle said. "Andre, you might have killed a woman last night. Don't you feel badly about that?"

"She was evil," Andre said. "I could feel that. And as I said she ran into my knife."

Gabrielle studied Andre's face, trying to read his thoughts. Behind her, a clock ticked, and a pair of finches chattered noisily. But it was dark in the living room, and the shadows cast through the picture window hid the expression in Andre's eyes.

"It all happened so fast," he said. "I just want to forget about it. You certainly don't care about this Flora, do you, who hurt you so badly?"

Gabrielle turned away from him and fixed her eyes on a silver-framed picture. No, she didn't care about Flora. But she did worry that Andre might be sent to jail for what he had done. And if that happened, maybe Kerry would be returned to the orphanage and maybe Jared would be taken away from her. She wouldn't think of her own fate.

She felt tears rising, and blinked them away. But Andre, sensing her fears, put his arms around her and held her close. She let the beating of his heart soothe her, snuggling into his chest.

"What if she isn't dead?" she whispered. "What if she finds me again? She did it before."

"You were alone then," Andre said, petting her long black hair. "There was no one to protect you. But I am here, and Emilie and Barry too. If Flora comes, we will fight her. She will not get near you."

"Andre," Gabrielle breathed. "I want so much to believe that."

She heard Jared crying upstairs, and pulled away from him.

"My son must be hungry," she said. She took Andre's hand and squeezed it. "I'll be all right."

Andre watched her walk out to the hallway, then went to the bar and poured himself some wine. From Napa Valley, not from his France. He smiled to think how much of an American Emilie had become. And Gabrielle? Could Gabrielle become a Frenchwoman?

That was a crazy thought. What would Gabrielle do in France? Why would he even take her? He hardly knew her!

And yet there was something about the girl, something he had felt even as he was helping her through the difficulties of labor. . . .

"Andre?"

Barry and Emilie had entered the room. Barry switched on a light and headed to a lounge chair with a mug of beer in his hand.

"You will want to ask questions, I suppose," Andre said.

"Just tell me what those two are doing here," Barry said.

Andre related a story he had made up in his own head, partially from Gabrielle's own. He left out all the horrible things, and anything connected with Flora Collins.

"They're runaways?" Barry asked.

"From an orphanage," Andre replied. "They were treated badly. The people there tried to make Gabrielle abort her baby."

"When I first saw them," Emilie said, "I thought perhaps it was yours. The middle name, and all."

"Of course it isn't mine," Andre said. "I haven't

been to America since last year. No, Gabrielle said it was some boy she thought she was in love with. Obviously, he cared nothing for her."

He said this in such an angry tone that Barry and Emilie exchanged glances. Barry set his beer down on a glass stand beside his chair. He pushed it back into a reclining position and folded his large hands over his turquoise belt buckle.

"Whatever," he said. "You should have made reports about any abuse, Andre. Now you could be accused of kidnapping."

"Those two were on the road for three weeks before I met them," Andre said. "If the orphanage didn't try to find them earlier, why should they do so now? Look, Gabrielle has a little baby of her own. They probably wouldn't want to be burdened with it."

"What about her brother?" Barry asked. "He's a minor, you know."

"Kerry will have to go to school," Emilie said. "If he doesn't, someone will surely become suspicious."

Andre leaned forward to reach his glass of wine.

"You are a teacher, Emilie," he said. "Can't you let him into your class?"

"What do I tell the administration about him?"

Barry sighed. "Well, we'll have to think of something. Okay—they can stay here until we do. But I assume no responsibility if you get caught, Andre."

Andre thanked him, knowing this was the best he could expect.

"You were always so kind to strays, Andre," Emilie said. "I remember how Mama used to roll her eyes when you'd bring all those puppies and kittens home. You still do it like that, don't you?"

Andre smiled at her, thinking that Gabrielle was hardly what he'd call a stray.

Lou Hunter shifted his mailbag from one shoulder to the other and stopped to look up the steep hill that would take him several blocks from his usual mail route. He caught the eyes of an elderly woman; the two exchanged smiles. Lou had one of those pleasant, non-descript faces that people immediately trusted. And that was what made him dangerous.

Today his task was far from innocent. He began climbing the hill at last, then finally knocked at the door of a blue-and-white Victorian house. The woman who answered was a petite redhead.

"You aren't our usual mailman," she said.

"No, ma'am," Lou said pleasantly. "But I found this letter in my bag and thought I'd drop it by. Thought it might be important."

He handed the envelope to her. Emilie glanced at it, and saw only an address.

"There's no name."

"Well, you can open it and figure out who it's for," Lou said. He glanced past Emilie's shoulder. "There aren't too many people living here, are there?"

As Emilie answered him, Lou caught sight of a young girl with dark hair. She stopped in the doorway to the foyer cradling a small infant in her arms. But, like an apparition, she quickly ducked out of sight after meeting Lou's inquiring eyes.

"Well, you didn't have to trouble yourself," Emilie said at last. "But thank you."

"My pleasure," Lou said with a tip of his cap.

He turned and walked down to the sidewalk, a smug expression on his face. Sure it was his pleasure! Flora Collins would be more than pleased with him when he called to tell her the girl was hiding in this house.

Meanwhile, Emilie carried the letter into her living room and ripped it open. Gabrielle was sitting on the couch, feeding Jared his bottle. She saw bewilderment on the Frenchwoman's face and asked what was wrong.

"This letter," Emilie replied. "Isn't it silly? Someone put a blank piece of paper in this envelope!"

Shrugging it off as some kind of joke, Emilie crinkled up the paper and tossed it in the trash can.

*   *   *

Because the Paulsens respected their privacy, Gabrielle and Kerry began to feel at ease around them. Gabrielle was still worried that Flora might come after her, but Andre constantly reassured her that he would take care of the woman if she did. So whenever thoughts of Flora crowded her mind, Gabrielle tried to concentrate on other matters. Most important was the care of her newborn son. Jared was growing bigger and cuter with each passing day. He was such a delightful child that even Barry noticed.

"That kid hardly ever cries," he commented one Saturday in early November. "If Emilie and I decide to have a kid, I hope it turns out just like that one."

"Thank you," Gabrielle said, flattered. She was sitting in the living room with Jared in her lap. Beside her, Kerry was busy with a TV game. "He really is good-natured, isn't he?"

I don't know how that can be, she thought, *considering what he went through before he was born. I wonder if I only imagined he could sense my fears?*

"Look," Barry said, "Andre and Emilie are back from shopping. And it looks like they hit every store in Union Square."

The two were chattering in French when they came through the front door. Barry immediately went to help Emilie with her parcels, and soon the window seat was overflowing.

"I started some Christmas shopping," Emilie said. "So don't peek at anything, Barry."

"I haven't even started thinking about Christmas, Em," Barry said. "It's six weeks away!"

"So?"

"What did you buy?" Kerry asked, the array of colorful packages diverting his attention from the TV screen.

"Kerry, don't be so nosy," Gabrielle said. The thought of Christmas made her feel depressed.

Emilie held up her hands.

"Oh, it's all right," she said. "In fact, we bought

some things for you. Look, Kerry, here's an outfit for you to wear to school on Monday."

Kerry wrinkled his nose.

"I don't wanna think about school," he said.

"But all little boys must go to school," Emilie pointed out. "And you will be in my class. You should like that, no?"

Andre gestured towards the window.

"It's such a beautiful day out," he said. "Why don't we go to Chinatown and forget about school? You haven't seen much of San Francisco, Gabrielle."

"I don't really feel like going out," Gabrielle said.

"But you've been in this house for so long," Emilie said. "You need some fresh air! And so do your baby and little Kerry."

Kerry, who hadn't ventured much further than a small park across the street, took up on the idea.

"Can we ride a trolley?"

"We will do that first of all," Andre said. "Please, Gabrielle. Is it not foolish to waste such a lovely day?"

"Well . . ."

"I'll buy you dinner in Chinatown," Andre coaxed.

"Say 'yes,' Gabrielle," Kerry begged. "I wanna try an eggroll!"

Gabrielle smiled crookedly at him.

"Oh, okay!" she cried. "Just let me get a sweater for Jared."

A short while later, she returned to the living room. She had dressed Jared in a striped stretchie that Emilie had bought for him. In fact, Emilie had furnished the baby with everything he needed. She commented on how cute he looked.

"He's smiling," she said. "He must like to be flattered."

"Probably just gas," Barry said. "Babies that young can't smile. They don't know what's going on."

Gabrielle held her head up, a proud mother.

"My baby knows," she said.

"And what makes you an expert on babies, Barry Paulsen?" Emilie asked, her hands on her hips.

Andre laughed, and took Jared while Gabrielle put on a light coat. It was a coat Emilie was about to discard, easily made like new by purchasing a full set of buttons and stitching the torn lining. It was a little short on Gabrielle, but the thought of someone caring enough to give it to her made her feel it was very special.

"We'll see you later tonight," Andre told his sister, kissing her cheek.

"Enjoy your chop suey!" Barry called after them.

Kerry was delighted at the clanging sound of the trolley bells, but disappointed that they didn't move very fast—even down the steepest hills. He watched a conductor pull a lever each time someone boarded. Andre pointed to a counter, and explained it was keeping track of the number of people riding.

"Here's where we get off," he said at last. "Grant Avenue. It's the most important street in Chinatown."

He helped Kerry and Gabrielle down, and they all headed into a bustling, colorful street of Chinese shops and restaurants. Boxes and tables laden with merchandise—everything from bamboo steamers to Chinatown T-shirts lined the sidewalks. The street was full of people, so many that it seemed like a holiday, and the air was thick with the smell of cooking food.

"Some of the things you see are—what do you say?" Andre stopped to think a moment, standing next to a tree with bright red flowers. "I know. Some of the things are junk. But we will see the beautiful things, of course."

At Kerry's suggestion, they stopped in every bakery to sample a different kind of Chinese pastry—black bean cakes, almond cookies, other indescribable treats. Finally, Gabrielle said they would spoil their appetites if they kept this up.

"Not me," Kerry said, licking plum sauce from his fingers. "I could eat tons of this stuff! Boy, we never had such good food at the orphanage."

"Let's not talk about that, Kerry," Gabrielle said. She had spotted a pagoda-shaped street lamp. Elaborate snakes swirled up its sides, making her think of the skull-and-snakes. She shivered and turned away.

"There's an interesting window," Andre said, pointing across the street. He led Gabrielle to a jewelry shop. The display glittered with gold and silver and precious jade, mixed with colorful bits of coral, ivory and ebony jewelry.

"Look at that pretty tree," Gabrielle said, indicating a bonsai with an ebony trunk and jade leaves. A miniature golden bird sat among the pink coral flowers, its head thrown back as if in the midst of a song. "It's so beautiful."

"Not as beautiful as you are," Andre said.

Gabrielle's eyes widened, and she turned to Andre in surprise. But, as if he had said nothing, the Frenchman moved swiftly away from the jewelry shop. A few stores later, he busied himself with helping Kerry pick out a souvenir. Gabrielle decided to let the matter drop. It had only been a spontaneous statement; it meant nothing.

As she passed a dark, recessed doorway, Gabrielle noticed a woman in a black kimono pull back into the shadows. But she thought nothing of it. She never saw the woman's face, so she didn't know that she had been the subject of keen observation ever since she set foot on Grant Avenue.

Twenty-one

Andre spent most of his time with Gabrielle, and she began to wonder if he'd forgotten his company in Europe. He'd explained all about Paget International, and she worried that she was taking him away from his work. But he assured her that things were going so well with the company that his brother, Henri, did not need his help.

"I had made plans to stay here with my sister for a few months," he said. "If Henri needs me, he will call."

"That means you'll be heading back to Paris, doesn't it?" Gabrielle asked. "I'll miss you. You've been so nice to my brother and me."

"I am not going back yet," Andre said. "It may be a long time that I stay here in America."

He looked at her in such a way that Gabrielle sensed he didn't really want to leave California. She was glad of that—Andre had become such a dear friend that she couldn't bear the thought of losing him to some far-off sporting goods company. But she decided she wouldn't think of that. It was more important to take advantage of the happiest days she'd ever experienced. It was hard to believe that nothing at all had happened since they left the Utah hospital. By the time Christmas week came, Gabrielle came to realize that Andre was right. Flora would certainly have found her by now if she wanted to! So, believing all the horror had passed, she let herself be caught up in the joy of the Christmas season. Barry had paid her to straighten up his files, and she decided to use the money to do some Christmas shopping.

Andre took her to Pier 39, a wonderful mosaic of shops located right next to Fisherman's Wharf. It was constructed of wooden decks, wet from a sudden downpour, and each level was clustered with interesting boutiques. Colorful hanging plants decorated the wooden beams. Christmas lights were strung everywhere.

"There's an amusement center here," Andre said quietly to Gabrielle. "If you want to shop for Kerry, I can take him there."

"Thanks," Gabrielle said. "I'll see you in a while."

As Gabrielle walked around, Jared seemed fascinated by the sights around him, and smiled his most adorable smile for anyone who looked his way.

"What an alert baby you have!" one woman commented, wiggling her fingers at Jared.

Gabrielle thanked her politely, then turned to walk away. The woman's expression turned grim as she watched the retreating figure. It was obvious the girl felt nervous around strangers, and that thought made the woman smile again. But this time, there was no sweetness in the smile. She watched until Gabrielle disappeared around a corner, then headed for the nearest pay phone.

When a woman answered after several rings, she said:

"She's alone, with the child. Should I . . ."

"No," came the quick reply. "Just watch her. The time is not right yet."

Unaware of all this, Gabrielle looked around herself for a place to start shopping.

She spotted a store that exclusively sold Christmas paraphernalia and bought a pretty porcelain unicorn for Barry and Emilie's tree. A nearby toy shop had an adorable stuffed lion for Kerry. Gabrielle watched the girl wrap it and recalled how much Kerry loved his stuffed raccoon—the one he had lost in the accident with Amy MacClellan. She hoped he'd like this animal as much.

Now, what to buy Andre? Nothing seemed right for him, at least nothing Gabrielle could afford. There were beautiful pocket watches and shaving kits and hand-tooled leather belts. But Andre probably had tons of that kind of thing. After all, he had more money than Gabrielle had ever seen. What do you buy a man like that?

What do you buy a man who was responsible for turning your life around?

She suddenly realized how ridiculous her thoughts were. What did it matter? He was just a friend—if a best friend. She didn't have to make an impression on him! And yet she wanted to give him something very, very special. Something to let him know she appreciated all his help.

She finally came across something in a store selling prints and posters. Knowing how much of an outdoorsman Andre was, she chose a picture depicting the Tour de

France. It was colorfully painted in an abstract way, the cyclists blending into the wind that brushed back from their bicycles. The frame for it nearly wiped out Gabrielle's funds, but she didn't care. She was certain Andre would like this reminder of his beloved France. She divided her packages between her two arms, and pushed Jared's stroller to meet Andre and Kerry.

Christmas came at last. Kerry was delighted with his new lion, and Emilie made a big fuss over the unicorn. To Gabrielle's surprise, the Paulsens had gifts for them, too: an electronic football game and Forty-niners T-shirt for Kerry, a new outfit for Gabrielle, and a jumper seat for Jared. It so overwhelmed the young girl that she ran from the room in tears.

There was a knock at her door, and Andre entered her room with a small red package.

"*Chéri*, you did not open my gift," he said. He stopped at the edge of her bed. "Why are you crying?"

"I don't know," Gabrielle said, sitting up. Blinking Christmas lights from the street outside played on her face as she wiped her eyes. "I'm sorry."

"You don't need to be sorry."

"I—I guess I didn't think I'd ever be this happy," Gabrielle said. "I started thinking about the farm in Kansas, and about Flora. . . ."

"You haven't mentioned her in weeks," Andre said. "Please, don't spoil a beautiful holiday."

Gabrielle nodded.

"I'm okay now," she said. "Let's go back downstairs. I can hear Emilie playing Christmas carols on the piano."

She started to get up, but Andre gently pushed her down again.

"Wait," he said. "I want you to open my gift."

"You didn't have to . . ."

"And you didn't have to buy me the poster," Andre said. "But of all the gifts I've ever received, it is the most precious, because there is true feeling behind it. Now, you unwrap this one."

Gabrielle did so, and gasped when she pulled back

the layers of tissue surrounding her gift. It was the ebony and jade tree she'd seen in Chinatown! Shaking her head, she gently touched the golden bird. She threw her arms around Andre and hugged him as tightly as she could.

"Thank you! Thank you so much!"

"I thought you would like it," Andre said. He pulled away. "Come now, we should return, shouldn't we? I haven't given Kerry his gift."

Gabrielle wanted to sit alone with him for a while longer, but he was already leaving the room. At that moment, she felt something grow warm inside her, a feeling for Andre she couldn't help but understand.

She was in love with him.

But he had kept their relationship at a strictly Platonic level, and though his attentions sometimes hinted at mutual feelings, he never let them go too far. *Well*, Gabrielle thought as she got up from the bed, *there was time for all that*. And the others were waiting.

No one said a word about her bloodshot eyes when she entered the living room again, but they all commented on the beautiful tree. Gabrielle set it down among the other gifts and sat back to admire the way the Christmas lights made its surfaces sparkle.

"Look, Gabrielle!" Kerry cried suddenly. "Real roller skates! The kind with shoes, and stoppers on the toes and ball-bearing wheels!"

"Hey, that's great," Barry said. "You could stand at the top of California Street and roll all the way down to the Ferry Building."

Everyone laughed, and Kerry sat down to try on the skates. He beamed up at Andre.

"They fit!"

"*Merveilleux*," Andre said. "We'll go to Golden Gate Park tomorrow to try them out."

Emilie, who had left the room, returned with a trayful of eggnogs.

"I would like to make a toast," Barry said, "even if there isn't a drop of brandy in these things."

"Not with an eight-year-old here," Emilie said.

Barry laughed, and raised his mug. "To many, many more days as happy as this one has been."

"I wanna say something, too," Kerry chimed in. "I wanna say thanks to you guys for being the best friends me and Gabrielle ever had."

"Thank you for all you've done," Gabrielle said.

They clicked the mugs and exchanged kisses of thanks for the gifts received, as well as the weeks of love and friendship that they had shared. Emilie smiled to see the way Andre was watching Gabrielle, and knew it was just a matter of time before he'd admit he was in love with the girl.

A light January rain pattered against the kitchen window as Andre sat with his sister and brother-in-law at breakfast. Emilie and he shared fresh croissants, while Barry devoured a huge stack of pancakes. The others hadn't woken up yet.

"The school board has begun asking questions again about Kerry," Emilie said. "I'm starting to worry, Andre."

"I had a feeling this would happen," Barry said, sipping at his coffee. "And I've been prepared for it."

"What do you say we should do?" Andre asked.

"I'll have my secretary type up a letter on some official-looking paper," Barry said. "We'll say the school was burned down, and that it will take a while before duplicates can be sent. You know how red tape is—it'll be summer before anything happens!"

"You are so smart, Barry!" Emilie said, leaning over to kiss him.

Andre wanted to know why Barry was suddenly so willing to help Gabrielle and Kerry.

"A few months ago, you were afraid of being called a kidnapper," he said. "But now . . . Barry, have you done something?"

The big man held up two hands.

"All right," he said. "I did a little snooping. Now, don't look so worried! I simply called the orphanage pretending to be a long lost relative. They said both kids had been adopted last year, and that they hadn't heard a thing about them."

"How did you know where to call?"

"A label in those sneakers Emilie finally made Kerry deep-six," Barry explained. "Get this—when I asked for a forwarding address, they said they had no record of the adoptions. I don't think they would have given them to me anyway. But if they were really runaways, don't you think their foster parents would have contacted the orphanage? The impression I got was that no one there seemed to give a damn about the Hansens."

"I don't understand," Andre said. "How could two young people be allowed to run off without anyone asking questions?"

Barry shrugged. "Beats the hell out of me. Anyway, this just proves that no one is going to come snooping around here looking for them. And I have to say that sets my mind at ease."

"I still wish you hadn't done it," Andre grumbled. "If they do come looking for her, I hate to think what they'll do to Gabrielle."

"You care a lot about her, don't you?" Emilie asked.

Andre clicked his tongue.

"She's just a friend."

"Of course," Emilie said, smiling. "A very beautiful friend, no?"

Before Andre could comment, the kitchen door swung open, and Gabrielle entered with Jared in her arms. Her face was pale, and it seemed something had frightened her.

"*Chéri*, what is it?" Andre said, hurrying to her. "What happened?"

"Jared talked!" Gabrielle cried, sitting down. "He called me 'Mama.'"

"Oh, but that's impossible, *ma petite*!" Emilie said. "He is only three months old! It is much too early for a baby to speak!"

Gabrielle shook her head. "No, he looked right at me and he said 'Mama.' I know he did!"

"Hey, babies always make funny noises," Barry said. "Probably just sounded that way."

"I *know* what I heard," Gabrielle said, defiantly.

Emilie tickled Jared's chin.

"Well, you're going to see his doctor today, aren't you? Ask him what he thinks."

In the doctor's office, Gabrielle did just that. Dr. Janovic listened with interest, then finally said he had to agree with the others.

"It isn't likely that a baby that age would speak," he said as Gabrielle dressed her son. "But I must admit Jared Andre is the most remarkable child I've ever seen. His development is far more advanced than the average for his age."

"What does that mean?"

"Well, I noticed a long attention span at his first examination, two months ago," Dr. Janovic said. "Babies usually don't concentrate on things that early. And just now, you were playing 'Peek-a-Boo' with him. I know babies of five and six months of age that haven't mastered that! More than this, he imitates the sounds I make at him."

"Then why don't you think he can talk?"

"There's a limit to how advanced a baby can be," the doctor said. "Ms. Hansen, why worry? You obviously have a very, very bright child. And he's healthy as all get-out too. Hasn't even had a cold, has he?"

"Is that good?"

"That's wonderful," Dr. Janovic said. "I wish all my patients were as cheerful, bright and healthy as your son!"

Thus reassured, Gabrielle decided to stop wondering if Jared had actually spoken to her. Over the next months, he showed more signs of advanced intelligence. He sat up earlier than most babies, then crawled and stood on his own as soon as his body was physically able to support him. And he *did* speak, saying little words so well that there was no denying he meant "Mama" or "Kerry" or "bottle."

But by all other appearances he was a perfectly average child. Perhaps he stood up before anyone expected him to, but he could only take a few steps before falling on his rump. Emilie and Gabrielle would run to fuss over him, but Jared would only clap his hands and laugh.

"It's hard to believe he's eight months old now," Emilie commented one day.

"I think it's harder to believe we've been here that long," Gabrielle replied. "Is it still okay?"

Emilie put an arm around her.

"Of course!" she said. "I told you before that any friend of Andre's is welcome here."

"But what if he goes back to France?" Gabrielle asked. "What if Henri needs him?"

"Does it worry you much that he might leave?"

Gabrielle met her eyes.

"I'd miss him so much," she said.

"You love him." It was a statement, not a question, and so to the point that Gabrielle admitted that she did.

"I don't know when I started to," she said. "There have been so many worries on my mind. But I know that I do now, and I want to stay with Andre forever."

"I understand, *ma petite*," Emilie said. "And do you know something? I think Andre loves you, too. But he's funny. He won't admit it. You don't worry about all this, though. If Andre leaves, I would bet he'll bring you to Paris with him."

"You really think so?"

"I am certain of it, yes," Emilie said. "Now, if you'll excuse me, I have some school papers to correct."

Gabrielle hardly heard her leave the room. She felt more elated than she had in months. It was nice to realize she felt she deserved love—a far cry from the frightened little girl she'd been just a year earlier. But Andre and the Paulsens were responsible for that. She couldn't help taking hold of her amulet and twisting it to make it catch the sunlight. Maybe someday she'd be able to take it off, believing she didn't need it anymore.

Jared, fascinated by the sparkles of sunshine, grabbed for the amulet and put it in his mouth. Gabrielle laughed and took it out, then covered her baby's face with kisses.

"Oh, Jared," she said. "I'm happy today. Really happy!"

She danced in front of the window with him, singing. On the sidewalk across the street, someone watched her, frowning to see her joyous mood.

Twenty-two

Towards the end of spring, Gabrielle decided to take Jared for another checkup. She called Dr. Janovic's office to set up an appointment, and learned the pediatrician was away on vacation.

"However," the nurse said, "we could have Dr. Gant look at your little boy. He's the new partner here."

"I don't know," Gabrielle said. "Jared was so comfortable with Dr. Janovic. When will he be back?"

"In two weeks," the nurse replied. "How about seeing us on, say—Tuesday the eighteenth?"

"I'll be there," Gabrielle promised.

But when she arrived, it was to receive sad news.

"Dr. Gant has taken charge here now," the nurse told her. "I'm sorry to say that Dr. Janovic met with an accident while on vacation."

"How awful," Gabrielle said. "Is he going to be all right?"

The nurse shook her head, tears coming to her eyes. Quickly, she shook them away.

"He had chartered a fishing boat with some friends," she said. "Somehow, the gas tank caught fire, and it exploded. There—there were no survivors."

Gabrielle shuddered. "That poor man . . ."

The nurse sighed, fidgeting with her appointment book.

"Well, thank heaven for Dr. Gant," she said. "Funny, how things work out. We only hired him a few days before Dr. Janovic left. He's really been a great help, taking on Dr. Janovic's patients as well as his own. I don't know what I'd do without him."

She smiled suddenly, indicating Jared.

"I shouldn't be talking like this," she said. "I can see your baby is frightened by this sad look on my face."

"I guess babies can sense when things are going on," Gabrielle said. "Don't worry, Jared. I'm sure Dr. Gant is as nice as Dr. Janovic."

Dr. Gant turned out to be a young man in his mid-thirties, with a pleasant smile and gentle voice. Usually, Jared would take immediately to such a person. But today, he kept a frown on his little face. He stiffened his legs and arms, making it very difficult for Dr. Gant to examine him.

"I'm sorry," Gabrielle said. "Jared, it's okay! C'mon, honey—relax!"

Dr. Gant tickled the baby's stomach.

"He just has to get used to me," he said. "Really, Mrs. Hansen, your baby isn't as bad as some of the others I've had."

He held up a bandaged finger.

"One little fellow bit me today!"

"Oh, Jared wouldn't do anything like that," Gabrielle insisted.

Dr. Gant smiled.

"Of course not," he said. "Well, you can dress him again. Everything looks great. You've got a really healthy, beautiful baby, Mrs. Hansen."

"Thank you," Gabrielle replied pleasantly. "And I

admire you for taking on so much extra work here. The nurse told me about Dr. Janovic."

"Ah, yes," Dr. Gant sighed. "That was a tragedy, wasn't it?"

He opened the office door, indicating he didn't wish to speak further on the subject. Understanding, Gabrielle thanked him again and left. Dr. Gant watched her from the partially opened door as she paid the bill, and when she had gone from the office he walked out to the nurse's desk.

"I've got someone I want you to get on the phone for me," he said.

The nurse read the slip of paper he handed her.

"Flora Collins?" she asked. "I don't recognize the name."

"She's an old friend," Dr. Gant said. "When she's on the line, connect her to my office. And see to it that I'm not disturbed."

"Well, now that school's over," Barry said to Kerry at dinner early one summer evening, "what do you want to do to celebrate?"

Kerry didn't hesitate with his answer.

"Go to Alcatraz!"

Andre laughed. "I thought little American boys considered school like Alcatraz."

"I think Kerry enjoyed my teaching," Emilie said in a defensive tone. She sighed. "But I'm glad it's over, too. Now there won't be any more questions about his records."

"So, can we go?" Kerry asked.

"I haven't been there in ages," Barry said. "Okay, since tomorrow's Saturday we'll take a trip there. Before the place is too overrun with tourists!"

The next day, everyone took the trolley to Fisherman's Wharf, and from Pier 41 crossed the Bay to Alcatraz Island. Gabrielle shuddered at the sight of the place, which resembled a worn-down army barracks with its cold lines and broken windows and barbed wire. She could almost imagine grim-faced guards mak-

ing certain no one disobeyed a sign stating only gov-
ernment boats were allowed within two hundred yards
of the shore. They were greeted by a young guide in a
ranger's uniform, who gave them a brief history of "The
Rock."

"We're goin' up some pretty steep inclines," the
young man said. "So I hope you're all in shape!"

He wasn't kidding, and each time he stopped at a
landing to tell a story the air was filled with the
sounds of heavy panting. Andre had no trouble at all,
and neither did Kerry. But Barry had let himself get
out of shape over the winter. The two women took
turns carrying Jared, which slowed them up. But at
last, they reached the prison itself. The guide explained
the actual procedures the prisoners went through upon
arrival: strip searches, showers, a doctor's examination.

"Wow, look how tiny those prison cells were!"
Kerry gasped as they entered a new section of the
prison.

The guard laughed. "You wouldn't want to stay in
one of those, would you?"

Kerry gave his head a broad shake.

"Well," the guide said. "We used to let people try
them out, but we don't any more because the doors
jammed once for four hours."

A rumble of comments ran through the crowd.

"One key opened all these doors," the guide went
on, "and when they shut, the noise was so loud that the
prisoners nicknamed this place 'The Slammer.'"

There were other nicknames—like Broadway and
Park Avenue. These cells were larger than the others,
but any cell was better than the horrors of solitary
confinement. Everyone listened in awe at tales of naked
men being forced to stay in dark, ice cold cells with
only a minimum of food to kealive.

"Sometimes, if the guard was in a good mood,"
the guide said, "he'd give a prisoner some toilet tissue
to put in those places where his body contacted the
metal floor. It helped just a little in keeping warm.

But just a little. Anyone want to see what it's like inside there?"

Most of the people nodded, eager to see what prison life was like. The guard explained that it would be so frightening that he would only keep the doors shut for twenty seconds.

"That's all you'll be able to stand," he said. "Now, why don't you choose a cell?"

Gabrielle stood back, not wanting to bring Jared inside. Beside her and the guard, there was only one other man. She thought nothing of this. She laughed when the guide said, "Watch out for rats," each time he closed a door, knowing he was only teasing. After he closed the last one, he headed straight to the first.

"Scary, huh?" the man beside her said.

"Looks like it," Gabrielle agreed. She nodded at Jared. "I wouldn't bring him inside."

Now she noticed that her son, who usually had a smile for everyone, was giving this man the nastiest look she'd ever seen. She scolded him for it, but the stranger only laughed.

Finally, the guide went to open the last door, and Gabrielle's shoulders heaved with relief. She didn't really like the idea of Kerry being stuck in the dark like that.

"How frightening!" Emilie cried as she walked out of the cell, her green eyes wide.

Barry put his arm around her.

"It wasn't that bad, was it?"

"I certainly wouldn't want to stay in there," Andre said.

Gabrielle made some agreeing noise and glanced past them to her brother, who had crouched down on the floor to tie his shoe. The guard stood near the door and said:

"Come on out of there, son. We want to get on with the tour."

"Just a second," Kerry said.

As he tied the shoe, he said:

"Gabrielle, it was so neat! It was really dark, and . . ."

He stood up to walk out of the cell.

". . . you couldn't see a thing!"

The guide stepped back a little, ready to close the door once Kerry was out. The little boy was no more than six inches from the threshold when suddenly the door flew out of the guide's hand and slammed shut with an echo that resounded along the entire hallway.

"Must have slipped," the guide said, moving to open it again.

But something was wrong. It wouldn't budge.

"Oh, dear," a woman said, "is that poor child stuck?"

"Can't be," the guide reassured. "These doors don't lock."

Gabrielle heard pounding noises as Kerry knocked at the door, yelling to be let out.

"Why can't you get it open?" she demanded.

The guide shook his head in bewilderment.

"It seems to be stuck tight," he said.

Andre and Barry stepped forward and offered their help. There was a small window in the door, and the guide made an attempt to open the cover over it. At least, that way, there would be light in the cell.

But it too was jammed tightly.

Inside the cell, Kerry leaned a shoulder against the door and listened to the sounds of someone trying to force it open. For the moment, it was an adventure to him, something he could brag about to the friends he'd made in Emilie's neighborhood. Imagine getting stuck in a real prison cell!

"Can't you work any faster?" Gabrielle demanded after a few minutes.

"I'm doing all I can, ma'am," the guide insisted. He backed away, wiping sweat from his brow with the cuff of his khaki shirt.

"Let me get a crowbar," he said.

As he hurried from the hall, Andre and Barry took

turns at the door handle and the window latch—to no avail.

"Don't worry," Emile said. "The guide will open it with the crowbar."

Kerry was growing impatient. What had started minutes earlier as an adventure was becoming a drag. Why didn't they just open the stupid door?

Clicking his tongue, he sank down to the floor and folded his arms, staring at nothing. He wished he could see something, even the blank wall. Being in such ink-like blackness was starting to make him feel as if there *were* no walls, as if he were lost in some void, like in an outer space movie.

And it wasn't so much fun any more.

"GET ME OUTTA HERE!".

"Andre, please do something," Gabrielle pleaded. "He must be scared half to death!"

The guide returned with a crowbar and proceeded to wedge it into the crack around the door.

"I can't figure this out," he mumbled.

The man who had spoken earlier to Gabrielle stood at the entrance to the hall, smiling to see the fear in everyone's eyes. He brought a fist up to his mouth to hide the smile, thinking it was only a taste of horrors to come. Only Jared noticed him. Only that little baby saw the skull-and-snakes ring he was wearing.

But Jared couldn't tell anyone. He couldn't tell anyone that the man had turned around and left the group.

"Look at him," Emilie said, taking Jared's tiny hand. "He's afraid for Kerry, too."

Gabrielle kissed her son and began to rock him, feeling tension in his small muscles.

Inside the cell, Kerry heard the squeaking noise of the crowbar. Putting his hand out to balance himself as he shifted his position to stand up, he felt something wet and cold against his wrist.

And then something furry brushed along his arm. Rats?

Watch out for rats, the guard had said.

But he was only teasing!

"GAAAABRIIIIEEEEELLLE!!!"

Kerry scrambled to his feet, his heart thumping loudly. He wasn't afraid, he wasn't afraid at all! There weren't any rats in here! No rats waiting in the darkness to bite him. . . .

The sudden appearance of light in the cell startled him so that he let out a little scream. But it only took a second for him to run out into the blissful light to throw his arms around Gabrielle.

"Thank God," someone said.

"Kerry, are you all right?"

She looked into her brother's wide gray eyes as he clutched tightly at her arms.

"There was a rat in there," Kerry gasped.

The guide looked into the cell, innocently empty.

"There's nothing there," he said.

"Yes, there was!" Kerry cried.

Emilie brushed his black hair from his eyes.

"*Mon petit*," she said, "if there had been a rat we would have seen it run out!"

Kerry pouted, realizing they probably thought he had just imagined it because he was scared. He knew there was no use in arguing with grown-ups.

"You shouldn't have made that remark before," Gabrielle said. "It put ideas in his head."

"I'm sorry," came the reply. "I'm really sorry. Nothing like this has ever happened before."

"Well," someone said, "now that it's over and the kid's okay, can we get on with the tour? I didn't pay three dollars for. . ."

The guide looked at Kerry, who nodded that he was fine. Maybe he *had* just imagined the furry thing that brushed his arm. . . .

With summer officially here, the horrors Gabrielle had experienced almost a year ago had now taken on the illusion-like quality of a bad dream. She hardly ever thought of Flora, and did not worry any more that the woman would come for her. The proof of her new self-confidence was in the fact that she didn't dwell on the incident at Alcatraz Island. She saw it as an unfortunate mistake—not as a means to frighten her.

She had grown up enough in the last year to have no qualms about staying home alone one day when the others decided to visit Golden Gate Park.

"You'll be all right?" Andre said. "I could stay home with you."

"No, you go ahead," Gabrielle said, fishing through her robe for a tissue. She'd caught a summer cold and was resting on the yellow couch in the den. "I don't want you to stay cooped up in here just because of me."

"No wonder you've caught a cold," Emilie said. "It was chilly on Fisherman's Wharf the other day, wasn't it?"

Gabrielle sneezed. "I'm okay. I'll just rest easy today."

When the others left, she used the remote control to click on the TV set, and watched an old Audrey Hepburn movie. Jared bounced happily in his jumper seat, making a set of chimes over his head jangle melodiously. But suddenly, the chimes stopped. Gabrielle thought her baby had fallen asleep, but when she turned she saw he was wide-awake.

He was staring at the telephone with round violet eyes.

"What's so interesting?" she asked.

When the phone rang, she nearly fell from the couch. Watching Jared's serious expression, she went to answer it. No one was on the other end. Gabrielle turned to the phone and snapped the cradle, trying to bring the connection back.

"Hello?"

She decided to hang up, and as she did so Jared suddenly began to scream, his face red with fury. Rushing to him, Gabrielle pulled him from the jumper and checked him all over, certain he had hurt himself.

"What's wrong with you?" she cried, finding nothing obvious.

Jared stiffened in her arms, crying so hard that he

started making choking sounds. His gaze was still fixed on the telephone.

"Did that frighten you?" Gabrielle said. "It's only a telephone!"

She walked back and forth with him, holding him close and talking to him until at last he had cried himself into an exhausted sleep. Making plans to mention this to Dr. Gant, she carried him upstairs to his crib.

The phone was ringing again when she returned to the den. She lifted it from the receiver impatiently. This time, a woman's voice greeted her.

"You thought that cell jammed shut by accident, didn't you?"

"What?" Gabrielle asked. She sneezed, and looked around for a tissue.

"It was no accident," the woman said. "I have found you, Gabrielle. I will have what is mine!"

The tissue was forgotten.

"Flora?"

No, it couldn't be, after so long! It's some crank . . .

"The Master wills this!"

Oh, God, it is Flora!

"Leave me alone!"

She wanted to hang up, yet she was frozen.

"You have had the child for too long," the woman went on. "You thought you could defy me, just as your mother did. But she was punished for her interference, as you will be! I will have what is mine!"

The line went dead. Gabrielle stared at the receiver, too shocked to even cry. How could this be happening? How could the horror start again when she was so happy?

Trembling, Gabrielle headed quickly for the stairs. There was a window in her room, where Jared slept, big enough for someone to crawl in through.

But Jared was still fast asleep, curled up with a stuffed lamb clutched in his tiny arms. Gabrielle laid a gentle hand on his back and felt the slight rise and fall of his chest. Then she bent down and kissed his warm, downy hair.

The gesture sent waves of anger through her. How could anyone dare to threaten her precious baby? She clenched her fists and walked to the window, gazing out at the Bay. A year ago, she might have given in to Flora's threats—she almost did so this time. But she'd been frightened and alone then, and too weakened by her pregnancy to defend herself. But she was no longer alone, and was certain she had gained an inner strength over the past months.

This time, she wouldn't crumble under Flora's evil.

She felt suddenly tired, worn out by her cold, by Jared's tantrum, and by her own fury at that phone call. She went to her bed to lie down, and soon fell fast asleep.

Only her nightmares would admit she was still very, very frightened.

She was a little girl of ten again. A little girl standing in the kitchen doorway of a diner in New Mexico, watching blood spurt from the mouths of patrons, hearing choking noises, seeing eyes go mad with terror.

Naomi turned to her. But this time, it wasn't Naomi—it was Flora.

"You mustn't look at this, my dear," she said, her voice sweet. "Your own punishment will be much, much worse!"

Flora started laughing, laughter that swirled through time and mixed with the terrified screams of a young girl.

"Gabrielle!"

A man's voice called to her through the darkness. A voice that she knew and trusted. Gabrielle stopped screaming and opened her eyes to look at Andre, who sat on the edge of her bed holding her by the shoulders.

"Andre?" Her voice was weak. "You're back already?"

"I couldn't stay out, worrying about you," Andre

said. "And I am glad I came home. You were having a nightmare, *chéri.* Do you want to talk about it?"

"No," Gabrielle said softly. "No, I don't want to talk about it."

She was so tired. She pressed her head against the cool fluff of her pillow and closed her eyes. Soon, she was asleep again.

Andre stood at her side, watching her, wanting to take her into his arms and yet afraid to disturb her. She seemed so very fragile at that moment, the way she had looked many months earlier when he saw her in the Utah hospital. What set this off again, he wondered? What had happened to make her have a frightening dream?

Finally, he kissed her softly, then pulled up a chair and sat beside her bed until the others came home. All the while he held her hand, feeling little jerking movements in her fingers as she struggled through more dreams.

Andre didn't tell the others about it. When Gabrielle didn't show up for dinner, he said he thought she was trying to sleep off her cold.

"She needs rest," Emilie agreed. "If she wakes up, I'll bring her something."

But it was nearly midnight before Gabrielle woke up. She came downstairs in her nightgown and robe, looking for something to eat. By then, everyone but Andre was in bed. He couldn't sleep for worrying about Gabrielle, and sat in the kitchen drinking a cup of tea. Surprised to hear the kitchen door open, he turned and saw Gabrielle standing there, pale and drawn.

"*Chéri,*" he said. "You shouldn't be out of bed."

"I'm hungry," Gabrielle replied, heading for the refrigerator. She pulled out a plate of leftover pork roast and poured herself a glass of milk.

"That's a good thing, being hungry," Andre said. "It shows me you're all right."

Gabrielle sat across from him and started to make a sandwich.

"I'm not all right, Andre," she said, her tone

matter-of-fact. "Something horrible happened while you were out, something that tells me it isn't over yet."

"What?"

"Andre, I got a phone call this afternoon," Gabrielle said. "It was anonymous, but I recognized the voice. Flora's caught up with me—even though it's been months, she hasn't given up."

"How can you be sure it was her?"

"Things she said," Gabrielle replied. She gulped down some of her milk, then slammed the glass on the table. "She wants my baby. But she won't have him! I'm not going to be weak like I was last year! I'm not going to let her frighten me!"

"Good for you," Andre said. "I promised you something, Gabrielle. I told you I would help you, and I will."

"I know that," Gabrielle said. "That's why I feel I haven't already lost this battle. I feel very strong."

"Perhaps not so strong," Andre said. "That horrible dream you had . . ."

Gabrielle breathed deeply, smelling the aromas of dinner that still lingered in the kitchen and becoming relaxed by them.

"That wasn't a dream, Andre," she said. "I was remembering something."

"Tell me," Andre coaxed, putting his hand over hers.

"When I was a little girl," Gabrielle began, "my mother and father and I moved into a town in New Mexico. I don't remember the name, but I know they started a diner there and were very, very happy. Kerry was born then, too. But my mother—well, my mother was usually in a sad mood."

She looked down at the amulet.

"I don't remember when she gave this to me," she said, "but it seemed very important to her that I never take it off."

"It's just a necklace," Andre protested.

"An amulet," Gabrielle corrected. "It's supposed to have powers. And I think it *has* protected me. But my mother should have had one, too. She needed protection more than I did, back then."

She had started crying, and wiped the tears away.

"My father died," she said. "He was attacked by wild dogs in the desert near our home. It's all very vague to me though. But one thing is too damned clear in my mind."

Andre took her other hand and held both while she continued.

"Mommy was working in the diner one day," she said, staring at her forgotten dinner. "I was taking care of Kerry in the back, and I remember calling to her for some reason. As she was standing in the kitchen with me, we heard a commotion in the front room. Mommy ran through the doors, and she saw that the people in the diner were choking."

She squeezed her eyes shut.

"She didn't know I was standing there," Gabrielle went on, her voice soft. "I couldn't turn away. I just watched those people spitting blood all over the place, watched them fall one by one to the floor."

"*Chéri,* you mustn't think about . . ."

"I have to," Gabrielle insisted. "I have to get it out of me once and for all. The sheriff came a while later. He spoke kindly to my mother, but she started acting . . ."

Gabrielle wiped her tears and met Andre's concerned blue eyes.

"The very last time I saw my mother," she said, "she was on the kitchen floor, rolling around like a mad woman. She kept screaming that she didn't do it. And I'm sure now that she didn't. But in the orphanage, no one would talk to me about her. Mrs. Macon said she was a monster, but I know she wasn't. My mother was a sweet, kind woman!"

She stood up and came around the table to sit on Andre's lap. Sobbing, she held fast to him for a few moments, letting words spoken in his native tongue soothe her. At last, when she had calmed down, Andre asked her a question.

"Why did you never tell me before of your mother?"

Gabrielle cuddled closer to him.

"I thought it was part of the past I was trying to forget," she said. "But when I received that phone call, Flora specifically said my mother was punished for her interference. Andre, I think she was set up to look like a murderess! Flora had something to do with that, and the only way I'll be able to fight her is to understand what kind of relationship she had with my mother."

Andre put both his hands on her wet cheeks and kissed her softly.

"You know I will help you," he said.

There was a pause.

"I love you, Gabrielle."

"Andre . . ."

But there was no need for words. There were no more tears. Just a long kiss and the warmth of arms entwined in a loving embrace. Gabrielle clung to the man she loved and felt strengthened.

She was safe as long as she had Andre.

Twenty-three

The next day, at Andre's suggestion, Gabrielle took Barry aside and told him about the phone call. As the big man listened, sitting in his lounge chair, she explained all she could about Flora Collins. When she finished the frightening report, Barry said in a quiet tone:

"What can I do to help you?"

"I want to find out more about my mother," Gabrielle said. "I don't think she killed those people, no matter what anyone says. I think Flora did. And if I know the truth, I can fight her."

Barry considered this, even as Andre assured him

he'd be paid well. He waved a hand at his brother-in-law.

"I'm not worried about the money," he said. "But there's something that puzzles me. You've been here since last October, Gabrielle. And a single phone call suddenly made you tell the truth about yourself?"

Gabrielle looked at her hands.

"I couldn't talk about it back then," she said.

"Under the circumstances . . ."

"Let me finish, Andre," Gabrielle requested. "I was afraid, Barry, that Kerry would be taken away from me and sent back to the orphanage. I was afraid Flora would find me here, and that she'd try to get at my baby. Not to mention what could happen to you and Andre and Emilie."

"I'm not worried about her," Barry said. He opened his hands and closed them again. "Go ahead."

"I'm not the weakling I was back then," Gabrielle said. "All the love you've given me made me realize I don't have to be afraid. So I want to face up to Flora Collins and end this once and for all. Will you help?"

Barry nodded without hesitation.

"But it'll mean going back to the orphanage," he said. "You realize that's the only logical source of information on your mother?"

"That's why I waited until Kerry wasn't here," Gabrielle said. "His biggest fear is being sent back there. But I'm sure you'll work out a way of getting the information I need without risking that."

"I can handle it," Barry said.

"Besides, there is no need to worry about that any more," Andre said. "I plan to go there with Barry to get your birth certificates."

"Birth certificates?"

"*Oui*," Andre said. "You need them for passports, *chéri*. After I adopt Kerry, and you deal with this Flora, I am taking you to France with me."

Gabrielle's eyes widened.

"Andre!" she cried. "You want to adopt Kerry? When—when did this idea come up?"

Andre shrugged, as if it were no big deal.

"It should have 'come up' long ago," he said. "I should have taken you from this country before the trouble began again."

"Oh, that would be wonderful," Gabrielle sighed. "To have a real home, and... But Andre, how do you know they'll give you the birth certificates?"

"Trust me," Andre said with a smile. "I know how to get what I want."

Barry and Andre left for New Mexico two days later. Emilie knew of their plans, but Kerry was led to believe they had gone off on a camping expedition. The little boy moped around the house until they returned, partly because he missed them and mostly because he felt left out. Why couldn't he go on a camping trip, too?

As for Gabrielle, she spent much of her time praying all would go well. This was such a big step to take, a risk that could get her in a lot of trouble. But she could no longer sit by and just let things happen, could she?

Finally, at the end of the week, the two returned. Barry and Andre sat on the steps in front of the house with Gabrielle while they told her what they'd learned. Kerry was busy skating up and down the street, and Emilie was off shopping. Andre held Gabrielle's hand as Barry spoke.

"First, you should know your Frenchman got those certificates," he began. "Certified copies, anyway."

"How?"

"It was easy," Andre said. "I bribed the new owner of the orphanage."

"New owner?" Gabrielle echoed. "What happened to Mrs. Macon?"

"She died of a heart attack," Barry said, "and her brother was more than willing to talk to me after I threatened to expose the way you two were treated while living there."

He brought one knee up a step and wrapped his arms around it.

"As you know, your mother was arrested for murder," he began. "It seemed she had put ground glass in the food she served that day at the restaurant—which, by the way, is located in a town called Freedom, New Mexico."

"She didn't do it," Gabrielle said darkly.

"Well, the authorities thought she did," Barry said. "There wasn't any other explanation. The companies that sold her the food were not related in any way, so it wasn't likely the glass had gotten into the different kinds of foods by accident. But whether or not your mother did it is beside the point. She suffered an emotional collapse and was declared mentally unfit for trial. She was taken to a mental hospital, where she died in a fire."

"I knew all that already," Gabrielle said in a disappointed tone.

"I'm not finished," Barry said. "I managed to locate one of the nurses who cared for Naomi at the hospital. Listen to this, Gabrielle. The one thing they remember about her is that she kept begging them to protect you and Kerry—from a woman named Flora Collins."

Gabrielle turned to Andre with a gasp, then looked back at Barry.

"Then she *knew* there was something wrong with that woman!" she cried. "Why didn't anyone pay attention to her?"

"*Chéri*, remember your mother was very ill," Andre said in a soft tone. "They probably couldn't listen seriously to her."

Gabrielle slapped the cement next to her.

"Well, damn it!" she said. "They should have asked questions!"

"You're asking them now, Gabrielle," Barry said. "I just wish I had more answers for you."

"You've given me a start," Gabrielle said. "And now that I know where the diner was located, I can go there and ask more questions."

"Do you think that's a good idea?" Andre asked.

"I can't just leave it like this," Gabrielle said. She

stood up. "We'll talk about this later. Kerry's coming back and I think I hear Jared crying."

She hurried into the house, where she found her baby standing up in his crib. Taking him into her arms, she walked with him for a few moments before laying him down on her bed to change him. But even after he was dry he went on crying.

"Damn that Flora," Gabrielle said. "She scares you, too, doesn't she?"

Jared grabbed for the dangling amulet and pulled hard on it, making Gabrielle cry out. She pulled it off and let him play with it. Almost immediately, he began to giggle and coo.

"You like that, don't you?" Gabrielle singsonged, grinning at the now happy child. "But don't you worry, Jared Andre. Pretty soon, we won't need that amulet to protect us."

The stewardess on flight 220 to Albuquerque stopped at Gabrielle's seat and commented on how adorable Jared was. Gabrielle felt herself go cold, something that hadn't happened in months. Flora's threats had made her frightened of strangers again. But she realized this woman belonged here and was only being nice. She managed a smile for her.

"If you need anything," the woman said, "my name is Angela."

"Thanks," Gabrielle said. She turned to Andre. "How much longer to Albuquerque?"

"Not long," Andre said. "And then we'll have to drive at least two hours to get to Freedom. Barry said he would phone ahead to the airport to have a car waiting for us."

"It was nice of Barry to help us," Gabrielle said. "He and Emilie are really great people."

Kerry, who had been visiting the lavatory, came back now with a plastic bag in his hand.

"The stewardess gave me a bunch of stuff," he said, climbing over the others to the window seat. He reached forward and flipped down his tray, then emptied the bag. "Look, Gabrielle! I got wings just like a captain wears!"

"That's nice, Kerry," Gabrielle said. "Maybe Andre can pin them on for you."

Andre obliged as Kerry explored his other goodies. Gabrielle was happy to see her little brother didn't feel any apprehension about visiting the town where their mother died. Everything had been explained to him, but he had shown little interest. *Well*, Gabrielle thought, *he was only a baby when we left Freedom. He doesn't remember any of it*.

As for herself, Gabrielle wished her memories were more clear. But she hoped when this trip was over, the mystery she had lived with for these past nine years would be solved.

Flora Collins stood at the base of Coit Tower in San Francisco and looked out at the lights of the city. The night air whipped her black dress around her, but she did not feel its chill. So, Gabrielle thought she could fight her? She thought she could run off?

She laughed out loud, making some nearby tourists look in her direction.

Let them run all they like, she thought. *I'll get them in the end! I'll win, as I always win. But first, I'll deal with that pair who dared to take them in and give them shelter. . . .*

It was evening by the time Gabrielle and the others came into the small town of Freedom, New Mexico. Vague memories washed over Gabrielle as she rode through the dusky, quiet streets. She thought she recognized a few of the stores and the adobe-style houses that surrounded them. But she couldn't quite place any of them. It was as if a door had slammed shut on this part of her life, only to be reopened ever so slightly to reveal bits of memory.

Had it really been nine years?

"Do you think the diner is still here?" Andre

asked, turning down a road that led to the town's only
motel.

"I don't know," Gabrielle said. "I don't really want
to see it tonight, though. I'm not ready."

"I understand, *chéri*," Andre said.

At the motel desk, he signed them in as Mr. and
Mrs. Paget. Gabrielle was surprised by this, but showed
no reaction. Now Kerry tugged at her arm and pointed
to two old ladies who sat on a couch behind them.

"They're staring at us," he said.

"Don't point," Gabrielle answered. "And I'm sure
they aren't staring."

But she had also noticed that the two old women
had turned their heads quickly away when she glanced
at them.

Don't be paranoid, she warned herself.

"Let's bring our things upstairs," Andre said, lifting
the suitcases. "Then we can see about having dinner
somewhere."

In the small town, there wasn't much choice but a
Mexican restaurant and a coffee shop. They chose the
coffee shop. The owner was very friendly towards Kerry
and Andre, but when he saw Gabrielle his expression
turned serious.

"Is something wrong?" Andre asked.

The man shook his head and led them to a table,
all the while staring at Gabrielle. Kerry stuck his tongue
out at him, making him turn away to busy himself with
something behind the counter.

"Do you suppose that man knows you?" Andre
whispered after their order was taken.

"He might," Gabrielle said. "But he doesn't look
familiar to me."

"Well, perhaps he is someone to ask your questions," Andre said. "But—let's worry about that tomorrow."

During their meal, Kerry talked in an animated
way about the airplane trip and the plastic wings pin
he'd gotten. He had both Andre and Gabrielle laughing
so much at his enthusiasm that neither of them noticed

the middle-aged woman who stared at them from a seat at the counter.

"MURDERESS!"

Gabrielle turned abruptly. She saw the woman jump from her chair and stagger towards her table, shaking a fist. Her hair was all unkempt, her dress stained by the coffee she'd just spilled on herself.

"Murderess!"

"Who are you?" Andre demanded.

Gabrielle backed away, her arms tightening protectively around Jared. She looked helplessly at the owner, who stood behind his counter and did nothing.

"How could they have set you free?" the woman cried. "You murdered my husband! You murdered him!"

"No, it wasn't . . ."

Andre reached across the table to take Gabrielle's hand.

"Please leave us alone," he said in a firm voice. "It's obvious you've made a mistake."

"I know you! I know who you are!" the woman raved. "I'm not crazy!"

The owner realized the woman's cries were distracting his other customers. He came over to her and said a few gentle words, leading her from the restaurant. Then he came back to the table.

"I'm sorry," he said. "But I can see why she made the mistake. You look *exactly* like a woman who murdered a half-dozen of our neighbors a decade ago."

Gabrielle caught her breath, but Andre shook his head at her.

"Of course," the owner went on, "it couldn't be you, could it? You're too young."

"Could you perhaps tell us the story?" Andre requested.

Eager to impress these outsiders with Freedom's biggest story ever, the man obliged.

"Her name was Naomi Hansen," he said. "Pretty woman—like I said she looked like you. Anyway, she had these two little kids and a husband, and she owned a diner just outside town. Well, one night she went nuts and killed off a bunch of people. Mrs. Allman's husband Joe was one of 'em. Now, this all happened just after Mrs. Hansen's husband died, so I guess she was touched in the head. They carted her off."

"What became of the children?" Andre asked.

"Well, Frenchie," the owner said, "no one really knows. I reckon they were put in a home. Hell, anything's better'n living with a crazed woman like that!"

Andre felt Gabrielle's hand stiffen in his, but still she remained silent. Now the door to the cafe opened, and a man in a sheriff's uniform entered. Seth Gallagher looked around himself, until he finally spotted Gabrielle. Mrs. Allman had come running to his station to say Naomi was back in town. He listened patiently to her drunken ravings, then promised to check the situation.

Damn! he thought. *If that's not her daughter, my name isn't . . .*

He dropped his cigarette to the floor and walked over to the table. When the owner saw him, he went back to his work. Seth leaned towards the table and said softly:

"You Gabrielle Hansen?"

She nodded. There was something familiar about this man, and she felt at ease in his presence.

"There's some things we should discuss," Seth said. "Would you come to the station with me?"

"All right," Gabrielle said.

Andre waved a hand at her.

"Wait," he said. "I'm not sure if . . ."

"There won't be any trouble," Seth assured him. "I was a friend of Naomi's."

"Please, Andre," Gabrielle said. "This is why we're here."

Andre consented, and ten minutes later they were seated around a wooden table in a room at the police station. Seth asked about the little boy, and was introduced to Naomi's son, Kerry.

"You were just a baby last time I saw you," he said.

Kerry made a face at him.

"I'm not a baby now," he said.

"No, I imagine you've grown up a lot these past years," Seth said. He looked at Gabrielle. "I knew both your parents very well. Paul and Naomi were fine people. I guess you know what happened to your father?"

"He was attacked by wild dogs," Gabrielle said.

"Well," Seth replied, "they found dog saliva when they examined him. But something bugged the hell outta me about that. What was a sensible man like Paul Hansen doing in the desert in the middle of the night? And there was something else, too. They found this weird object in his hand. Some kind of metal disc with a design stamped on it. It was a skull, with snakes around it."

"Oh, no," Gabrielle said softly.

Flora had gotten to her father, too?

"You recognize it?"

"Please go on," Gabrielle urged.

"I was here when the accident happened a few days later at the diner," Seth said. "I say 'accident' because I've always believed in Naomi's innocence. There wasn't a cruel bone in that woman's body! But no one else believed her. Six people were dead. So they sent your mother to a mental institution, and you and your baby brother to an orphanage."

One word echoed in Gabrielle's mind: "innocence." At last, she had found someone who also believed Naomi didn't do those horrible things.

"I came back to the diner a few weeks after the funerals," Seth went on. "Just wanted to make sure there was no vandalism—you know how people can get. I saw something shining in one of the yucca plants outside the door. It turned out to be a metal piece just like the one your father had in his hand. Now, I had *that* one, and the place had been combed thoroughly after your mother's arrest. There was no way she could have put it there."

"What did you do?" Kerry asked.

"I intended to bring it to the state police," Seth answered. "I hoped they'd be able to use it as proof of Naomi's innocence. But it was too late."

"My mother had died in that fire," Gabrielle said, her voice nearly expressionless.

Seth shook his head.

"I opened my door one December night and found this woman standing there in a ragged grey dress," he said. "She had soot all over her face, but I recognized her. She'd come to me because I was the only friend she had in the world."

He paused long enough to light a cigarette.

"Gabrielle, Kerry," he said. "Your mother is still alive."

Twenty-four

Emilie Paulsen climbed from her bed, moving carefully so as not to disturb her husband. Barry had been so busy all day trying to catch up on the work he'd left when he'd taken Andre to the airport. He needed his sleep, so she wouldn't bother him with the fact that she'd heard something downstairs.

She pulled a gun from the armoire beside their bed and carefully headed towards the sound. It sounded like someone singing, in a monotonous voice. Emilie told herself it was probably just a radio—maybe the kitchen window was open—but still she wanted to check.

The downstairs was empty and quiet suddenly except for the chattering of her pet finches. She spoke in French to them, then headed back to her bedroom. It had only been her imagination.

Someone was standing at the foot of the stairs.

Someone in a dark hooded robe. In her horror, Emilie demanded in French to know who it was. But when she saw the knife go up, her words turned into a scream.

"BAAAARREEEEE!!!!!"

Caught under an evil spell, her husband didn't hear her.

"I have to warn you," Seth said as they drove up into the Rockies, "your mother isn't the same woman you remember. She's been through a terrible ordeal."

"I just want to see her," Gabrielle said. "Do you think she'll want to see me?"

Seth smiled at her. "She's been waiting a long, long time for this, Gabrielle."

Gabrielle turned to look out the window, rubbing her arms. She was trembling all over, her feelings an amalgam of nervousness and excitement. What would the reunion with her mother be like?

She wished that Andre was with her. But it had been late when they left the sheriff's office, and both Kerry and Jared were falling asleep. Andre had volunteered to take them back to the motel, but Gabrielle had decided she couldn't put off seeing her mother.

"Here we are," Seth announced, turning onto the sandy bank of the road. "We have to walk the rest of the way—it isn't far."

The little shack glowed in the moonlight, looking cold and unloving. Gabrielle stopped to look at it, unable to believe her mother was living under such conditions.

"It's all right," Seth said. "I know this place looks bad, but I've fixed it up pretty nice and your mother's been comfortable."

Seth went to knock at the door. But Gabrielle wouldn't move, prompting the sheriff to turn and say:

"You want to come back tomorrow?"

"No," Gabrielle said, walking to him. "Is she there? Why hasn't she answered?"

"She never leaves," Seth said. "But she needs time to get . . ."

An old woman answered the door, squinting through the moonlit night at the pair. Her face was sagged and wrinkled, her lips slack, her shoulders hunched. Stark white hair hung like straw to her shoulders, and the eyes that watched them were filmy gray.

"Naomi," Seth said gently. "I've brought someone here to see you."

Gabrielle backed away, covering her mouth. This wasn't her mother! This was some old lady, and her mother could only be about thirty-five now. And she'd been beautiful. Gabrielle remembered her mother was beautiful!

The woman pointed to her amulet.

"Gabrielle?" she asked uncertainly. "You never took the amulet off, did you?"

Gabrielle shook her head at Seth.

"You made a mistake," she said. "That isn't my mother!"

"Gabrielle, this is . . ."

"NNNNOOO!!!!"

Screaming, Gabrielle turned and ran down the twisting path that led to the sheriff's car. Seth put his hand on Naomi's shoulder.

"She'll be back," he said. "She just needs time."

"Gabrielle," Naomi said. She looked at Seth. "Where did you find my daughter?"

"She found me," Seth said. "I'm sorry, Naomi. I promise I'll bring her back."

Before Naomi could say another word, Seth headed back to his car, leaving the woman standing in the doorway in stunned silence. It had all happened so quickly that now she wasn't quite sure if it had been real or another dream. She had so many dreams about her children. . . .

Climbing behind the wheel of his car, Seth said:

"I'm sorry. I should have made things more clear to you."

"Why did you play such a horrible trick on me?" Gabrielle demanded, staring at her lap. "How could you tell me my mother was still alive?"

"Honey, I'm afraid that *was* your mother," Seth answered. "Or what became of her after the hell she went through. She's been living in fear all these years, and it's taken its toll."

"But she's an old woman," Gabrielle argued as the car turned onto the road.

"Naomi isn't old," Seth said. "But your father's death, and the murders, and the fire at the institution aged her. Please, Gabrielle. The only thing that's kept her alive is knowing that some day you'd come back to her. Don't let her suffer further. Let me bring you tomorrow, and you'll see I'm not lying."

Gabrielle slid her feet down to the floor and straightened her back. She waved her hands in front of her.

"Please, just bring me back to the motel."

Seth did this, escorting the young girl up to her room. When Andre answered the door, Gabrielle's tears began anew, and she threw herself into his arms. Andre looking over her at Seth, who simply shook his head and walked away.

"Come inside, *chéri*," Andre said.

"It was awful," Gabrielle choked as she let him sit her on the bed. Kerry and Jared slept in another room, so she was free to talk without disturbing them. "There was this old woman. And the sheriff says it's my mother."

"Is it?"

Gabrielle started to shake her head, then nodded, then shook her head with a definite "no."

"You don't seem certain."

Gabrielle bowed her head.

"I don't know what to think!"

"Shh," Andre whispered, taking her into his arms. "If you can't think, there is no reason to do so tonight. Come, let's get into bed. I'll hold you."

"I'm glad you're here, Andre," Gabrielle said.

"I will always be here," Andre said. "*Je t'aime,* Gabrielle."

"I love you, too," Gabrielle said.

They held onto each other for the rest of the night. Numbed, Gabrielle wasn't able to think straight, though she tried to convince herself it was possible the old woman *was* her mother. She had witnessed the results of evil before this.

But she could not collect her thoughts, and finally let them float free. As Andre said, there was no need to think of it tonight. . . .

Barry sat in his lounge chair, staring out the picture window, a still unopened can of beer in his hand. He was wearing his pajamas, just as he'd been when the police came early this morning to answer his call. After sending the critically-wounded woman to the hospital, they had questioned him about the attack, receiving only monotonous replies. Barry could only think how slim Emilie's chances of survival were.

They think I did it, Barry said to himself. *They think I almost killed my wife*.

It was only pure exhaustion that let Gabrielle sleep without dreaming, until the warm rays of the sun woke her up just after dawn. She lay quietly next to Andre. His face, half-buried in the lumpy pillow, had a strained expression. Gabrielle wondered if he'd spent the night worrying about her.

A whimpering sound from the adjoining room told her Jared had awakened. Gabrielle climbed from the bed and went to the diaper bag that sat on a luggage stand. Pulling out a can of formula, she filled a bottle and carried it in to her son.

"Good morning," she said with a grin. Just looking at her darling baby made her fears fly away. She lifted her arms and smothered him with kisses.

Jared took hold of the bottle and popped it in his mouth. Then his eyes rounded, and he grabbed for the amulet. Gabrielle took it off and gave it to him, and was about to take a seat nearby when something occurred to her.

Last night, that old woman had pointed to the amulet. She had said: "You never took the amulet off, did you?"

Who else but her mother would say such a thing?

Gabrielle sank into a lounge chair and buried her face in her hands.

"Oh, Mommy," she whispered. "What did Flora do to you?"

But I don't want that to be my mother!

Still, as Naomi's words echoed over and over in her mind, Gabrielle became more certain it *was* her mother. Even after all these years, she still recognized the woman's voice. It had been heard so much through her dreams that it seemed she had never been apart from her.

Yet last night she had run away from her.

She had run away from her mother....

"Is it time to get up?"

Gabrielle looked over at Kerry's bed to see her brother half-sitting up, his eyes blinking and his hair in a mess.

"It's early," Gabrielle said. "Go back to sleep."

She took the amulet from Jared and left the room, entering her own room just as the phone began to ring. Andre moaned in protest, but took the receiver before she could reach it. In a moment, he was sitting up on the edge of the bed, his eyes wide. He looked over at her.

"Who is it?" Gabrielle whispered.

She saw him mouth the word "Barry."

"I don't understand," he said into the phone. "What do you mean, Emilie's been hurt?"

He heard Barry sigh.

"I slept through it all," Barry said. "I *slept*."

"Barry, you'll have to explain this," Andre said.

This time, there was no answer. He heard what seemed to be sobs, and then abrupt silence.

"Barry? Barry are you there?" Andre asked, his tone rising. "What's the trouble? What happened to Emilie?"

Now there was a scream, a scream so loud that even Gabrielle heard. A look of concern washed over Andre's face.

"Andre?" Gabrielle asked.

Andre went completely pale as he heard the sound of a gun being fired, and Barry's faint cry. But he would not accept the possibility that Barry had been shot. He slammed down the receiver.

"Barry said Emilie's been hurt," he told Gabrielle.

"Hurt?" Gabrielle said. "What does that mean?"

"I don't know," Andre replied. He had a sick feeling that he did know, but wouldn't tell Gabrielle. He wouldn't tell her the last thing he heard before hanging up was a deep, ugly voice whispering: "You're next to die."

He stood up and headed for the bathroom.

"Andre!" Gabrielle cried. "Is that all you're going to tell me?"

Stopping at the door, Andre said:

"I have to get back to San Francisco, Gabrielle. I have to be certain my sister is all right."

He hurried into the bathroom and turned on the shower before she could ask questions. When he came out, she had already dressed, and had gotten Kerry out of bed. As the little boy shuffled to the bathroom, she said to Andre:

"I don't want to leave here without seeing my mother again."

Andre studied her. He was too caught up in his own worries to ask when she'd decided that it *was* her mother she saw last night. Finally, he nodded.

"All right," he said. "Get your things packed. We'll see her on the way to the airport."

As she crossed the lobby of Albuquerque's small airport, Flora Collins had a smug expression on her face. By now, she thought, Roger and the others had taken care of Barry Paulsen. That meddling fool and his wife had paid dearly for what they'd done. Soon, she would have the baby, just as the Master planned long ago. Then, and only then, would she deal with the others. . . .

*		*		*

"I'm not so sure about this," Gabrielle said to Andre as they approached the little shack.

"You will never know unless you talk to the woman," Andre said. He didn't want to waste time here. He just wanted to get back to California as quickly as he could.

Gabrielle gave both Andre and Kerry a hug, then turned to rap on the door. She stood back and waited for it to open, imagining the next scene. Would Naomi cry out in joy to see her? Would she throw her arms around her daughter, then run to smother her little boy with kisses?

But strangely, as if it were all part of a dream, Naomi merely stared at the group in front of her home. Morning sunlight colored her face pale pink, but still her eyes were as dull as the previous night. Without a word, she backed away and beckoned them into her home.

"I hope I'm not . . ."

Gabrielle cut herself off. She looked back at Andre, who held Jared in his arms. Kerry, frightened of the old woman, hugged Andre's legs and looked at her with wide eyes.

Now the woman went to the shelves that lined her walls, and pulled down the family portrait she had cherished over the years taken while they were visiting a lakeside resort. She brought it to Gabrielle, and by way of greeting her at last said:

"Do you remember that vacation?"

Gabrielle studied the picture. There was no glass over it, and she touched the image of herself as a little girl. She had been so happy back then. . . .

"Oh, Mommy," she whimpered.

She threw her arms around Naomi and began to cry as the woman petted her hair.

"I knew you'd come back," Naomi said in a soft voice. "I always believed I'd see you again."

"I—I thought you were dead. Why did they tell me you were dead, Mommy?"

Naomi tightened her arms around Gabrielle.

"They wanted to hurt me," she said. "Flora wanted

to hurt me, and I had to hide here. I couldn't come for you!"

She looked across the room.

"Kerry?"

The little boy ducked further behind Andre.

"He's Kerry," Andre said. "He's bewildered, I think."

"Oh, my baby!" Naomi cried. "Please, come to me!"

Kerry shook his head.

"Mommy, what happened to you?" Gabrielle asked, pulling away. "What happened?"

Naomi put both her hands on her daughter's cheeks, holding her.

"It's a long story," she said. "I never thought I'd be able to tell it to you."

She pulled her daughter to her again.

"My little Gabrielle," she said. "I can't believe you're here again. I feel as if I've awakened from a bad, bad dream. . . ."

Twenty-Five

Manhattan, 1965

Seventeen-year-old Naomi Hansen held a paper cup of soda with both hands and listened to her best friend rave about a new movie. She stood with a group in the gymnasium of St. Martha's High School, transformed that afternoon with balloons and streamers for the dance they were now attending. In one corner, a band of long-haired boys in turtleneck sweaters and double-breasted jackets sang a Beatles tune.

"What do you mean, you haven't seen *Dr. Zhivago* yet?" Denise Simons squealed. "It's such a *great* movie. That Omar Sharif!"

"I haven't had the chance," Naomi said, brushing her bangs from her eyes.

A boy in the group leaned forward a little and tapped her arm.

"Don't worry," he said. "I haven't seen it, either."

Everyone looked at Joey Collins, the new boy in school. He hooked his thumbs through the loops of his black denim trousers and grinned at Naomi. The other girls giggled.

"Don't tell me you like Omar Sharif," Naomi said.

"I'll take Julie Christie, thanks," Joey said. "I don't really like those long movies, anyway. I go for westerns."

"That's where Joey's from," Denise explained, since Naomi hadn't been formally introduced to him. "Out West. He lives here now with his aunt."

"I'd like to see the real West someday," Naomi said.

"Maybe you will," Joey replied.

He looked around, and found the others in the group had suddenly gone off to dance. Then he turned back to Naomi and smiled, a smile so radiant that she felt her heart swell.

"Oh, he was handsome," she told her daughter. Gabrielle sat in a chair next to hers, holding her mother's hand as she listened to her story. Across the room, Andre and Kerry had sat down at a wooden table.

"The other girls couldn't stop talking about him," Naomi went on. "I remember a few saying they would give anything to be his steady. But he decided he wanted to go out with me."

"That's because you were beautiful," Gabrielle said, trying to see beyond the ragged old woman that her mother had become.

"No, it was part of a plan," Naomi said. "But I didn't know that then. I was just about your age, and it's very hard to see straight when you're infatuated by someone." She sighed. "Joey and I grew closer every day, and were very much in love. Well, it finally led to

our—to our sleeping together. I became pregnant with
you then."

"What did you do?"

"My parents wouldn't help me," Naomi said. "So I
turned to Joey's aunt—to Flora Collins. She lived across
town in a brownstone."

Naomi clenched her fists.

"I should have wondered why she was so willing to
take me in," she said bitterly. "I should have wondered
about the dead animals I often saw on her property, and
that awful midnight chanting, and Joey's refusal to
discuss any of it . . ."

Naomi stood near a window in her bedroom at
Flora's house, looking out at a dark back yard. Someone
was down there, holding a candle and walking circles
around what appeared to be a dead dog. Naomi wrapped
her arms around herself and felt her baby kick hard.
Then she turned away with a moan of disgust.

"I don't understand why your aunt doesn't call the
police," she said to Joey. He was sitting cross-legged on
her bed, dressed in a white T-shirt and jeans, and
smoking a joint. "God, I've seen enough dead animals
around here! What's next—people?"

"You're the only one who's seen them," Joey said.
"So maybe my Aunt Flora is right—it's just your imagination." He patted the bed. "Sit down."

She did so, and he started to rub her back.

"Crazy things happen all the time in the city," he
said.

"I've lived here since I was a little girl," Naomi
pointed out. "And I don't remember anything so bad in
this . . . Oh, Joey!"

"What's the matter?" Joey asked, alarmed. "Did I
hurt you?"

"No—no," Naomi stammered. "I think it's the
baby."

"I'll get my aunt," Joey said, putting the joint out
and hiding it in a drawer. "She's got Dr. Sunn's number."

"Hurry back!"

Naomi went to lie down as another pain came. But it was a long time before anyone came to her room. Flora entered alone, and went to stare at her with a grim expression. Feeling afraid of her for some reason, Naomi pulled her covers up to her chin.

"Are you going to take me to the hospital?"

Flora simply shook her head.

"Why not?" Naomi demanded. "And where's Joey?"

"Joey isn't here."

"What do you mean, he isn't here?" Naomi asked, her voice panicky. "Where did he go? How could he—"

Flora answered her as she fought another contraction.

"I sent him away," she said, her voice dull. "I no longer need him."

"*I* need him!"

"Lie still!"

Naomi screamed again, trying to roll from the bed. Something was wrong. She should be on her way to the hospital. Joey should be here! Why wasn't Flora helping her?

"JOOOOEEEEE!!!!"

Nobody heard her. Nobody but Flora and the two big men who suddenly burst into her room. Naomi thrashed and fought with all her might, but they were too strong. She couldn't resist as Flora put something over her mouth. Something that smelled of spices . . .

"When I came to," Naomi said, tears streaming down her pale face, "my baby had been born. That was you, Gabrielle. I was exhausted and terrified, and couldn't help falling asleep again."

"Did Flora let you see me?"

"Flora wasn't there," Naomi said. "No one was in the room, and you were lying in a blanket beside me. You were so beautiful, Gabrielle."

She smiled sadly at her daughter.

"I was awakened near dawn by a horrible scream," she continued. "The kind of scream you hear all the time in the city, but you ignore. Except that this one was too familiar, and I got out of bed to see what it was."

She rubbed her eyes.

"It wasn't an animal, this time," she said softly. "It was Joey, screaming because Flora was pulling a knife over his throat. I can still see the way the backyard light reflected off the metal. . . ."

Naomi burst into tears, and it was a few minutes before she could go on.

"I could think of only one thing—escape," she said. "So I grabbed what I could and bundled you into my arms. No one saw me leave the building, and I headed for the nearest subway stop. I—I think I finally collapsed in a train I had been riding. The next thing I knew, I woke up in some clinic."

"Then you contacted your parents?" Andre asked.

Naomi shook her head. "I couldn't. My father made it very clear I was no longer welcome. I found shelter at a home for unwed mothers. I lived there for two years, Gabrielle, and then I married one of the workers there. Paul Hansen was his name. We moved to the Southwest and started a new life, opening that little diner together.

"I was so happy there, with my little family. And when I learned I was pregnant again, I was certain the past was really behind me. It had been *years* since I last saw Flora Collins. But when Kerry was born, all I could think of was that horrible night in New York. I couldn't find the strength to care for the baby, and I became very withdrawn. The doctor said it was post-partum blues, but I knew better. I knew it was the past haunting me."

"So you told Daddy what happened?"

"Yes, I did," Naomi said. "And he decided something should be done about it. He kept talking about calling the police, but he never got the chance. They found . . ."

Gabrielle cut her off. "I know what happened to him. And I can guess the rest. Flora set you up for those murders, didn't she?"

"Yes," Naomi said. "And no one believed my story. No one but Seth Gallagher, who has been my dearest friend these past two years. You see, when the rest home caught fire, I managed to escape unnoticed. I walked for three days before reaching his house. Seth built this shelter for me, here in the mountains where no one would ever know I existed. Hiding here was the only way I could save my life."

She stood up, and Gabrielle stood with her.

"It's over now," Gabrielle said, embracing her mother. "We're back together again, and nothing can change that."

"But Flora . . ."

"We can fight Flora," Gabrielle said with a determination brought on by anger at her mother's misfortunes. "Andre is going to help us. He's going to take us to France with him!"

Naomi looked through her tears at the handsome Frenchman.

"France?"

"First, we must go back to my sister's home in San Francisco," Andre said. He looked at his watch. "I didn't realize we were here so long. Can you pack your things quickly? I must be on my way at once!"

"I don't . . ."

"Mommy, please come with us," Gabrielle begged. "We can't stay here with Flora after us, and we won't leave you!"

Naomi looked at her surroundings, her eyes full of fear.

"I've never left this place in two years," she said.

Kerry, who had listened in wonder to her tale, stood up now. He still didn't understand what was going on, but if Gabrielle believed this was his mother, then it had to be. He ran to her and threw his arms around her waist.

"We don't want to leave you, Mommy!" he cried.

Naomi bent down and hugged him as tightly as she could.

"My baby," she said. "My baby—you do know me, don't you?"

She looked at Andre.

"All right, I will come with you," she said.

Seth Gallagher walked out the front door of the motel and headed for his waiting car. The desk clerk told him that Gabrielle and the others had left a while earlier, but did not say where they were going. Seth didn't have to take long to guess.

He got into his car and started to drive towards the outskirts of town, planning to check in on Naomi. But about halfway there, someone suddenly ran in front of his car, forcing him to slam the brakes. It was Mrs. Allman.

"What're you gonna do about Naomi Hansen?"

She leaned into his window, filling the air around him with whisky breath. Seth backed away a little.

"Now, Mrs. Allman," he said. "You know that wasn't Naomi at all."

"It *was* her!"

Seth groaned.

"All right, hop in and we'll go down to the station and talk about it."

Mrs. Allman did as she was told, rambling on about Naomi all the way back to the station.

"I never believed in miracles until today," Naomi said, limping across the room.

"Well, we aren't free yet," Andre said. "Come quickly, I want to get to the airport."

He opened the metal door of the shack and walked outside, carrying a small bundle that held Naomi's few possessions. She had had Gabrielle write a note to Seth, hoping he would understand her sudden departure.

"Come on, Mom," Gabrielle said. Holding Jared, she walked out of the little house. In a moment, though, she realized Naomi wasn't with her. She turned, and saw that her mother had stopped at the top of the path. Naomi had a look of pure terror on her face, staring at something just beyond Gabrielle's shoulder. Gabrielle nearly screamed when she saw what had frightened her mother.

"FLORA!"

The woman began to laugh, moving closer to Gabrielle.

"You thought you could escape me, didn't you?" she said.

Gabrielle ran to Andre's side, hiding behind him.

"How could you be alive?" Andre demanded. "I stabbed . . ."

"It was a trick," Flora said. "You could never harm me! I *let* you escape!"

"Leave these people alone," Andre commanded. "They've done nothing to you!"

"Fool!" Flora hissed. "You will pay for your interference!"

She lunged forward suddenly, grabbing for Jared as Gabrielle screamed. But Andre easily blocked her, slamming his body against hers. It was like hitting a brick wall.

"Give me the child!" Flora cried.

Without a word, Andre swung his fist back and brought it around to punch the woman's jaw. Flora stumbled a little, but did not fall. She glared at Andre with glowing green eyes.

"The child is mine," she hissed. "The Master wills this."

"The Master?" Gabrielle echoed, holding her wailing son tightly. "Who is the Master?"

Flora shook her head.

"WHO IS HE?"

"*Satan!*" Flora screamed. "Satan is the Master!"

Andre said something in French, swearing at the woman, thinking she was completely out of her mind. He signalled Gabrielle into the car, but there was no way Gabrielle could do that without Flora getting to her.

"Flora Collins," she said in an even voice that hid her fears, "tell me what this is all about. Tell me what you could possibly want from my mother and me."

Andre looked over at her.

"Gabrielle, we must get out of here," he said. "Don't waste time talking to this maniac!"

"Andre, I have to know!"

Flora smiled sweetly.

"Of course you have to know, my dear," she said. "You should know why you are going to die!"

As Kerry and Gabrielle huddled behind Andre, and Naomi waited several yards away, Flora told them all a bizarre story.

"Over a hundred years ago," she said, "a poor young girl made the mistake of falling in love with an important man. She lived on a manor outside of London, and when he came riding by in his fancy clothes, on his fine horse, she thought she had seen a god."

Gabrielle saw the woman clench her fists.

"He seduced her!" she went on. "He used her young body for his vile passions, making her believe he loved her. But he didn't! He didn't love her! When she came to be with child, he tossed her aside like a rag. He laughed at her when she begged him for help after her family threw her into the streets!"

"I don't understand what this has . . ." Andre said.

Flora glared at him.

"*I* was that young girl!" she cried. "*I* was the one Oliver Tallinger used like some hussy!"

"That's impossible!" Gabrielle cried. "You said that story happened over a hundred years ago!"

Flora laughed at her.

"Satan's power has kept me alive all these years, so that I could seek vengeance!"

"Vengeance for what?" Gabrielle demanded.

Flora screamed her answer.

"*Oliver murdered my baby! He murdered my little boy!*"

She steadied herself, speaking now through gritted teeth.

"I saw him running away from my home one afternoon," she continued. "And when I entered, it was to find that he had smothered my child. I knew nothing but hate from that moment, hatred that grew so strong that the Devil took me as a disciple! I vowed that the Tallingers would pay, and they are paying. Oh, God, they are paying!"

"You are insane!" Andre said. "Gabrielle, we don't have to listen to this. We can go to the police, and..."

"No, Andre," Gabrielle said softly. "I'll never rest until I understand the whole story." She looked at Flora. "Who is Oliver Tallinger? What has he got to do with us?"

"He was your ancestor," Flora said. "And his descendants will pay forever for his crime!"

She folded her arms.

"I made a pact with Satan," she said, her voice steady now. "I was allowed to take the first-born male of every successive Tallinger generation. I raised those boys as my own, loved them as my own—until the next baby was born. I stole from the Tallingers what Oliver had taken from me—the first-born sons. And when they reached maturity, I gave them to Satan."

She laughed maniacally.

"Your own father is in hell now!" she cried. "In hell! Serving the Master for eternity as the pain of fire surrounds him!"

Naomi screamed.

"Oh, but he isn't alone," Flora said, sweetly. "He had friends there—all the other boys I took from your family. They tried to defy me once. Virna Stossel and her husband tried to cross the Atlantic to escape me. But I followed them! I followed them, and took what was rightfully mine! As I will have Jared!"

Gabrielle backed away a little.

"I don't understand any of this," she said, tears forming in her eyes. How could this all be happening? "You said you took the first-born male of every generation. And yet Kerry..."

"Kerry has no Tallinger blood in him," Flora said. She turned to Naomi, who stood with both hands over her mouth. "There was another child at Gabrielle's birth. A son, Naomi. Gabrielle's twin!"

"What?" Naomi gasped.

"I had a twin?" Gabrielle said, her voice high. "What happened to him? Where did he . . ."

She stopped herself as reality struck her.

"The boy with dark curls on the farm," she said.

Flora nodded.

"Your brother," she said. "Didn't you see how you two resembled each other? Dark hair, fair skin . . ."

"I . . . I remember feeling something when I met him," Gabrielle choked. "Flora, where is he?"

"Dead!" Flora cried. "Dead, as you will be!"

Just then, Naomi saw a familiar figure approaching. Needing her best friend, she didn't hesitate to run out to him.

"SETH!"

Flora glanced at the sheriff, then turned to see Naomi running towards her. She pointed a heavily ringed finger at Naomi.

"NNNNOOOOO!!!!"

A great explosion knocked Seth to the ground, and pushed the others against the side of the car. When they were able to steady themselves, it was to witness a horror beyond anything they had experienced before.

Where Naomi had stood just seconds earlier, there was now a screaming column of fire.

"WHAT HAVE YOU DONE?" Gabrielle screamed.

Seth pulled himself to his feet, and he and Andre ran as fast as they could to Naomi.

But there was nothing left of her.

In a matter of seconds, amidst flames and smoke, she had turned to ash.

"God," Seth whispered, shaking his head as the smoke cleared away. "I've never seen anything like . . ."

Andre ran over to Flora, grabbing her.

"How did you do that?" he demanded. "What kind of evil person . . ."

She laughed mockingly at him and, as if he were a small child, lifted him up and threw him several yards.

"Now, I will finish my work," she said, moving slowly towards Gabrielle.

"NNNNOOOO!!!!"

"Leave my sister alone!" Kerry screamed, watching this all through bewildered tears.

Seth knelt to the ground and reached for a blackened hand, all that was left of Naomi Collins.

Not even bones...

"God help me," he gasped. He pulled himself to his feet.

"Stop where you are!" he ordered, pulling out his gun.

But Flora kept moving towards Gabrielle as if she hadn't heard him. Seth fired, a shot at such close range it should have gone right into her arm, wounding her.

The bullet made a black mark on her sleeve, but she didn't even flinch.

"STOP!"

"You can't hurt me!" Flora cried. "I have the power of Satan with me! I will have what the Master wills!"

Gabrielle raced around the car, putting it between her and the insane woman who wanted her baby. But Flora moved with incredible speed. Andre, reaching her again, tried to grab her away from Gabrielle. But Flora suddenly had Jared in her arms, wrenched from Gabrielle's tight embrace.

She began to laugh.

"I've won! I've won! You can't..."

Seth put his gun at his side now, unable to risk shooting now that she held the baby. But Flora had stopped ranting, and was staring into Jared's wide eyes. He seemed to be glaring back at her, no tears on his face, an expression of pure hatred that seemed unnatural for such a tiny child.

Suddenly, Flora let go of him, dropping him to the ground.

"Jared!" Gabrielle cried, rushing to pick him up. She smothered him with kisses, crying with relief to have her son back again. But Jared seemed unaware of her. He was pointing a tiny finger at Flora, who had collapsed to the ground.

She began to writhe on the sand, tearing at her hair, ripping it out in huge chunks. As Gabrielle and the others watched in stunned silence, she rolled onto her stomach, then on her back.

What they saw was the face of an old, old woman.

Something like an animal growl came from Jared's mouth as he glared at her.

"What *is* he?" Flora gasped.

There were no teeth left in her mouth.

As the hot sun glared down on her, she rolled back and forth, screaming in pain. Her skin seemed to turn into leather, darkening and wrinkling. Her eyes flicked back and forth wildly, her bony arms and legs flailed.

Then, suddenly, the eyes fixed themselves on the sun above. At that same instant, Jared began to cry, like a normal baby.

"Andre?" Gabrielle whispered.

He put his arms around her.

Seth Gallagher readied his gun and slowly approached the woman. But as he bent to touch her, her chest caved in, and suddenly she was no longer there. Her body disintegrated into ash, ash that was carried off by the mountain wind.

Seth looked up at the others.

"Naomi was always afraid something evil would happen to her," he said softly. "She was right, wasn't she?"

Gabrielle did not answer. She pressed herself closer to Andre and buried her face in his chest, closing her eyes tightly. But she did not cry.

The time for tears was over.

"Come, *chéri*," Andre said, his voice hoarse on the mountain wind. "Let's get the hell out of here. There is nothing more we can do."

Seth Gallagher backed away and watched them climb into their car, nervously fishing through his pockets for a cigarette. In the heavy air, the sound of the engine seemed muffled, as if he were hearing it through a dream.

This whole damn thing's been like a nightmare, Seth thought as he struck a match. *And I'm not going to try to understand it.*

The car backed away and turned onto the road. But suddenly it stopped, and Seth saw Gabrielle roll her window down. He went to the side of the car. Gabrielle's eyes were dry now, but her face was pale and drawn. She reached out and took his hand, squeezing it.

"Thank you," she said softly. "Thank you for helping my mother the way you did."

Before he could answer, she rolled the window back up, and as the car drove down the road she rested her head against Jared's downy soft hair.

Epilogue

Paris, France, two months later

Andre poured a small bottle of seltzer into a glass of lemon syrup, then stirred it and handed it to Kerry. The little boy thanked him for the *citron pressé*, and picked up the glass. He sat with Andre and his sister outside a *café* along the Boulevard St. Michel. Gabrielle had a cup of *café au lait* in front of her, which she hadn't touched.

"You are thinking about your mother again, aren't you?" Andre asked.

Gabrielle stared up at him, frowning. She didn't answer.

"I wish that you wouldn't," Andre said. "It's been a long time, and it was enough to have to attend my brother-in-law's funeral without dwelling on it. Thank God Emilie is still alive though."

He thought for a moment of his sister, who was recuperating at their aunt's house in Normandy.

Almost as if she hadn't heard him, Gabrielle kissed her baby son and dangled her amulet in front of him.

"I can't believe he's going to be a year old next month," she said.

She looked back at Andre.

"What happened, back there in the Rockies?"

"I don't know," Andre said. "We'll never know."

"But how could Jared have been the one to save us?" Gabrielle asked. "How could a little baby fight that evil woman, when we couldn't?"

Kerry put his glass down and reached for a croissant.

"Maybe Jared's special," he said. "Maybe he's got magic powers, like Superman!"

Gabrielle began to rock her son, who giggled happily as he played with the amulet. There was no indication whatsoever of the child who had defeated Flora Collins. Only an adorable little baby with bright eyes and a happy smile.

"He's just a baby," Gabrielle insisted. "There isn't anything 'special' about him."

After a few seconds, she met Andre's eyes, and said in a worried tone:

"Is there?"

ABOUT THE AUTHOR

CLARE MCNALLY attended the Fashion Institute of Technology in New York City where she studied advertising and communications. She has worked on a children's wear magazine, freelanced as an advertising copywriter and edited a technical magazine. She now devotes all her time to writing novels. Her first occult thriller was *Ghost House*, followed by *Ghost House Revenge* and *Ghost Light*. She is currently hard at work on her fourth novel of supernatural terror.

Ms. McNally lives on Long Island with her husband.

THE ASTONISHING #1 BESTSELLER
IS COMING IN PAPERBACK

THE VALLEY OF HORSES

by Jean M. Auel

author of *The Clan of the Cave Bear*

Here is an unforgettable odyssey into a world of awesome mysteries, into a distant past made vividly real. In a novel that touches the very core of the human spirit, Jean Auel carries us back to the exotic, primeval world we experienced in *The Clan of the Cave Bear*— and to beautiful Ayla, the bold woman who captivates us with her fierce courage and questing heart.

Read THE VALLEY OF HORSES, on sale September 1, 1983, wherever Bantam paperbacks are sold.

Hair-raising happenings that guarantee nightmares!

You'll be fascinated by unearthly events, intrigued by stories of weird and bizarre occurrences, startled by terrifying tales that border fact and fiction, truth and fantasy. Look for these titles or use the handy coupon below. Go beyond time and space into the strange mysteries of all times!

☐	23518	THE DISCIPLE by Laird Koenig	$2.95
☐	22687	THE TRUE BRIDE by Thomas Altman	$2.95
☐	23356	HOUSES OF HORROR by Richard Winer	$2.95
☐	22616	THE DEMON SYNDROME by Nancy Osborne Ishmael	$2.95
☐	22748	MOMMA'S LITTLE GIRL by George McNeil	$2.95
☐	22634	THE AMITYVILLE HORROR by Jay Anson	$3.50
☐	23755	HAUNTED HOUSES by Winer & Osborn	$2.95
☐	23670	WHAT ABOUT THE BABY Clare McNally	$2.95
☐	23834	GHOST HOUSE by Clare McNally	$2.95
☐	23065	GHOST HOUSE REVENGE by Clare McNally	$2.95
☐	22520	GHOST LIGHT by Clare McNally	$2.95
☐	20701	THE EXORCIST by William Blatty	$3.50
☐	22740	HALLOWEEN by Curtis Richards	$2.95
☐	20535	50 GREAT GHOST STORIES by John Canning, ed.	$2.95
☐	20799	50 GREAT HORROR STORIES by John Canning, ed.	$2.95

Prices and availability subject to change without notice.

Buy them at your local bookstore or use this handy coupon for ordering:

Bantam Books, Inc., Dept. EDA, 414 East Golf Road, Des Plaines, Ill. 60016

Please send me the books I have checked above. I am enclosing $_____ (please add $1.25 to cover postage and handling). Send check or money order —no cash or C.O.D.'s please.

Mr/Mrs/Miss_____

Address_____

City_____ State/Zip_____

EDA—9/83

Please allow four to six weeks for delivery. This offer expires 3/84.

DON'T MISS
THESE CURRENT
Bantam Bestsellers